THE Elevator

BOOKS BY CLAIRE COOPER

WRITING AS C. J. COOPER

The Book Club

Lie to Me

bookouture

Published by Bookouture in 2023

An imprint of Storyfire Ltd.
Carmelite House
50 Victoria Embankment
London EC4Y 0DZ

www.bookouture.com

ISBN: 978-1-83790-757-1
eBook ISBN: 978-1-83790-756-4

For Dad, with love. Thank you for helping me chase rainbows.

PROLOGUE

Four hours from now

She's too close. The scent of her chokes me.

But it's not just here, in this metal box. She'll never be far enough away. Never sorry enough. Never lonely enough. Never hurting enough for what she's done.

So this is where it ends.

She watches me, thinking she's won. Thinking she has me cornered.

She's wrong.

When the doors open, only one of us will walk out. And though she doesn't know it yet, that person will be me.

ONE

NEW YORK

Now

I lean into the chrome and glass door and feel the heat hit my face as I step outside. The sunlight blasts off the pavement – no, *sidewalk* – and I screw up my eyes. I should have brought my sunglasses, but I'm not going to be out here long. I just need a break, a few moments alone to prepare.

I slip my jacket from my shoulders and breathe deep, but the air is thick and treacly. In London, I like to think I'd have left the office ten minutes earlier and strolled to Victoria Tower Gardens, sat on a bench overlooking the river. I wouldn't have, though. It wouldn't have occurred to me back then to take that kind of mental break. I made my trips to the gardens during lunch, nibbling on a sandwich there when I felt like a bit of peace and quiet. It was a different time, before everything went wrong.

I inhale again, count to three, exhale, repeat, the way my therapist has shown me. A therapist. I'd never have imagined I'd have one of those. I try to remember what we talked about at our last session. 'Your circumstances don't create your feelings,' Dr Welmar said, peering at me earnestly through her large, black-framed spectacles. 'It's your thoughts that create your feelings. So we need to work on changing your thoughts.'

It won't be like last time, I think, obediently. *This is completely different. I can handle it. I know what I'm doing. I'm in control.*

Beside me, the bank of swing doors open and close constantly, disgorging men in suits, women in high heels. The corporate uniform. I look just like them, I'm almost sure of it. The new, short haircut, the smart trouser suit. I barely recognise myself when I look in the mirror. That's the aim.

I check my watch: thirty-five minutes to go. I'll take just five more and then go back inside. That way there'll be plenty of time to give the room a once-over, make sure everything's set up just right. Cassie will have done it perfectly, the way she does everything; but it doesn't hurt to double-check. The bottle of water, the three glasses. A box of tissues, placed somewhere discreet yet convenient. You never know if you'll need them, even with a man.

This time, everything will go smoothly.

A strand of hair sticks wetly to my forehead and I brush it back with one finger, careful not to smudge my foundation. I can't allow a chip in the veneer of my polished professionalism; who knows what they'd see underneath.

For a moment I allow myself to imagine the day going differently. Breezing in, asking Cassie about her weekend. Saying yes to the next invitation to lunch or after-work drinks. Sitting in a bar or coffee shop with a person, instead of my laptop. Talking to someone, anyone, about something other than recruitment or training budgets. Letting them in. Making a connection. Maybe even having a laugh. It feels like so long since I did that; I'm not sure my facial muscles are even capable of it anymore.

But then I remember – it has to be this way. This is my punishment. And God knows, it's less than I deserve. I straighten my shoulders and head back into the lobby.

Just a few minutes outside and the A/C is already a relief. I let the cool air slide over my skin before threading my arms into my jacket once more. The nerves are fluttering in my stomach now, but still this space makes me pause and catch my breath, the way it always does. The double-height ceiling, the black granite monolith that serves as the reception desk. Floor-length windows combine with overhead lighting to scatter diamonds across the glossy white floor. It's been over two months since I first set foot in this building, and I'm still not used to it. Maybe I never will be.

But there's someone else who doesn't belong here – the British vowels carry across the space. 'I *have* an appointment,' she's saying.

There are plenty of Brits at Pearl Associates, so it isn't the accent that's drawing the attention of the other people in the lobby. It's the agitation in her voice, the floaty linen shirt and trousers in the midst of the pencil skirts and sharply pressed suits. And even though the security guard at the gates is staring grimly ahead, watching me as I reach for my pass, I slow down to take a closer look at her.

'There's clearly some mistake,' she says. 'I've travelled a very long way—'

The receptionist is smiling at her, one of those fixed, bright smiles that let you know the person wearing it would very much like you to go away. 'If you'll just take a seat, ma'am...'

'It's Maeve—' the woman starts to say, crossly.

I've dawdled and paid the price. A gaggle of suits have cut in front of me and are applying their passes to the gates, a chorus of beeps drowning out the rest of the British woman's reply. I check my watch again before I can help myself: twenty-nine minutes. There's no need to panic.

I position myself behind the gate with the fewest suits – but one of them is having a problem with his pass. It beeps angrily, a red light illuminating the Perspex barrier instead of the green one that precedes the gate swinging open. I suppress a sigh as the security guard goes to check his credentials, and swap to the next gate.

'Sir! Sir!'

The suit in front of me now is having problems too. The security guard is beginning to look harried.

'Can you just let me through?'

'We're all together.'

'This is making me late...'

The security guard turns away and says something into his radio. A pause, then he places his own pass on the barrier. The gate opens and the man ahead of me walks through, the guard already off to the next gate, repeating the process.

I press my pass to the glass panel and step forward. That angry beep. A red light. I fight to stay calm. I don't need this. Not today.

A second guard has appeared and waves me to the gate at the end. The suits are still 'Sir, sir'-ing his colleague, and I smile in what I hope looks like sympathy. 'Looks like you're having a bit of a day,' I say, but he just gives my pass a cursory glance and waves me through.

'Mine's not working either,' says a voice behind me. The British woman. She's got past the receptionist after all. She's reaching into her shoulder bag. 'Oh! I've just put it away. Do I need it again?'

The guard sighs as she rummages in the depths of her bag, and with a look of immense weariness opens the gate once more.

I hear her footsteps following as I cross the lobby, aiming for the lift at the far end on the right. This one serves even-numbered floors between 20 and 30, and for some reason, doubtless involving a complex algorithm I don't understand, it usually opens its doors approximately ten seconds after its twin on the left. Time it right, and it's often empty. As it is today.

I step inside and immediately jab the button for the 26th floor. There are still suits milling around, and I don't want to take the chance that they're heading the same way. I need the space to think, to run through my script in my head. The doors are sliding shut and my mind is already turning to the task before me when that voice rings out again.

'Excuse me!'

The woman behind me stretches her arm between the doors and they open again.

'Does this go to floor 26?'

I nod, but she's already turning away, her gaze fixed on the door. At least she's not a talker.

I push the button and the doors slide shut.

Only your thoughts create your feelings, I remind myself. *It's just one other passenger, and it's only for a minute.*

It could be a whole lot worse.

TWO

LONDON

Maeve, seventeen years ago

Maeve was thirsty. It wasn't surprising. She'd been sitting on the bench for two hours and eighteen minutes, with nothing to drink since the pub lunch with Alistair. A glass of orange juice and a coffee, that was all she'd had then. She'd been trying to set an example. Alistair had drunk two pints all the same, though he'd originally said, 'Just the one,' like a kid asking for a chocolate biscuit. But he'd been fine when they parted. So was she. Would be fine still, if it hadn't been for that stupid woman in the shop.

She stood up and stretched her legs, took a couple of steps to the left, walked back again. She couldn't risk taking her eyes from the door. A couple of people had come out wearing the uniform, confirming that she'd correctly identified the staff exit. They'd stood around smoking, before going back inside again. There'd been no change of shift yet, but she didn't care. She could wait.

She fingered the flimsy piece of paper between her fingers, allowing herself to feel the burning anger again. Across the top were printed the words 'Credit note'. It wasn't the money; it was the *principle* of the thing, the sheer injustice of it. She'd never worn that top. She hadn't had time to try it on when she'd bought it, cutting short her shopping in order not to miss the train back to Bristol. But when she'd put it on at home, she could see instantly that it was all wrong. Too short in the arms, tight across the chest. And the colour didn't suit her either, turning her skin from pale to anaemic, her hair from honey blonde to straw. She'd taken it off straight away and stuffed it back into its bag, complete with receipt, waiting for her next visit to London to return it.

She realised she was grinding her teeth and forced herself to relax her jaw. She'd known from the moment she saw the woman in the shop that she was going to be trouble.

'Next,' she'd called, without so much as a 'please' or a smile. She had dyed black hair pulled back into a severe ponytail and hard lines around her mouth, though she couldn't have been more than twenty-five.

Maeve placed the bag on the counter and explained that she needed a refund. She was polite, saying 'please' because she wasn't a savage, and even though she was the customer, and was supposed to be always right.

The woman prodded at the top. 'This has been worn,' she said.

'I tried it on, then took it off again. Like I told you, it didn't fit.'

The woman pointed to the neckline with an acrylic nail. 'There's no tag.'

'Oh, isn't there?' Maeve looked at where she was pointing. 'They must have taken it off when I bought it.'

'We don't do that. You need the tag for returns.'

Maeve took a breath, tried to ignore the building irritation. 'Well, I have the receipt. That has all the details.'

'That's not the point. I can't accept a return without the tag. If I did, you could just wear that top, then bring it back for a refund.' The woman tilted her head sideways and regarded Maeve through narrowed eyes. 'Couldn't you?'

Maeve could feel the stares of the other customers warming the back of her neck. 'No,' she said, straightening, 'I couldn't do that, because I'm not a liar or a cheat.' She heard a muffled gasp of delight from the spectators behind. 'And secondly, as I've already told you, the top didn't fit. Now are you going to give me a refund, or are you going to get your supervisor?'

But an older woman had already materialised behind the counter, fussily examining the top. Maeve was dimly aware that she was talking to her, but she kept her eyes fixed on Acrylic Nails. 'Store policy' – the woman was saying – 'circumstances... condition...' Acrylic Nails stared back at her, her upper lip curled as though Maeve had stepped in something unpleasant.

'...On this occasion,' the supervisor's pitch indicated that she'd reached her denouement, 'I'm happy to offer you a credit note as a gesture of good faith.'

There was a piece of paper on the counter. Maeve could see it in her peripheral vision, placed there like a white flag. She slid her hand over it, her eyes still on Acrylic Nails, drinking her in, making sure she'd recognise her again. Then she looked directly at the supervisor and smiled. 'Thank you for being so helpful,' she said.

Now her eyes flicked to her watch. Just gone 4.30 p.m. The shop didn't shut until seven. Would there be a shift finishing before that? But even if there was, that didn't mean Acrylic Nails would leave then. She could be there until closing, or even later. Perhaps she'd have to tidy up changing rooms, restock clothes rails.

You could just let it go, said a voice in her head. But she knew who it belonged to, and she wasn't about to listen to it. Letting things go led to all kinds of trouble. Her mother had learned that lesson the hard way, and Maeve wasn't about to repeat her mistakes. She turned her head from side to side, loosening up the muscles in her neck, and settled back on the bench.

It was 4.47 p.m. when the door opened again. The first to emerge were two young women, matching poker-straight hair, heads bent together over a phone. Maeve sat forward and pulled the strap of her bag further onto her shoulder, ready to go.

And then she saw her.

Acrylic Nails was wearing a short red jacket over bootcut jeans, her black hair still pulled into its painful ponytail. She was alone, walking briskly as though she had somewhere to be. Maeve watched as she reached the corner then turned right, towards the high street. She left the bench and followed her.

The pavements were still crowded with Saturday shoppers, but Maeve wasn't concerned. The red jacket and dye job were easy to keep in sight as she threaded her way around gaggles of teenagers, young families, women meeting for shopping and coffee. Was Acrylic Nails on her way home, perhaps planning to shower and change before a night out? Perhaps she was rehearsing the story she'd tell her friends about the snotty cow she'd humiliated earlier that day. Perhaps she thought they'd be impressed.

The crowd thickened at the top of the steps to the Tube station. Maeve caught a flash of the jacket and pressed forward. She could tell from its position that Acrylic Nails was going to take the stairs. A longer journey, then. Home, almost certainly.

She made her way swiftly through the crowd, grateful for her years of experience in navigating London, her ability to spot the spaces just large enough to slip through without drawing complaints, not wanting to risk losing sight of her quarry.

What are you going to say when you catch up with her? said the voice in her head. *What exactly do you hope to achieve?*

I'm going to embarrass her, she responded silently. *I'm going to make her understand that she's rude and ignorant, and she can't just talk to people that way. I'm going to make her apologise in front of a whole bunch of people she doesn't even know.*

Into the ticket hall now, and there was Acrylic Nails at the gates to the Central line. Maeve slid her travelcard into the reader and slipped through the barriers. Acrylic Nails was already on the escalator, walking down the left-hand side. Maeve skirted around a dawdling middle-aged couple and followed a few steps behind. She'd wait until she reached the platform to confront her, wait until there'd be a captive audience.

They'd reached the bottom of the escalator now and Acrylic Nails turned left, towards the eastbound platform. Maeve caught a glimpse of her face as she turned the corner, those thin lips set in a sneer. That was how she'd looked at Maeve when she'd accused her of lying about wearing the top.

As if I was something on the bottom of her shoe, thought Maeve, and her fists clenched.

She'd walk up behind her so she didn't have time to prepare. Tap her on the shoulder. Then she'd let her have it with both barrels. There, on neutral ground.

The platform was busy: the board said the next train would be in four minutes. Acrylic Nails was still walking, presumably heading for wherever the doors would open nearest the exit at her destination. Maeve was closer now. She watched the stupid ponytail swinging back and forth. If she reached out, she'd be able to grab it.

Abruptly, Acrylic Nails stopped and stepped to the side. She'd spotted a gap in the line of people waiting at the platform edge. Maeve checked her pace and slotted in behind her. The board now showed three minutes to the train. Enough time to give her a piece of her mind.

Maeve reached out to tap her on the shoulder.

'Sorry, can I just—?'

Something hit Maeve's left foot and she turned, her hand half-raised. A woman with a buggy containing a podgy-faced toddler was trying to get to the front of the platform, ignoring the implicit queue.

'Oh God, sorry! Was that your foot?' The woman looked hot and flustered, the toddler on the verge of tears.

'It's fine,' Maeve mumbled, sorry for her. She moved to try to create more space. The number on the platform indicator changed from three minutes to two.

In front of the buggy, a tall man in a tan jacket turned around. 'You all right, love? Here, let me.' He tried to shuffle to the side, but there was only room for him to take one step. Other people looked around wearing expressions of sympathy, but the platform was too packed for them to do more.

Except for one person.

Acrylic Nails could move to the right. There were a few inches of clear space. It wasn't much, but it would give the woman with the buggy just enough room to squeeze in. Enough room to let her get on when the doors opened, instead of being pushed to the back of the tidal wave of passengers. But Acrylic Nails was staring straight ahead, ignoring the situation.

Maeve felt the anger bubble up inside her again. *Of course* this horrible woman wasn't going to move. *Of course* she was going to stand there, pretending she couldn't see the buggy. If Acrylic Nails moved to the side, she'd have to allow the woman with the toddler to board first. She might lose that golden opportunity to get the one remaining spare seat. And what, after all, were good manners in the face of such a risk? What was the value of common decency against sitting down for an extra five minutes on her way home?

There was no point trying to talk to someone like that. Maeve should have known better. The ponytail was right in front of her, dangling against the red jacket, every last strand tucked tight, tight, tight into a bright pink band. It was the same colour as the nails that had tapped the neckline of the top. *This has been worn.*

Maeve glanced to either side. No one was looking at her. It would take only a second. She could feel it now, the sharp edge of bony shoulder blades beneath the cotton jacket. The brief moment of resistance then release.

You can't do this, Maeve.

The voice was as clear as if he'd spoken in her ear. But she didn't have time right now to worry about how he'd react.

She checked over her left shoulder, then her right. There was the CCTV camera. If she aimed low, the movement would be hidden by the crowd. The small of the back, then, not the shoulders. Just one small push.

You can't do this. You promised.

Maeve clenched her fists then opened them, flexed her fingers.

You promised.

Just one small push.

THREE

NEW YORK

Now

As soon as the lift starts to move, carrying me closer to the meeting, I realise I've already messed things up.

I should have insisted on a pre-meeting with Leo, made it clear how I wanted things to go. I tried, but not hard enough. He managed to put me off without too much effort: the look of surprise that implied I was making a big deal out of nothing. 'I'll just follow your lead,' he said. 'I won't say anything unless you ask me to.' That smile, the perfect teeth they all have here.

I let him get away with it, and it's too late now. Because what if Jay asks him a question? It's what I would do. I'd make him explain himself. We should have gone through it all, practised what he'd say. Made sure it would hit the right note.

Floor eight intones the lift. Elevator, I mean. What's that quote about two countries separated by a common language? Using the wrong words makes me stand out – that and the accent, but I can't do much about that. They remind people where I'm from. That's the last thing I want.

Focus.

I check my watch again: twenty-six minutes. Plenty of time.

Twenty-six minutes. The 26th floor. That's where the other woman is going too. I study the back of her head. She has blonde hair twisted into a chignon. It's held in place with a plain silver clip that's not quite straight. When my hair was long, Matt always preferred it loose.

Matt. I can't believe he called me, last night of all nights. All this time without a word, and then, out of nowhere, asking how I am, how I'm settling in. It threw me, hearing his voice again, and despite it all I could feel myself almost giving in to the temptation to respond, just to talk to someone who knows me. The real me, I mean, not just my job description. I didn't do it, though. I made up some excuse about having to go, dinner with friends. 'Sorry to disturb you,' he huffed, which brought me to my senses.

The lights flicker. At least I think they do. I look up to the ceiling. Nine spotlights gleam back steadily, reflecting against the stainless-steel walls. That's the look in this building – brushed metal, shiny metal, lots of white, hard edges, brilliant surfaces. It's nothing like Holbrooke and Dean back home. Maybe they'll give the London office a makeover in time. Or maybe they'll just close it. Matt was always convinced that was the plan, though it never made any sense to me. 'Why would they buy up a London firm just to shut it down?' I asked him in one of our many conversations about it. 'It's not as if we're poaching their clients.'

'Let's just wait and see,' he replied, trying to sound enigmatic. But by then I'd worked out that, with Matt, enigmatic usually meant he didn't know what he was talking about.

The lights flicker again. I'm sure of it this time. The other woman is looking up now too.

Floor f-f-fourteen, stutters the elevator voice.

The woman turns, and I try not to look alarmed. 'Is this normal?' she asks.

'I'm sure it's fine,' I say, somehow slipping into the role of host. 'Probably just a glitch of some—'

And then the lights go out.

FOUR

BRISTOL

Maeve, seventeen years ago

Maeve turned the heart-shaped charm on her bracelet, avoiding looking at the man sitting opposite her as she decided how to frame her answer.

'I get very angry sometimes,' she said. 'I'd like to be able to control that better.'

It's what had made her pick up the phone after the incident on the Tube. She'd lain awake that night, replaying those moments on the platform, how close she'd come. She could almost hear the screams, the screeching brakes, almost see those shiny nails reaching for the platform edge. Part of her was disappointed that she hadn't pushed that woman. She'd deserved it, after all.

But she knew it wasn't right to feel that way. She'd seen the damage that kind of anger could do. And though she was completely different – she didn't pick on people who were smaller or weaker than she was, people who'd done nothing wrong – she knew Ali worried about it all the same. She could see it in his eyes sometimes, the way he looked at her when she was getting worked up about something. As if she reminded him of someone else. The thought of that made her feel sick.

She'd called the office of Dr Paul Morgan first thing the next morning, his website the first of the AltaVista search results for 'psychotherapist, Bristol'. She wondered now if it had been a mistake.

'Do you feel you're not able to control your anger?' He sat across from her, studying her with an intensity that made her shift uncomfortably on the leather chair.

She nodded. Surely she'd already said as much?

'Why do you feel that way?'

She cleared her throat, giving herself time to choose her words. 'Sometimes I lose my temper.'

'Sometimes or often?'

'Sometimes.'

'Doesn't everyone lose their temper sometimes?'

He was smiling at her. Was he taking her seriously? Or was it possible he was deliberately baiting her? Trying to see what it took to make her angry?

'Probably. But I don't enjoy it when it happens. Like I said, I'd like to learn to control it.'

'Tell me about the last time you lost your temper.'

His eyes were blue, she saw now. There were lines at the edges as if he laughed a lot. His shirt was white and crisp. Everything about him was clean.

She said, 'I was waiting for a train.'

He nodded as she talked, occasionally making a note on the pad balanced on his lap. She wondered what he was writing there. *Mad as a box of frogs*, probably.

When she'd finished, he said, 'And you'd never seen this woman before?'

'No. She was just in front of me on the platform.'

He made another note. 'You said she was "inconsiderate" towards the woman with the buggy. Was that what made you angry?'

She nodded. 'There was no need for it. She could have helped so easily. She just needed to move half a step to the side. But she didn't care. All she cared about was herself.'

'Have other people in your life behaved like that? As if all they cared about were themselves?'

She stiffened. 'What? No. I mean, I don't see how that's relevant.'

A pause, then, 'Did that question upset you?'

She tried to laugh. 'I'm not upset. I just don't see how it helps. I told you, all I need are some tips, some techniques—'

'To get your anger under control, yes.' He was silent for a long moment before continuing. 'Let's go back to the woman on the platform. Tell me how you felt when she didn't move.'

'Like I said, it made me angry.' He waited, apparently wanting more. 'I felt like I should do something.'

'Do something?'

'To make her see she shouldn't behave like that.'

'So what did you do?'

'I...' Her fingers felt for her bracelet, touched one of the silver hearts that hung from its length. 'Nothing. I didn't do anything.'

'And yet you're here,' he said, 'telling me you want to learn to control your anger.'

He leaned back in his chair, laid his pen on his notepad, covered it with one hand. His fingernails, she noticed, were straight and short. He was older than she'd thought at first, threads of silver at his temples.

A silence formed between them. Should she fill it, tell him what she'd thought and felt as she stood on that platform? It felt terrifying, opening herself up that way. But what was the point in coming if she didn't give him the chance to help?

She swallowed. 'Okay, you're right. I thought about hurting her.'

She waited for him to say something but he just nodded, motioned for her to continue.

'She was right in front of me, right on the edge of the platform. I thought about pushing her.'

'And what did you do then?'

She looked down, adjusted one of the hearts so it lay flat against her wrist. 'It was just for a second, but it – it shook me. I felt like I'd been close to really doing it, just reaching out and giving her a shove. So I left. That's when I decided I should get help. Talk to someone about it.'

Saying it was a relief, she realised. She'd handed over her problem. And this was a professional, someone who understood these things. He could tell her how to make it right.

He uncrossed his legs. 'That's all we have time for today, Maeve. But you've made the right decision. Tell them at reception that I'd like to see you again in a week.'

She stared at him. 'That's it?'

'Just for now. You've made a great start. I think we're going to work really well together.' He smiled at her again then, with what looked like real warmth. The lines at the corners of his eyes crinkled, the way she'd known they would. Despite herself, she felt a glow as she walked to the door.

'Maeve?'

She turned to see him standing behind her, his hand held out. In the centre of his palm nestled a small silver heart with blue enamel in the middle, one of the charms from her bracelet.

'You dropped this.'

She took it from him. His skin was warm and dry against her fingertips, and the contact went on a microsecond longer than it needed to. At reception, she made an appointment for the following week.

FIVE

NEW YORK

Now

A shudder, metal rasping against metal. I make a grab for the handrail, but it's already over. The lights flicker back on. The lift has stopped moving. Completely.

The other woman stands in the corner diagonally opposite, her arms outstretched, palms flat against the walls.

'Are you okay?' I ask her.

She jumps at my voice, pushes away from the wall and grabs her bag, cradling it to her chest like it's a baby she needs to protect.

'Sorry, sorry,' I say, though I'm not sure what I'm apologising for. 'Are you okay?' I ask again.

'Yes, fine.' Though it's accompanied by a tiny shake of her head. She's still clutching her bag. Perhaps she thinks I'm going to mug her.

'You're British?' she asks, and it sounds like an accusation.

I nod, though I'm not sure our mutual nationality is the

number one priority right now. On the wall there's a digital panel that a moment ago displayed an arrow flashing rhythmically above a number. Now it's blank. That can't be good.

'It'll start up again in a minute, I'm sure,' I say, as much to reassure myself as her.

'How do you know?'

Her voice is sharp, and I try not to react. She's worried, that's all. I can't blame her for that.

'This building is really hi-tech. Everything's monitored. They'll have an engineer on it straight away. We'll probably hear from them any second.'

We both look expectantly at the control panel. There's a speaker set into the top, above the double column of buttons. A second passes, two, three. It stays silent.

'I'll ring the alarm to be on the safe side,' I say. I release the handrail. It's not as if the lift is going to plunge several floors just because I've let go of it. Is it?

I cross to the control panel, trying to look confident, and stab the button with the bell on it. Nothing happens. I press again and hold it down this time, count to three before releasing it.

'It's probably ringing in the control room,' I say. 'It's just that we can't hear anything here.'

I don't turn around to see whether she looks any more convinced by that explanation than I am. Instead I lower my head to the speaker. 'Hello?' I say, feeling foolish. Surely there's a microphone. There has to be; everything in this building is state of the art. But there's no reply.

'Is there a camera?' She's staring at me, that bag still clasped to her body. Something in her expression seems off in a way I can't quite identify. Could she seriously be worrying I'm going to make a grab for it if there's no surveillance?

I follow her gaze up to the ceiling. The spotlights glitter back at us. It's so small that at first I don't see it. But there, right in the corner: a disc extends from the ceiling, the sides finished in the same brushed metal as the walls of the lift. From beneath it protrudes a glass orb.

I point to it. 'They know we're in here.' I wave at the camera and smile, as if to prove I'm a good person, someone worthy of being rescued from a stuck lift. It's probably true of the other woman, at least.

'Is it working?' She takes a step closer. She's clutching the bag so tightly her knuckles are white against the leather. 'Shouldn't there be a light or something?'

I move back, closer to the camera, keeping the distance between us in a way I hope signals I'm not a threat. She's right, there's no light, but does that mean anything? I have no idea. I reach into my jacket pocket for my phone and hold it up. 'I'll give reception a call.'

I find the number in my contacts and press the screen to dial. There's a long pause in which I hold my breath. Then it rings, and relief floods through me. I smile across at the blonde woman. 'What's your name? I'll let them know you're in here too.'

'Pearl Associates. How may I help?'

I recognise the voice. 'Sheri, it's Cerys here. Don't laugh, but I'm—'

'Pearl Associates?'

'Hi, Sheri. Can you hear—?'

'I'm sorry, caller, I can't hear you.'

I take the phone from my ear and look at the screen. There's only one bar. I step to the other side of the lift and try again. 'Sheri, it's Cerys. Cerys—'

But she's gone. At the top of the screen, I see the time. Twenty-two minutes until the meeting. Unease settles like lead in my belly.

'There's hardly any signal,' I say, trying to reassure her, realising too late that I've probably done the opposite. I raise the phone towards the ceiling and squint at it. The single bar disappears altogether.

She watches me silently, but she's released the bag. It hangs from her shoulder, apparently no longer at risk. Maybe the phone call, unsuccessful as it was, has at least established my non-mugger credentials.

I circle the lift, my body turned away from her just in case she's still on edge. Three steps to the rear wall, three to the side, three to the front, and back again. I raise and lower the phone as I go. The bar is there, not there, there again.

Below the camera, we're back to one bar. I try again, but this time the phone gives up before it even rings, a dull beep that roughly translates as 'Not a hope in hell'. I bite back a curse.

'Do you want to try yours?' I ask, worried now. What if I'm stuck in here and Leo goes ahead with the meeting without me? What if he doesn't handle it right? What if Jay walks out of that door and...

'My phone's dead,' she says with a frown. 'I thought I'd charged it last night, but my adapter can't have been working. I tried to check my texts downstairs, but it wouldn't even switch on.'

The reminder of the scene in reception distracts me for a second. *We need to interrupt the cycle of negative thoughts*, that's what Dr Welmar is always telling me. So I pick up the thread.

'I saw you at reception. It sounded like you were having problems.'

She looks at the floor. 'It was a misunderstanding.'

'It's funny,' I say, 'two British women stuck in a New York lift. Sounds like the beginning of a joke.'

She gives the ghost of a smile, but her eyes are guarded. I can tell she's avoiding telling me what was going on. It piques my curiosity, so I persevere. 'You said you'd come a long way. You haven't flown all the way from the UK for a meeting?'

I note again the loose linen clothing, the long hair pinned up. That bag she's so worried about. I'd guess she's a few years older than me, and she doesn't look like the corporate type. But there's an air of determination about her that's at odds with her casual appearance. I remember the conversation in the lobby, and it occurs to me that perhaps she doesn't have an appointment after all. Not that it's any of my business. Sheri will deal with any unexpected visitors. Polite but firm, that's her style.

'How about you?' The question interrupts my speculation. 'Do you work here?'

She's trying to deflect, but that's fine with me. I nod, checking the phone again. Still no signal.

'Have you been here long?'

'A while,' I lie. Then, to put her off asking more, 'It's a great city.'

'Is it strange, though, working in another country?' She looks genuinely interested. 'I mean, do you work with any other British people?'

I force a smile. 'You'd be surprised. Pearl Associates bought up the firm I used to work for last year. We were based in London. Quite a few of us have come over since then. It's good for integration.'

I say the words as if they're my own, but I can see Grace now, leaning back in her chair as she made the case. 'It's a level down, but it's an expanding team. Good, interesting work.' The silver Montblanc pen twisting between her fingers. 'You could put all this behind you.'

The British woman is watching me intently. 'Lots of Brits here, then,' she says. 'And you're Cerys, did I hear that right?'

There's something in her expression that's a little weird. 'That's me,' I say, and offer my hand to shake. It's awkward, but no more awkward than standing there with her staring at me.

She takes my hand, grip firm. 'I'm Maeve,' she says.

SIX

LONDON AND BRISTOL

Maeve, sixteen years ago

Alistair was looking well. Really well. It made Maeve's heart swell to see it.

The café he'd picked was small and busy, oilcloth on the tables and a big whiteboard behind the counter listing jacket potatoes and variants on an English breakfast. Every so often a man in a white apron bellowed a number in the voice of an opera singer, and someone got up from a table with a look of delight, as if they'd just won a gameshow where the prize was cod, chips and mushy peas. No licence. No alcohol on the menu. It was a good sign.

'How's work?' she asked him.

'Good. Great, actually. If things keep going like this, I'm going to need another person. Long hours, too.'

He didn't need to say it; she knew what that meant. Coming home late, tired. No time to sit alone and remember. Things to look forward to. The anxiety she wore like a corset loosened a fraction.

He finished his chips and reached across for one of hers. 'But what about you and this Paul bloke?'

He was trying to keep his voice light, but it didn't work. She sighed. 'Please don't start with this again.'

'I'm worried about you, Maeve, that's all. What kind of shrink asks out his patients? There are rules about that kind of thing.'

She glared at him. 'He's a psychologist, not a shrink.'

'Same thing. And it's not on.'

'I told you, he'd already referred me to someone else.'

Alistair rolled his eyes. 'Yeah, right. And I wonder why he did that.'

It was sweet, really, she told herself, that he was questioning her like this. It showed how far he'd come that he was able to worry about her, confident enough in his own judgement to query hers. But she didn't have to put up with it, all the same.

'Look, Ali, I don't need your permission to see someone. I had two appointments with Paul. Two, that's all. We'd already agreed I wouldn't see him again, and we went for a coffee. We got on. We got together. It's not a big deal.'

'But you're over there all the time. Every time I call you, you're there. I don't even know anything about him.'

Perhaps this wasn't the time to tell him she'd as good as moved in. Instead, she said, 'What would you like to know?'

'How old is he?'

She hesitated. 'Forty-six.'

'You've got to be kidding me.'

'Oh come on—'

'What do you mean, "come on"?' He held his hands out as if expecting the answer to drop into them. 'He's old enough to be your dad!'

She stared at him, jaw tight, daring him to continue. But he knew better than to go there. He passed his hand across his forehead. 'Look, I know I'm a useless brother, but I'm your brother all the same. I just don't want to see you get hurt.'

Something inside her softened. 'You're not useless. But you don't need to worry about me, I promise.' She reached out and squeezed his hand. His fingers were greasy from the chips.

She smiled. 'Let's change the subject. Tell me what Kirsten's been up to.'

She saw him considering whether to let it go, but the lure of complaining about his least favourite flatmate was too strong.

'Jesus,' he said, 'have I told you about the hair in the shower?'

Later, on the platform at Paddington, he pulled her into a hug. 'Just take care of yourself, Maeve,' he said. 'This Paul guy. I know you think it's okay, but I don't like the sound of him. Promise me you'll be careful.'

She held on to him for a moment, enjoying the scent of his freshly laundered clothes. Then she pushed him away. 'Don't worry, little brother,' she said with a smile. 'He's the one who needs to be careful.'

Something shifted in his expression. 'That's what I meant,' he said.

It was dark by the time she got off the train at Temple Meads. Paul had offered to meet her at the station, but she'd put him off, telling him there were signal problems and she wasn't sure what time she'd get in. She didn't want to start giving in to that kind of thing: she'd always looked after herself, and that wasn't about to change. No matter what Alistair thought, she was in control. She was going to make sure it stayed that way.

She called in at the off-licence on her way back, buying a bottle of red twice the price of the kind she'd get for an evening on her own. Paul had been used to the finer things, she knew that from the comments he made now and then. But that was before he was paying rent as well as a mortgage, before whatever else he gave that woman every month. And still it wasn't enough for her. Still she wouldn't let him go.

Back at the flats, Maeve turned her key in the lock and crossed the concrete-floored foyer, placing the bottle on the bottom step as she took a mirror from her bag. She checked her eye make-up and added an extra smear of lip gloss. Then she climbed the stairs and let herself in.

He was there the moment she stepped across the threshold, so fast she knew he'd been waiting for her. And as he pulled the door shut behind her and pushed her against it, his hands in her hair and the hardness in his jeans against her stomach, she knew: whatever he'd given up, she more than compensated for it.

She looked out towards the horizon. The sea sparkled in the sunshine, but the waters were deep, too deep to see what was below the surface. She didn't want to go in, but that didn't matter. Paul was next to her and they didn't need to leave the beach. It was warm here, and safe. But that bee – where had it come from? It buzzed in the air near her face, but she was too tired to lift her arm and wave it away. Buzz, buzz. She had to make it stop. With an effort, she raised her hand—

Her fingertips brushed something flat and cold, and in an instant she was awake. She pulled back her hand from the glass of water she kept on the nightstand. It was lucky she hadn't spilled it. The mattress shifted as Paul turned to the other side of the bed. The buzzing of his phone on the bedside table came to an abrupt halt.

'For God's sake, Bethan,' he whispered fiercely, 'it's three in the morning.'

Maeve rolled towards him, but he was already getting out of bed. He turned back to her, flapping his hand in a gesture that told her to stay where she was. She sat up, indignant.

'You can't keep doing this,' he said, more softly, and Maeve rolled her eyes. Apparently, his wife disagreed. This was the third early hours call that week. Paul had urged Maeve to be patient, telling her Bethan was upset. *Fragile*, he'd called her, as if she was a bird with a wounded wing, not a grown woman who got pissed and embarrassed herself by phoning her ex in the middle of the night.

He left the room and she could hear him pacing in the hallway, sentences cut off before they got anywhere. Bethan was crying, probably, trying to get under his skin. For a psychologist, Paul seemed amazingly susceptible to his wife's tactics. Maeve had tried to point out that she was manipulating him, trying to make him feel sorry for her. Guilty enough to go back. 'You should just put the phone down on her,' she'd told him. 'Make her realise it's not going to work. It's the kindest thing in the long run.' But he wouldn't do it. He still wanted to be the good guy, she supposed, that was all it was. Still believed there was some way for him to get everything he wanted: his new life with Maeve, and a comfortable equilibrium with an ex-wife and kid happy to accept that the marriage had simply run its course, that there was no blame on either side.

She listened to his voice rise and fall, trying to ignore the hollow feeling in the pit of her stomach. She was the one Paul had chosen, she reminded herself. They had a connection – he'd recognised it (so he'd said) the moment they met. He wasn't going to turn his back on that for some woman who called up half-cut at 3 a.m.

No, she didn't need to worry. Bethan was history. And it was high time she realised that.

SEVEN

NEW YORK

Now

Eleven minutes before the meeting. I'm feeling sick, and I can't afford that. At any minute this useless, pointless, stupid, crock-of-shit elevator might finally decide to move, and then I'll have to be there, in that room, on my game. Assertive but kind, firm yet reassuring. Calm. Chilled as a bloody ice cube.

Oh God, I wish I had an ice cube. On top of everything else, it's getting hot in here. The other woman, Maeve, looks like she's feeling it too. The neckline of her linen top has developed a crinkled patch at the front where she keeps pulling it away from her chest.

I hold up the phone again. The single bar is back. I select 'PA Reception' from my contacts and stab at the screen once more. I've lost count of how many times I've tried.

Maeve has given up watching me. Her bag lies beside her on the floor, one hand resting lightly on top.

The phone is ringing. 'Hello—'

I cut her off. 'Sheri, just listen. It's Cerys. I'm supposed to be meeting Leo at eleven, but I'm stuck in the lift, and I keep losing the signal. Tell him if I'm not there, he needs to postpone. Tell him not to talk to Jay without me. Have you got that, Sheri?'

There's silence. I snatch the phone from my ear and stare at the screen. No signal. Somewhere in that monologue I've been cut off.

'Shit!'

Maeve looks up, surveys me mildly. 'They can't blame you for being stuck in here,' she says.

I shake my head. She doesn't understand that I'm not worried about getting into trouble. It might even be a relief if they sacked me. I could finally give up pretending everything's okay and go and hide under a rock somewhere. Perhaps that's what I should have done in the first place.

'Have you tried texting them?' she asks.

'The number I've got is a landline.' But then her words sink in, and in a flash I realise what an idiot I'm being. 'But I could email instead. The message might get through when the signal is stronger.'

I tap out an email, not bothering to correct the typos. As long as it can be understood, that's good enough. Every second I haven't pressed 'send' is a second when the signal could be strong enough for it to pass through the ether. I finish typing and press the little grey arrow. The image changes and I see the word 'sending' in red. Seven minutes to go. I force myself to tear my eyes away.

'Sounds like you're missing something important?'

My smile is like elastic. I feel it reach its limits and snap back. 'I haven't missed it yet.'

She turns to the control panel and presses the button with the bell again. 'Hello? Hello?' She waits, but it stays silent.

I say again, 'They might be able to hear us, even if we can't hear them.' I stand next to her and lower my head to the speaker. 'Can you get a message to Leo Kliver at Pearl Associates? Please tell him Cerys is stuck in the elevator and it's looking like I won't make it to the eleven o'clock meeting. Tell him I'll rearrange it as soon as possible, but not to go ahead without me.' I pause. 'That's really important. He mustn't hold the meeting without me. Please pass it on. Thanks so much for your help.'

I keep my ear to the panel, hoping for some kind of acknowledgement. Nothing.

I look back to Maeve. The nervous energy of earlier has gone, but she's looking rough, there's no two ways about it. She's pale, and there's a sheen of sweat on her brow.

'How are you feeling?' I ask. 'It's a bit warm in here.'

She nods, and I see her throat move as she swallows. If only I had my own bag with me, I'd at least be able to offer her the battery-powered fan I carry around. Summer in New York isn't like it is in London. Some days, it's like walking around under a hairdryer. I'm not built for it. It doesn't look like Maeve is either.

'I don't like small spaces,' she says.

I hope the horror doesn't show on my face. The lift will be moving again soon, it's bound to be, but the last thing I need is a claustrophobic companion freaking out on me before it does. I need to be calm when I get to that meeting room, ready to talk everything through in a measured way, to keep the emotional temperature nice and low.

'Try not to worry,' I say, scanning the ceiling in case there's some kind of ventilation shaft. There's always a hatch in films, isn't there? But the smooth metal surface is giving nothing away. 'We'll be on our way any moment, I expect.'

'I might just sit down for a minute.'

She slides down the wall, her eyes half-closed. It feels uncomfortable, looking down at her, so I bend my knees and follow suit, resting my back against the side of the lift. I look up at the camera in the corner. They'll be able to see Maeve is ill, surely. It will make them hurry. They won't want her becoming unwell. That kind of thing can be expensive here.

'It won't be much longer, I'm sure,' I say again. Her eyes are shut, and she doesn't reply. I can hear her breathing. I wish I had some water to give her. And I wish I hadn't thought that: now I'm noticing how dry my own tongue is.

'Are you over here for long?' I ask, hoping to take her mind off things. She shakes her head, says nothing more. The silence fills the space between us. Somehow it makes everything worse, emphasises how alone we are. 'Have you got family to get back to?'

The personal question slipped out; I shouldn't have asked it. I am careful, usually, about such things. Ask about someone's life and you invite them to reciprocate. 'It's okay,' I say, hurrying to repair the damage, 'we don't need to talk.'

But it's too late. 'No family,' she says. Then, inevitably, 'What about you? Are you married?'

I hesitate, but then, 'No,' I reply. 'I was going to be, but it didn't work out.'

The words take me by surprise. Why did I tell her that? But I know the answer. It's been so long, and I've been so alone. And then Matt calling last night, that almost overwhelming temptation to talk, to share how it's been these last few months. It feels good to tell this woman something real; there's the tiniest sense of something loosening.

She's opened her eyes. 'That sounds hard,' she says.

That flash of human empathy. I feel something inside me respond, like a flower turning towards the sun. Would it be so wrong to enjoy it, just for a few minutes until the lift starts moving again? Until I have to put the mask back on?

'It wasn't a big deal,' I say.

'I doubt that's true.' There's compassion in her voice. Or perhaps I imagined it. I'm not sure I care about the difference.

'Why don't you tell me what happened?' she says. 'It's not like you're going to see me again.'

I haven't come all this way to let down my guard – but surely it wouldn't hurt to talk a little? Not with this woman who knows nothing about Holbrooke and Dean, who can't connect me to what happened there. No way of putting the pieces together the way my colleagues here could do. Just a friendly ear for a few minutes before we go our separate ways.

'Please,' Maeve sighs. 'I could do with thinking about someone else's problems for a change.'

She looks so ill. It would be a kindness to distract her.

'I'm not sure I know where to start,' I say.

*

NEW YORK

Maeve, now

There's no need to panic.

I was ready. Focused. Certain that no matter what happened, it would be over today.

And now I'm stuck here. So close, yet not close enough. For a moment, when I heard that woman's accent, I even wondered – but no. I was too keyed up. Too ready to react, to jump at shadows. Perhaps this is for the best. A pause. A chance to regroup before the final step.

She's talking now. She was asking questions, so I did the same. The best way to deflect attention from yourself is to ask about the other person.

I am surprised to find her voice soothing – it's been a long time since anyone talked to me like this. The sense of companionship is skin-deep, but it's no less seductive for that. After today, I won't experience it again.

I let her words wash over me, try to steady my breaths. In, pause, out, pause. I reach out, touch the bag, reassure myself of its presence.

Don't worry, Ali. It won't be long now.

EIGHT

LONDON

Nine months ago

I've thought about this a lot, when it started to go wrong for Matt and me. If you asked him, he'd say it was later. He'd probably say I pushed him away when everything happened. Perhaps I did, but the truth is the rot had set in long before that. He knows that too, but telling the truth would make him look bad, and that's not the kind of thing Matt does.

But I think it all started that autumn, the conference he went to in Edinburgh. We'd been living together just over a year and a half by then, engaged for fourteen months. We hadn't set a date for the wedding, but I told myself that wasn't a problem. The takeover had been completed a few months earlier and we were both busy at work, wanting to show the new bosses we were worth keeping. There wasn't any rush.

The conference was a two-day thing, scheduled to finish early on the second day so all the Sassenachs could get their trains and be home in time for dinner. Matt had told me Alistair was going too, but that didn't worry me. It had been a long time since Alistair and I had worked together, longer still since I'd done the thing we didn't talk about. He'd never referred to it since, and I saw no reason he'd feel the need to unburden himself to my fiancé. But even so, when Matt got back that evening, and I'd ordered the takeaway – his favourite curry, an unspoken apology for having got home too late to cook – and he was ensconced on the sofa, remote control in hand, he said the words and something inside me vibrated with the understanding that, somehow, all was not well.

'That Alistair Douglass is a bit of a weirdo, isn't he?' he said, flicking through the channels too fast to see what was on any of them.

'Oh?' I said, wishing he'd slow down so we could actually pick something to watch. 'I've never thought so.'

He grunted. 'He was asking if we'd set a date for the wedding.'

I looked across at him, but he was staring at the television. 'Well, people do ask about that sort of thing when you're engaged, Matt. What did you tell him?'

'I said we hadn't settled anything yet, but it wasn't going to be a big thing, what with your family situation.'

'Okay,' I said; but there was the vibration again, my brain racing several steps ahead, seeing how the links might join together. 'So what was weird about that?'

'He said he knew about your mum. But I said your dad had passed not long afterwards, and he looked like I'd told him his house had burned down or something.'

Matt never referred to my parents as 'dead'. When we talked about them, which wasn't often and usually to do with some practical, wedding-related issue – who'd send out the invitations, that kind of thing – he used euphemisms like 'passed away' or, my pet hate, 'not around anymore', which made it sound as if they'd upped and abandoned me for a new life somewhere exotic.

But I had no idea why any of that would affect my former boss. 'What do you mean?' I asked.

'I don't know how else to describe it. He looked shocked. And I hardly got a word out of him afterwards. He just sat staring out of the window all the way from Newcastle. Like I said, weird.'

I stared at the TV, not paying attention to what was on the screen. I had no idea what it meant. Perhaps Matt had imagined it, but that didn't seem likely. He wasn't given to picking up on subtleties. If he'd thought something was up with Alistair, he was probably right.

'I think he's got a thing for you,' he said.

I snorted. 'Don't be ridiculous. I've known Alistair for years.'

'And you've never – you know.' He was looking at me now, male pride roused at the scent of competition. 'Not even a casual thing? I wouldn't mind if it was ages ago,' he lied. 'I just want to know.'

I got up from my chair and joined him on the sofa, snuggling into him in a way I hoped was reassuring. 'No, never,' I said firmly. 'I didn't date people at work until you came along.'

I felt him relax and he kissed the top of my head. 'Because I was irresistible.'

'Because you were persistent.'

I lifted my face and kissed him on the mouth, and we didn't talk any more about Alistair that night. But looking back, I think that was when the seed was planted. And when things started to go wrong, Elise was there to help it take root.

NINE

NEW YORK

Now

Maeve is looking at me through half-lidded eyes.

'There's not much to tell,' I say. 'We worked at the same place.'

'In London? What was his name?'

And suddenly there's an alertness to her, as if the answer matters. Unaccountably, it makes me uneasy, and I hesitate – but there's no need to keep it a secret. 'Matt,' I say, wondering if she'll ask for a surname.

But her eyes close again and she smiles. 'An office romance.'

'I'm afraid so. I'd been working there for eleven years when he joined the firm. I'd never gone out with anyone from work before. I tried to keep that side of my life separate.'

'But he swept you off your feet.'

I can't tell whether she's laughing at me. 'I think I was lonely.' The words are out before I realise I was thinking them. It's something about being here, in this small space, the time trickling away.

I'm going to miss the meeting with Leo and Jay, I know that now. Perhaps that too is contributing to my sudden candour. The knowledge that everything may be about to fall apart, and there's nothing I can do to stop it and there's nothing I can do to stop them.

Maeve says, 'I know how that feels.'

I look up at the corner of the lift, where the camera is. Is anyone listening to us? Maeve's head is tipped back against the wall, her skin an unhealthy shade of grey in the stark lighting. Someone earwigging on my embarrassing relationship stories is the least of my worries right now. I need to keep talking, keep her mind off being stuck in this breathless box.

'He asked me out four times before I said "yes",' I tell her. 'I was flattered that he kept trying. We went for dinner, and it was fun. We had plenty to talk about. It was easy to be with him. A few months later the lease was coming to an end on his flat and I had plenty of space, so it made sense for him to move in. He proposed on our first anniversary.'

Maeve raises her hand wearily and plucks at the front of her shirt. 'That's pretty quick.'

'I suppose so. My parents were together less than a year before they married. That didn't end well either. I guess I should have learned from their experience.'

Something passes across her face, as if she's in pain; but it's gone so fast I might have imagined it. 'It's not easy to learn from our parents,' she says. 'So when did it go wrong for the two of you?'

I try to order the narrative, work out how to tell the story so it stays away from the thing I can't think about. I'm afraid that if I get close to it, I won't be able to step away in time, and then all this effort I'm making to keep everything together will be for nothing, and it will spill out, wet and stinking, contaminating this place I want to be new and unsullied.

'I think he got bored,' I say. 'Not just of me. He wanted

promotion, but there weren't many opportunities. The firm wasn't big enough. Dead men's shoes, you know? He started to resent it.'

Maeve nods. 'Sounds like he was hard to live with.'

It's true, but it's not the whole story. 'I wasn't exactly a picnic, either. I had some difficult stuff going on at work.'

'And he didn't support you?'

'He tried to, but I couldn't talk to him about it.' I realise she might misunderstand me, and I add quickly, 'I mean, it was confidential. It wouldn't have been professional.'

I wonder if she understands this any better than Matt did. 'Why do you have to be so secretive?' he'd demand. 'It's not like I'm going to tell anyone. Besides, they probably *expect* us to talk about things like this.'

He never understood what my job was like. As director of HR, I had to be trusted to keep certain things private. Anyone having a problem with a co-worker, an illness affecting their work, a request for a raise, a discreet warning about internet use – all these were my domain. How could I tell him things about people who were his colleagues too? Even if he'd been the soul of discretion – which he most certainly was *not* – I couldn't have people worrying they might be the subject of our pillow talk. I had to be above suspicion.

And of course, when it came to Alistair, I had even more reason to keep my mouth shut.

I look across at Maeve. She's still pale, but her skin isn't sweaty any longer. Perhaps talking like this really is helping.

'Matt didn't get it. He thought I didn't trust him. It started to become a thing. He'd hear about something that had happened and he'd ask me about it. I'd have to tell him I couldn't discuss it, just like he knew I was going to. He'd get pissed off. I'd get angry. And by the time things got really bad and I needed him in my corner, he'd given up.' I take a breath before I can continue. 'He was seeing someone else behind my back.'

Maeve doesn't say anything. Her eyes are still closed; maybe she's asleep, or just stopped listening. It makes it easier to keep talking.

'I knew her too, the other woman. That made it even worse.'

I stare down at the floor. It's covered in a thin carpet with a small geometric pattern. Shades of grey repeating over and over.

'When I found out is when I realised it was over. Not because I was angry and humiliated, although I was. Maybe those feelings would have faded in time. But he betrayed me. I knew there was no coming back from that.'

Maeve isn't asleep after all. 'I couldn't agree more,' she says.

Silence falls between us, and this time I don't try to fill it. I pull out my phone and look at the time: 11.06. And even though I thought I'd already resigned myself to this, something cold turns over in my gut.

Leo will have got the message, I tell myself. *And even if he hasn't, he won't have the conversation without me. He'll have told Jay we need to rearrange. It's going to be all right this time. Nothing bad will happen.*

I look up at the glassy orb in the corner of the lift. It looks back at me blankly. That's when I hear the shriek of metal against metal, and the bottom falls out of my stomach as the lift drops.

TEN

BRISTOL

Maeve, fifteen years ago

Maeve scraped the plate into the bin. The chicken slid through its pool of congealed sauce, disappearing into the folds of black plastic, leaving a yellow smear in its wake. Asparagus spears and new potatoes followed. Two and a half hours of cooking, the first time she'd ever tried to make a meal like this, something properly grown-up, and everything was ruined.

She threw the plate into the sink on top of the one that was there already, half-hoping it would smash. There was a clatter, but it didn't break. From the other side of the wall, she could hear Paul's voice murmuring on. If he'd heard the evidence of her distress, he obviously didn't care enough to end his call.

It was another twenty minutes before he returned to find her sitting at the table, all traces of what had been supposed to be their romantic meal cleared away. He rubbed his palms over his face. 'I'm sorry, Mae,' he said. 'She was in a state. I couldn't just hang up on her.'

She didn't answer. They'd had this conversation too many times.

He pulled out the chair opposite her and sank into it. 'I'm worried about what this is doing to Anna.'

How about what it's doing to me? she wanted to cry. But she knew she wasn't supposed to think that way. Maybe if she'd seen the psychologist Paul had tried to set her up with, she'd be handling all this so much better. She'd never contacted him, though. She'd told herself Paul had wanted her more than he'd wanted to treat her; wasn't that proof that there was nothing wrong with her?

'It's a crucial time for her,' he continued, his brow furrowed.

'She'll be fine, Paul.' She tried to keep her voice low, soothing. 'It's her last year of uni. She has so many other things to think about.'

'That's what I'm worried about. How is she supposed to concentrate on her finals when her mother's falling to pieces?' He pinched the bridge of his nose. 'Bethan said she's talking about packing it in.'

Maeve shook her head. 'She won't do that. And how do you know that's even what she's thinking? For all you know, Bethan could be making it up.'

He looked up sharply. 'She wouldn't lie about something like that.'

Of course she wouldn't.

'I just wish she'd talk to me.'

'She's upset, that's all. She'll come around. Just give her time.' He didn't reply, and Maeve reached for his hand. 'We can't go on like this, Paul. I know it's hard, but we have our own lives too. Bethan calling you all the time, upsetting you like this. It needs to stop.'

He pulled his hand away and got to his feet. 'I need some air,' he said.

. . .

She was still awake when he came to bed. She turned towards him and nuzzled his neck, reminding him why he was there. He rolled over to face her and she hooked her leg over his hip, bringing him closer. He pushed her onto her back and then his tongue was in her mouth, and it was as good between them as it always was.

'Say it,' she said as he moved inside her, needing to hear the words.

'I want you,' he said. 'Only you.'

And then the phone on the bedside table began to buzz.

It was still dark when she slipped from the bed, just enough light creeping around the edge of the curtains to make out the lines of his face. His eyes were closed, lips slightly parted. He didn't stir as she collected her clothes from the chair, but she went to the bathroom to dress anyway, not wanting to risk waking him.

In the kitchen she found an old envelope and wrote a note for him on the back. With any luck it wouldn't take long, and she'd be back before he even saw it. But she wasn't going to hide what she was doing. He was too tender-hearted to do what was necessary; she should have realised that long ago. She'd speak to Bethan herself, sort this out properly, one woman to another.

She'd only been to Paul's old house once, waiting in the car while he dashed in to collect books and papers. The time had been carefully chosen in the expectation that Bethan would be out, and that had suited Maeve just fine. Until that moment, she'd resolutely avoided looking for photographs of her, even steering clear of that new website, the one where you could look up people you used to go to school with; and if Paul had taken any family pictures with him when he'd moved out, he'd kept them out of sight. It wasn't that she wasn't curious, but something deep in Maeve understood that it would be better to keep Bethan an unformed presence in her life, a shadow that could prompt neither comparison nor sympathy. And yet, when Paul had pulled the car up outside the neat white semi, with its block-paved driveway and planters outside the front door, the desire to see the woman who'd lived there with him had struck her with a force that was almost physical.

It hadn't happened, though. He had returned no more than five minutes later, a carrier bag stretched with books and folders in each hand. He'd driven away fast, as if leaving the scene of a crime. The urge to see what Bethan had looked like hadn't left her since, but she'd been successful in suppressing it. Well, she wouldn't need to do that any longer.

In the hallway, she took Paul's keys from the hook beside the door. She didn't want him waking too soon and overtaking her in the car. She didn't much like driving herself, and she wasn't sure that Paul's insurance covered her anyway. That was probably something they should talk about. Sharing a car was the sort of things couples did.

Outside, the air carried the chill of dawn and she wrapped her jacket more tightly around her as she walked. It was too early yet for most commuters, too early for parents taking their children to school. It occurred to her that Bethan might still be in bed, sleeping off the effects of the night before. Well, she'd just have to wake her up. Give her a taste of her own medicine.

It was hard, unfair almost, that in finding Paul she'd let another person with a drinking problem into her life. And when Alistair finally seemed to be getting himself together too. But, she reminded herself, nothing worth having ever came cheap. She'd have to be strong just one more time, and Bethan would be out of their lives for good.

There were only a few houses in his street and there was no sign of life at any of them. She turned into the driveway and strode straight up to the front door. To one side there was a small plastic button in a brass surround. She pressed it but didn't hear anything, so she grabbed the knocker over the letter box and rapped it hard against the wood.

Her eyes wandered to the planters on either side of her as she waited. Crocuses raised their golden heads above the frozen soil. Bethan would have planted them, she was sure. She couldn't see Paul doing anything so middle-aged as gardening.

She turned back to the door and knocked again. There was no sound of movement inside. It was just as she'd thought: Bethan was dead to the world. She could bang a hole in the door and the woman probably wouldn't hear her. She tapped her foot. Maybe she should go home, try again another time. But no. She'd come all this way. She wasn't leaving before she'd said her piece.

She reached into her pocket and lifted out Paul's keyring. His car key, a silver Chubb – for the back door, perhaps – something small that looked like it might open a padlock, and two brass Yales. She selected one of the Yales and pushed it into the lock. It turned smoothly.

The door swung open into a small hallway with a floor covered in terracotta tiles. Maeve looked back over her shoulder. The street was still deserted. She stepped inside and closed the door behind her with a gentle click.

ELEVEN

NEW YORK

Now

We're falling.

I scream, a note of terror so shrill that even in the moment it draws me up short. And as I tell myself not to lose it, there's another sound, a long metallic scrape. It's followed by a crash, and I'm thrown forward and then back again. My head strikes the wall behind me hard, and I see flashes of dark and light.

Everything is still.

I can't move. I can only sit here and listen to my ragged breathing. In and out, the oxygen streaming into me as if I've run a marathon. Slowly, I raise my hand to my tender head. It hurts to touch, but my fingers are dry. No blood. No lump that I can feel.

Cautiously, I straighten my neck and look around me. Everything looks as it did before. Everything except Maeve.

She's bent over, her head between her knees, hands clawed in her hair. I'm about to crawl over to her when white noise erupts from the control panel. I scramble to my feet and rush to the speaker, pressing my face against the metal.

'Hello?' I shout. 'Can anyone hear me?'

There's another crackle of static.

'Hello? Hello?' I slam my hand against the wall. 'You need to get us out of here!'

Silence. I press the button with the bell on it again, holding it down. 'Do you hear me? Is anyone there?'

But there's nothing, not even static.

'There's no point.'

Maeve has raised her head from her hands. I look down at her and almost recoil in shock. Her skin is grey and there are beads of moisture on her forehead. Her lips are edged in white, as if all the blood has drained away.

'It doesn't matter if they can hear us,' she says, and I'm alarmed to hear the whistle in her voice. 'They know we're in here. We can't tell them anything that's going to get us out any quicker.'

Her words may be calm, but I see the tendons standing out like cords in her neck. She reaches into the oversized shoulder bag on the floor next to her, pulls out a clear plastic bottle and holds it out to me.

Water. *Thank God.*

I unscrew the top and hand it back to her. She tips it up and I see her swallow twice, three times, before passing it back to me. 'Want some?'

I take it gratefully and have to stop myself from gulping down more than a mouthful. Who knows how long we're going to be in here – as long as we don't plummet to the ground before they get us out.

'Thanks,' I say, pointing to her bag. I force a laugh, trying to cover up my fear. 'I don't suppose you've got an emergency ladder in there too?'

She doesn't smile. 'What do you think is going on? Could it be terrorists?'

'No, I can't imagine—' But I stop. Who would have imagined such a thing any of the times it's happened? I try to remember the other tenants in the building. There are other consultancies, though they all have names like Bloggs and Partners, and I don't know what kind of work they do. There's an insurance firm. Some sort of think-tank. An advertising agency. Would they be targets? Or could the building alone, the capitalist symbol of its multi-storeyed granite and steel splendour, be target enough?

Maeve takes another sip from her water bottle. I want to tell her to stop, but I keep quiet. I won't add the worry of dehydration to everything else.

'I need to get out of here,' she says. She's not looking at me, is staring at the wall of the lift. Her fingers flex, curl into fists, flex again.

'Try not to think about it,' I tell her, as if that's going to help. 'Let's talk about something else.'

But her eyes remain fixed ahead. 'I need to get up there.'

'You will,' I say, trying to reassure her. 'They'll get us out soon.'

Now one of her hands has slipped beneath her other sleeve, her fingers circling her wrist. Back and forth, she twists them, back and forth.

I bite my lip, searching for something to say. My mind has gone blank.

But then her hands stop moving and she turns to me. 'Tell me about your family,' she says. 'Are they in Britain? Do you miss them?'

The abruptness of it throws me. It's as if some switch has been thrown inside her, brought her back to herself. It's a little eerie, but I go with it. What else can I do?

'I miss them very much,' I reply, and although my throat

closes around the words, it isn't the way she's probably imagining.

'Did they get on with your ex?'

'They never met him.' She doesn't say anything to that. 'I think my mum would have liked him, though. She always had a soft spot for a charmer.'

If she notices the past tense, she doesn't comment.

'He phoned me last night.' It must be the shock of the falling elevator that's doing this, making me overshare this way. It's shaken everything loose, like a bottle of fizzy drink with the cap popped off. I suppose it doesn't matter. What does she care anyway?

'You mean Matt?' she asks. 'What did he want?'

'I think...' *Come on, you know what you think.* 'I think he might want us to get back together.'

'Don't do it,' she says. And although that whistle is still there, her voice is firm.

'I'm not going to—'

'You're thinking about it. I don't even know you and I can tell. Don't do it.'

I know she's stressed, but I bristle all the same. Who is she to tell me what to do? And although I have no intention of letting Matt back into my life – no, not even though I'm so lonely sometimes it's as if my insides have been scooped out with a spoon, as if I'm not even a real person anymore, just a sad, pale phantom people can look straight through – what makes her an expert on our relationship?

'You've only heard my side of the story,' I say, swallowing down the irritation. 'If you talked to Matt, you might feel differently. You might be telling him to stay away from me.'

'You said you needed him, and he wasn't there for you. It doesn't matter what else happened. You felt like you were on your own.' She turns to me, and her eyes are blazing. 'You can't stay with someone like that. Someone who breaks their promises.'

I look down and see her fists are clenched, her knuckles white. And suddenly I'm no longer sure that it's Matt and me she's talking about.

TWELVE

BRISTOL

Maeve, fifteen years ago

The house was still and silent around her, as if holding its breath. The air carried a faint scent Maeve knew only too well. She wrinkled her nose in disgust.

Opposite the front door, a staircase with white banisters led to the first floor. She stood on the bottom step and called up. 'Hello? Hello?'

She waited for the running footsteps, the shriek of horror, the demand for her to explain why she was trespassing. But there was nothing. Bethan must have gone out after all.

In front of her, a short hallway ran alongside the staircase towards the back of the house, a half-open door at the end. To her right, another door. She shouldn't do it – but she was here now. What harm would it do to look around? She pushed the door to her right gently and stepped through.

At first the room looked ordinary: a cream three-piece suite, a low coffee table in the middle, pale blue curtains at the bay window. An oak sideboard stood against the far wall, a collection of framed photographs on top. But the smell was stronger here. Her eyes scanned the room a second time, taking in the details she'd missed on the first pass. A wine bottle stood on the floor next to the sofa. An empty glass lay next to it on its side, a purple crust running from base to rim. There evidently hadn't been much liquid left when it had spilled onto the carpet. The stain was small but livid against the pale wool.

There was a telephone on the coffee table. So this was where Bethan had sat when she'd phoned Paul. Maeve could imagine it all too clearly. Bethan watching TV, some weepy film perhaps, feeling sorry for herself as she drained the bottle. Then picking up the phone, not caring what time it was, not caring that she had no right. That was what people like her did. They didn't think about anyone else. All they cared about was themselves.

The base of the phone sat empty on the sideboard. Maeve crossed the room and stared down at the photographs next to it. There were three in silver frames, another face down, patches of white fluff dotted across its velvet back. The one standing in the middle was a school photo, a slim teenage girl in a white shirt and green blazer, long dark hair curled over her shoulders. She was smiling, a little self-conscious, a dimple on her left cheek. This, then, was Anna.

The photo must be a few years old; Paul's daughter was, Maeve knew, only a few years younger than her. Paul had looked embarrassed about that when he'd revealed it. But as she'd said to him then, what did age matter? This girl didn't look much like him. The dark hair was his, maybe, something in the shape of the eyes.

The photo on the right showed an older couple holding a baby. Grandparents, perhaps. On the left was an image of a young girl, laughing up at the camera as she kneeled on the floor, her arms around the neck of a dog with shaggy fur. The hair, the eyes, the dimple on her left cheek: Anna again, perhaps eleven or twelve this time.

Maeve reached out for the frame that was face down, half-knowing already what it would show. Sure enough, it was a wedding photo, taken outdoors, the happy couple standing beneath a tree. She pulled it towards her, drinking it in. There was Paul, smart in a grey suit and silk tie, a ruffled triangle of handkerchief sticking out of the top of his breast pocket. He was looking down at his new wife, his face wreathed in smiles. And even though the longer hair and smooth cheeks belonged to a man twenty years younger than the one who shared her bed, she felt something stab at her insides.

The woman next to him was blonde, hair a shade lighter than Maeve's, the strapless gown she wore displaying upper arms with a hint of extra flesh. She was pretty, with the same dimpled smile as her daughter. She was laughing up at Paul as she held his hand. They looked happy, the pair of them. When had that changed?

Paul had been wearing his wedding ring the day he'd asked Maeve out. He hadn't tried to disguise it. At the end of their second session together he'd announced simply that he thought she'd be better served by another psychologist, a specialist in anger management. She'd been surprised, remembering what he'd said before, that he thought they'd work well together. But as he passed her a card with the name of another doctor, he said, 'I'm about to finish for the day. Fancy joining me for a drink?' His tone had been casual, but his eyes met hers as he spoke, and suddenly it all made sense.

She'd hesitated, but only for a second. There was something about him, a combination of the known and unknown that intrigued her. At their session he'd asked her about her family, and this time she'd talked about Alistair, about the worry she carried around with her, that at any moment he'd slip from the tightrope he walked and fall so far and so fast she couldn't catch him. He'd asked about her parents too, but she'd answered with as few details as possible, and he hadn't pressed. Even so, something in the way he'd listened as she told him how responsible she felt for her brother, how she'd always needed to stand up for him, told her he guessed enough. She wondered whether his own father had been like hers; or perhaps it was simply that he'd heard her story too many times before.

They'd gone to a wine bar at a hotel around the corner. Over drinks, he had talked more than she had, perhaps feeling there was a deficit to be filled. He apologised for inviting her, asked her not to think badly of him. 'I couldn't help myself,' he said. 'I related so much to what you were saying.'

It was his wife, he'd told her. She'd always been fond of a drink, but in the last year or so it had gone beyond that. He'd started dreading going out with her, made excuses not to accept invitations from their friends, worried that she'd go too far. Once, he said, she'd fallen into a table and broken a vase that had been a family heirloom. Another time, she'd vomited in a neighbour's garden pond. He'd tried to get her to seek help, he said, 'But she tells me I'm overreacting.'

Now, Maeve peered more closely at the woman in the photograph, trying to imagine her heaving into a pond. She supposed she should feel sorry for her, but she could still smell the alcohol on the carpet and all she felt was revulsion. It was the daughter she pitied; but at least Anna had her grandparents. She replaced the photograph face down, the way she'd found it.

At the back of the room, patio doors led to a garden. To their left, a second door was closed up tight. Maeve paused with her hand on the doorknob, listening. Nothing. She twisted the knob and stepped through into a large kitchen.

This, she imagined, must have been what attracted them to the house. It was bright and spacious, a glass-ceilinged area at the end, perhaps a later extension, a dining table and chairs bathed in sunlight. A family home. Contrary to what she'd expected, it was clean and tidy. She opened cupboards, inspected the contents of the fridge. A half-empty bottle of milk next to two full bottles of white wine, a carton of yoghurt, a few tomatoes in the salad box. Nothing to make a proper meal.

She found the empties in a recycling bag tucked down between a pedal-bin and the wall. She lifted it onto the worktop and counted them out: four wine bottles, a small flat bottle of vodka, three beer cans. Perhaps Bethan mixed it up once in a while. Or perhaps she'd had company.

Maeve replaced the bottles and cans and put the bag back where she'd found it. Crossing to another door, she found herself back in the hallway. There was a cupboard under the stairs, and she opened it. Carrier bags hanging on hooks. A vacuum cleaner and a clothes dryer. An iron tucked onto a small shelf. Everything was neat and orderly. *A functional alcoholic*, she thought. Bethan was trying to keep it together, perhaps hoping Anna wouldn't notice what was going on when she came home.

She looked down and a breath caught in her throat. Three pairs of wellington boots stood in a line. One large enough for a man, a few splashes of dried mud on the toes. The other pairs were smaller, one black with a buckle around the calf, the other lilac. They huddled together, unbearably intimate. She closed the door on them and headed for the stairs.

At the bottom, she slipped off her own shoes so as not to leave marks on the carpet and padded softly upstairs. On the left of the landing, a single door stood open. To the right, three more, all shut up tight. Maeve took the one on the left and stepped into a bedroom.

The room was in semi-darkness, a gap between the curtains Bethan hadn't bothered to open properly. The bed was unmade, the duvet pushed back to reveal a crumpled sheet. And here was the smell again, stronger this time: the stale odour of alcohol distilled through the pores of human skin.

This, then, was the bed Paul had shared with his wife. Who could blame him for wanting to leave it?

She turned slowly, taking in the rest of the room. The furniture was similar to that downstairs, modern, pale oak, well-made but bland. She opened the wardrobe and gasped.

She'd thought Paul had cleared out his clothes when he left, but apparently she'd been wrong. About a quarter of the space was taken up by men's shirts, jackets, some kind of hanger draped with ties and belts. Shocked, she turned to the chest of drawers next to it. The top drawer was women's underwear. She pushed it shut again quickly, but not before she'd seen scraps of silk and lace at one end, kept apart from the everyday cotton. *She wore those for him.*

The next drawer held more women's clothing, the same for the one beneath. But the bottom drawer contained more of Paul's things. T-shirts on one side, jumpers on the other. There was room left over – presumably he'd grabbed a few things from the top. But why had he left so much behind? She'd have to talk to him about it, find a way to raise the subject. He needed to clear out his stuff properly. Leaving it here like this would be giving Bethan false hope, fuelling her fantasies of a reconciliation.

She was about to push the drawer back in when she froze. A noise – running water. She straightened, her heart thudding. But everything was quiet again. It must have been the central heating, water trickling through radiators.

She'd seen enough. It was time to go.

She closed the wardrobe doors and scanned the room, checking she'd left nothing out of place. Out on the landing she pulled the door behind her, leaving it open the same distance as it had been when she arrived. Bethan had probably been too out of it this morning to notice any difference, but it didn't hurt to be careful.

From behind one of the closed doors came the sound of a toilet flushing.

She swung around, the blood leaping in her veins. Was there time to make a run for it? Get back down the stairs and through the front door before she was seen?

But along the landing a door was already opening, a figure in a bathrobe with tousled blonde hair emerging before her. The sight brought a sudden calm. This was what she had come for, after all.

'Hello, Bethan,' she said.

THIRTEEN

NEW YORK

Now

We need air.

Or rather, Maeve does. I can hear her wheezing softly in the corner. Her eyes are screwed up tight, her shoulders tense. I expect she's trying to imagine being somewhere else, somewhere spacious and cool. I hope she's succeeding.

I look at the ceiling for about the fiftieth time. The polished metal surface is divided into nine panels, one spotlight in the centre of each. One of the panels must surely be a hatch, but I can't tell which. And even if I could, I don't know how I'd reach it. The lift is about seven feet tall, and the only thing to give me a boost is the handrail that runs along the back wall. It's cylindrical, brushed metal, less than a couple of inches across. There's no way I could balance on that.

If Maeve could just hold my weight, or perhaps she could balance on my shoulders – but that's not going to happen. The way she looks right now, I'd be surprised if she could stand at all.

'It's not terrorists,' she says, her voice sharp. It catches me by surprise; I'd thought she was miles away. 'It's not,' she says again.

'Okay,' I say, hoping to sound soothing.

'The security gates weren't working.'

She looks at me as if she's challenging me to argue. I expect it's her way of hiding her fear. I keep my voice low, calm. 'You think it's connected?'

'You said everything in this building was controlled by technology. Perhaps something's gone wrong with it. Some kind of bug in the system.'

'A virus, you mean?' It makes sense, but that still doesn't mean someone didn't put it there deliberately.

'Or a crossed wire. A fault somewhere.'

I frown. 'Surely there'd be fail-safes?'

She doesn't reply, and I'm annoyed with myself. I can see what she's trying to do: if she identifies the problem, she can imagine the solution, how long it might take them to get us out, to get somewhere she can breathe again.

'I expect you're right,' I say, trying to backtrack. 'Maybe we just have to wait for them to switch it off and on again.'

She stares at me, as if unsure whether I'm taking the piss. But then I see her breathe deep (another whistle, which I try to ignore) and she gives me the ghost of a smile. 'You've worked in an office too long,' she says.

I smile back, wanting to keep her talking. 'You may be right about that. I came to Holbrooke and Dean straight after uni.'

She raises her eyebrows, and I imagine what she's thinking. That I'm too cautious, too unimaginative to try new things. Or perhaps that's only what I've thought so often myself.

'I liked it,' I tell her truthfully. 'And I've moved around departments, done different jobs.'

'What do you do now?'

'HR,' I say. 'Recruitment, training, that kind of thing.' And other things too, but I'm not going to talk about those. 'But I started out as an environmental consultant.'

'What made you change jobs?'

'I did a project with HR. They were reviewing the induction programme and I was asked to help. I was new enough to remember the process, established enough to know the company. They agreed with my recommendations, made some changes. I think that's what made the difference.'

Maeve looks at me shrewdly. 'You thought if you worked there, you'd be the one making the decisions.'

I nod. 'That's the problem with being a consultant. You do all this work, and you tell clients what they should do, and then you move on and you never know what happens afterwards.'

'Didn't you have to retrain?'

'Yes, but I enjoyed it. I carried on working while I studied. My boss was very supportive.' The words slipped out unthinkingly, and from nowhere I feel a stab of pain. *Alistair.*

'Are you okay?'

Maeve is looking at me curiously. I realise if I answer her, I'm going to start crying. I turn away, but these shiny surfaces offer no privacy. She waits silently.

I take a few deep breaths. *Your thoughts create your feelings*, I remind myself. *So think of something else.*

I turn back to her. 'I'm sorry,' I say. 'I think being stuck in here is getting to me more than I realised.' I look up at the camera. Maybe they can see us, even if the microphone isn't working. 'You need to get this thing moving,' I say, enunciating clearly, hoping they can read my lips. 'It's as hot as hell in here.'

'Take this,' Maeve says, holding out the water bottle. 'Have another drink.'

I take it from her and swallow, trying my best to push the memories back down deep where they belong.

'Anyway,' I say, desperate to think of something else, 'Enough of all that. Isn't it time we talked about you?'

She closes her eyes again, and now I feel she's shutting me out deliberately. 'I don't think so, Cerys,' she says. 'There's really nothing to tell.'

FOURTEEN

BRISTOL

Maeve, fifteen years ago

Maeve tried to slide the key into the lock on the door of the flat, but her fingers trembled and it skittered across the surface. She took a shuddering breath and then a second. She had to keep it together. If she kept it together, everything would be all right.

She raised the key again, but before it reached the lock, the door was swinging inwards. Paul stood there, waving a piece of paper in her face.

'What the hell do you think you're doing?'

His anger flicked a switch inside her, the armour clanging into place, covering the soft places. 'Can I get inside before you start shouting at me?' she said, pushing past him into the narrow hallway.

He followed her, still clutching the note she'd left behind. 'You took my bloody keys! I was going to come and stop you, but I couldn't find the keys!' He looked at her sharply. 'Tell me you didn't take the car. I've told you, I need to change the insurance before you can drive it.'

She took the keys from her pocket. 'Is that really what you're worried about, Paul? No, I didn't take the car.'

She headed to the kitchen and filled the kettle at the tap.

'I can't believe you went over there,' he said. 'What the hell were you thinking? What did you say to her?'

She placed the kettle on its base and flicked the switch. 'For God's sake, calm down.'

'Calm down? What do you mean, "calm down"?' He'd gone red, and a vein was bulging at his temple.

He's not himself right now, she thought. *This isn't the man I did this for.*

'She wasn't there.'

He deflated, as if someone had pulled a stopper out of his backside. With a sigh of relief, he sank into a chair. 'Thank God for that.' But then he looked at his watch. 'Then where have you been? You've been gone ages.'

'I went for a walk. Thought I'd stretch my legs.'

He was re-reading the note she'd left. 'So you didn't speak to Bethan?'

'I've told you I didn't. Anyway, I was glad in the end that she wasn't home. It needs to come from you.'

He nodded, conciliatory now. 'You're right. I've been putting it off, and I'm sorry.'

How many times have I heard that? Maeve wondered. But the disbelief must have shown on her face because he got to his feet, adopting the stern expression of someone who meant business. 'I won't go over there now if she's out. But I'll do it this evening. Make sure she understands the way things are.'

Her mind was racing as he moved towards her, wrapping her in an embrace. 'I *will* do it, Mae,' he wheedled.

He held her and pressed his lips to hers. But when he tried to deepen the kiss, she pushed him gently away. 'Thank you,' she said softly. 'I know this is hard. But perhaps it's not the right time, after all. For you to see Bethan, I mean.'

He raised his eyebrows quizzically. 'But I thought—'

'She was the worse for wear last night, wasn't she? If she's had to go out today, she'll be feeling it. She won't be in the right frame of mind for a sensible conversation.'

He frowned. 'If I have to wait for her to be calm and sober, it'll never happen.' But she detected the edge of relief in his words. The confrontation would have been too much for him, she'd been right about that.

She buried her face in his chest. 'Just give her another day. There's no point trying to talk to her if she's got her head down a toilet bowl.'

Except that wasn't where her head would be. She squeezed her eyes shut, as if that could block out the image.

His arms tightened around her. 'You're too good for me,' he said, but she knew he didn't mean it.

'I know,' she said, and did.

She'd thought she wouldn't sleep that night, but by ten thirty her head was so heavy on her shoulders she could barely hold it up. It was the stress, probably; all day long her nerves had been stretched so tight she could hardly breathe. Every sound had her jumping, and twice she went to the front door, convinced she'd heard a knock.

'Are you all right, Mae?' Paul had asked the second time. 'You seem on edge.'

She'd got a grip of herself after that, slipping out to the kitchen while he was reading through case notes, taking the half-empty bottle of wine from the fridge and drinking it straight down, not bothering with a glass. *Careful of that*, said a voice inside her head. But she knew she didn't need the warning. Her father might not have given her much, but watching him had taught her one thing: she'd never leave her self-control at the bottom of a bottle. It was a pity Alistair hadn't learned the same lesson – but things had been different for him, she reminded herself. It wasn't his fault.

Paul had followed her to bed expectantly, but she'd put on her least alluring pyjamas and kissed him chastely on the cheek, declaring herself exhausted. If he was disappointed, she didn't see it. She was unconscious almost as soon as her head touched the pillow.

She woke early, sleep leaving her as abruptly as it had arrived. There was a cold hard pebble lodged somewhere in her chest. She watched herself in the mirror as she cleaned her teeth. She should look different, she thought. There should be some mark of what she'd done. But if it was there, she couldn't see it.

When Paul got up, she half-expected him to announce he would be leaving immediately; but his eagerness to confront his wife had apparently departed in the night. Yesterday, she'd wanted to delay him. Now, she yearned for it to be over. She considered prompting him, but every time she tried to say the words they lodged in her throat. No, it was surely better to wait. Let him think she'd forgotten all about it.

The day dragged. She wanted to leave the flat, get out into the open where she could breathe. But what if news came when she wasn't there? She couldn't afford to miss it. She drifted from room to room, opening windows, unable to settle. Eventually, in desperation, she reorganised the kitchen cupboards, taking everything out and cleaning the shelves with antibacterial spray and scouring pads, scrubbing until her fingers were raw.

She was putting the mugs back, lining them up neatly so the handles were all facing the same way, when the doorbell buzzed.

The mug she'd been holding fell to the floor, the handle catching the edge of the worktop as it went down, slicing it clean through. She stared at the fragments on the lino. Paul called out, 'Are you all right?', his voice mingling with the buzzer as he pushed the button to unlock the entrance to the flats. She tried to speak but no sound came. An echo from outside, heavy footsteps on the concrete stairs, the click as Paul unlatched the front door.

'Dr Morgan,' said a voice. And she knew they'd come for her.

FIFTEEN

NEW YORK

Now

I check my phone again: 11.24 and still no signal. If this lift is the only problem in the building, Leo could be talking to Jay right now.

Maybe he didn't get my message. Or maybe he did, and he's decided to ignore it. He'll think he can handle it, that I'm worried about nothing. Or perhaps he's got wind of what happened in London – it's possible, after all, despite Grace's promises. And if so, he'll probably think I shouldn't be doing this job at all, not after what I did. Maybe he's right. Either way, there's nothing I can do about it now. Not until this lift starts moving.

Maeve hasn't said a word since I said we should talk about her instead of me. I'm more certain than ever that she hasn't got an appointment. She's probably worried I'm going to ask her why she's here. That I'll tell security to escort her out the minute the doors open.

I eye her speculatively, and I remember her words when the lift stopped. 'I have to get up there,' wasn't that what she said? Whatever she's here for, she thinks it's important. But she doesn't look like our usual clients, not with those clothes, that aura of focused intent. And then, at last, it dawns on me, and I wonder why I didn't see it immediately: she's an activist. Someone wanting to protect great crested newts or lesser spotted woodpeckers on a site we're assessing. Concerned we've been paid to tell the authorities what the developers want them to hear.

No wonder she's being evasive. Maybe I should ask her about it, let her know she needn't worry that I'll get her chucked out. Like she said, she's come a long way. And I'm impressed she's put herself out for a cause she believes in. It's strange, though; I'd have expected a UK project to be run from the London office. The developer must be American, someone who already has a relationship with the team here.

Some of the colour has returned to her cheeks. Maybe staying quiet is better for her after all. Perhaps I've been kidding myself that I've been trying to take her mind off things. The truth is, it's my own mind I'm worried about. Sitting here in the silence, it's all too easy to start thinking of things I'd rather forget. Like Matt. Like Alistair.

Like trying one more time to pinpoint the moment it all began to go wrong.

LONDON

A year ago

Ever since their conversation on the train back from Edinburgh, Matt had had some kind of bee in his bonnet about Alistair. It didn't help that Alistair was behaving oddly too. I'd see him from time to time, in the staff kitchen or passing in a corridor. Usually, we'd exchange a few pleasantries in the way of people who have a history and no regrets about leaving it behind. But a few days after he and Matt had returned from the conference, I strolled into the kitchen to see him with his back to me, rinsing his cup at the sink. I called out my usual greeting and he jumped so hard the water arced through the air and splattered the worktop. I made a joke about it, but he just mumbled something and left. He hadn't even dried his cup.

I toyed with asking if I'd done something to upset him, but it felt too awkward so instead I told myself I was imagining things. That evening, when I met up with Matt to go home, I made the mistake of mentioning it to him, and the bigger mistake of hinting that perhaps he was to blame – that maybe he'd said something tactless to Alistair and he'd taken offence.

'So he's arsey with you and it's my fault?' he spluttered as we reached the lobby doors, irritable, and not entirely without cause.

'I just don't get it,' I said. 'What exactly did the two of you talk about? You said he asked about the wedding. I don't see what could have annoyed him about that. You didn't say anything about the guest list, did you? Tell him he wasn't invited?'

He sighed. 'I told you. I said it was going to be a small thing, but he was all right about that. I explained it was because of your mum and dad being – you know.'

He shifted uncomfortably, the way he always did, as if my dead parents were some kind of personal failing I should be embarrassed to have pointed out to me. I bit down the familiar surge of annoyance.

'So what did he say to that? Come on, Matt, there must have been *some*thing. He's being really weird.'

'No change there then,' he said, but when he saw I wasn't

going to bite, he gave another exasperated sigh. 'I don't know. I mean, I got the impression he thought it might have been recent, your dad, you know...'

I couldn't help myself this time. 'Dying,' I said.

He nodded unhappily.

'I told him it was ages ago, not long after your mum passed. He asked me if he'd been ill.' Matt wrinkled his brow, trying to remember. 'I told him it was an accident.'

We were nearing Charing Cross by then and I had to stop talking to navigate a crowd of grey-haired couples dressed up for the theatre.

By the time we'd got to the other side, Matt's attention was elsewhere.

'Have we got anything for dinner,' he said, 'or do you fancy YO!?'

I tried to forget about it as we sat at the conveyer belt, watching the brightly coloured plates of sushi circulate in front of us. But as Matt complained about every other dish involving aubergine, my mind kept returning to it, picking over the scraps.

I wondered if Alistair thought I should have told Matt about Dad: that excruciating day we'd had what I still thought of as The Conversation. It hadn't seemed like an omission at the time. I'd already had to turn myself inside out, expose too much that was bloody and raw. I doubt it even crossed my mind to mention the accident. Alistair didn't need to know every detail of my life; he was my employer, not my priest. Besides, I'd been concentrating too hard on keeping the tears under control to think about much else.

Thirteen years ago, and I could still remember how I'd felt sitting in that chair, desperate to appear composed and capable, like someone who'd made a mistake but with the best of intentions, someone who still had something to offer.

He'd taken pity on me then, but perhaps now he thought he'd made a mistake.

Perhaps that conversation with Matt had made him think I'd been keeping things back deliberately, that even when honesty was the only thing I had left to save myself with, I hadn't been telling him the whole story.

I ran into him a couple of times after the incident in the kitchen, once in the lift lobby, once as I was leaving for the day. Neither was the right time or place to ask him what was going on – or that's what I told myself anyway. It was obvious from the way he scurried off that he didn't want to talk to me. He wasn't dishevelled, exactly; but there was a looseness about him, something a half-step removed from his usual poise.

The second time, I thought I caught a whiff of alcohol as he passed.

I pretended I was mistaken, but I should have done something about it there and then. I was the HR director, after all.

More than that, I'd been his friend. If anyone should have seen it, had a quiet word, it was me.

But I put it off.

I let things go too far.

And that's why I'm here, in this *fucking* lift, and it's all too late for both of us.

SIXTEEN

BRISTOL

Maeve, fifteen years ago

Afterwards, Maeve would find it hard to remember exactly what they'd said. It was as if the voices of the police officers were coming to her from underwater. She watched their lips moving, and she gave a little start when Paul cried out; but the details were blurred, dreamlike.

He'd been more upset than she'd expected. She'd realised, of course, that it would come as a shock. He'd been married to Bethan, after all. But she'd expected part of him to have been, if not happy, at least relieved. Grateful that they could move forward in their new lives without his wife's unhappiness like a millstone around their necks. She'd even imagined that, when the dust had settled, she might tell him the truth, and he'd understand, and she wouldn't have to carry the weight of another secret all alone. But that was never going to happen, she saw that now.

He'd jumped up from the sofa when they told him. 'Anna,' he said. 'Oh God, Anna.'

One of the officers, a woman – did they always send women for jobs like this? Maeve wondered – stood too.

'Miss Parry has spoken to your daughter,' the officer said.

Paul looked at her blankly. 'Siân knows?'

Siân, it turned out, was Bethan's sister. She'd been the one who'd found her. Anna, the female officer told them, had called her that morning from university, having failed to get a reply on either her mother's mobile or landline number. Siân had gone to the house that afternoon – other things to do first, perhaps; or more likely, Maeve thought, she knew her sister well enough to suspect an unanswered phone might mean a morning recovering from the night before. It was she who had called the police.

'Please take a seat, Dr Morgan,' the second officer said, and something in his tone made it clear it wasn't a request. 'If it's okay with you, we'd like to ask you a few questions.'

After they'd finished, it was Maeve who showed them out, who thanked them for coming. Her heartbeat had slowed by then, and she pitched it just right, she thought: the confusion, the shock, the earnest desire to do whatever she could to help.

'Thank you for coming, officer,' she said to the man – what was his name? Dickson? Dickenson? – and he smiled at her; but the woman paused in the doorway.

'We'll be in touch,' she said, in a way Maeve wasn't sure how to read.

When she returned to the sitting room, Paul was already on his phone, pacing up and down. 'She's not answering,' he said. 'I have to go over there.'

Maeve went to him, took his hand. 'Anna won't be there yet. She's probably still on a train. Wait a bit. You can't talk to her with the signal going in and out.'

But he wasn't listening. He shook off her hand, his fingers on his phone again. 'Siân? Siân, the police were just here—'

And then he dissolved, his shoulders shaking. Maeve stared at him, trying to ignore the loneliness that clamped an iron band around her heart. *It will be okay,* she told herself. *He just needs time.* She watched a tear drip from his chin, then she turned and went back to the kitchen.

She'd cleaned up the broken mug by the time Paul emerged, his eyes red. It had been good to have some time to herself: she felt better now, back on an even keel. Already, she looked back on the thoughts that had been tumbling through her head when the police rang the doorbell with surprise. It must have been the shock, she realised; she hadn't been thinking straight. There was no reason to think they would connect her to what had happened. Why would they?

'How was Siân?' she asked.

He shook his head. 'In pieces.' He took a shuddering breath. 'She blames me.'

'I'm sure that's not true,' she said, knowing it probably was.

'She said it was my fault Bethan was drinking. My fault and...' She saw him force himself to stop talking. He wanted to say it, she realised. *My fault and yours.* He was bursting with it. He thought if he shared out the guilt, he'd find the burden easier to bear.

'It must have been terrible for her, finding her sister like that.'

'She says Anna doesn't want to talk to me.'

'Oh, Paul.'

He leaned over the worktop, buried his head in his hands. 'She told me to stop calling her.'

'Perhaps that's for the best, just for now. Perhaps—'

'I'm her father!'

Maeve winced. The harshness in his voice, the anger that came from nowhere. And from inside her, even now, the answering chord of fear.

He looked up at her, eyes narrow slits between puffy lids. 'I'm sorry, Mae. I just... I want to be there for her. I can't stand it.'

He reached for her and she went to him, pulled his head onto her shoulder and let him sob. He needed her, she told herself. He was hurt, and he needed her.

He came up for air. 'Why were the police asking questions? That stuff about Bethan drinking, okay, I get that. But they said she fell, right? Why do they need to know where I was?'

Maeve shifted so she could look at him properly. 'They said it was routine. I expect it's just something they have to do.'

He studied the worktop. 'I keep remembering what she said.'

'What do you mean?' she said, although she knew. This was what she'd been waiting for since they left.

'DC Laker. About the b—' He broke off and cleared his throat. 'About how Bethan was lying.'

The silence between them stretched and swelled. She could hear the dull murmur of a TV in the flat above. Paul's fingers drummed against the wooden worktop. 'I don't want to, but I keep imagining it. And it... it doesn't make sense.'

Should she pretend not to understand? She watched her hand reach out and stroke his arm. 'What doesn't?'

'She was at the bottom of the stairs, right? But DC Laker said she was lying on her back.'

Her fingers moved gently over the cotton shirt. She could feel the warmth of the skin beneath, the heat of the blood flowing through his veins. How fast was it moving? How long did it take for someone to bleed to death?

'I don't understand,' she lied.

His brows knitted together, his gaze still fixed on the worktop. 'Her tripping and falling, I can see that. Especially if she'd been drinking. But she'd be on her front, wouldn't she? If she'd fallen as she came down the stairs?'

'Paul—'

'I mean, she'd be falling forwards' – he pulled away from her, holding out his arms, trying to demonstrate – 'she'd put out her hands to save herself—'

'Not necessarily.'

'I mean, that's what that policewoman was saying. I could tell, she thought something was wrong.'

'I don't think—'

'That's what those questions were about. Where was I, when did I last talk to her. They think it wasn't an accident.'

'Paul, stop!' She grasped his upper arms and stepped in front of him, forcing him to look at her. 'You're not making any sense. You've had a terrible shock, and your imagination is running away with you.'

He shook his head. 'You're not getting it. Just think about what I'm saying.'

'I know what you're saying—'

'If she slipped, she'd have fallen forwards.'

'Unless her foot slid out from under her.'

He frowned. 'What?'

'Like this.' She stepped back from him and mimed the action, leaning back as she kicked out with her foot. 'Maybe she was coming downstairs and misjudged the step, caught the edge with her heel and slipped.'

'But then she'd just slide, wouldn't she? I don't see how—'

'And she'd be lying at the bottom of the stairs, face up, just like they said.'

'But that wouldn't have been enough to—'

'Or maybe she twisted as she fell. Tried to grab a banister, or...' *Arms flailing, mouth stretched wide open, the anger turning to horror...* Maeve blinked, took a breath. 'We can't know what happened, Paul. But she was drunk, they as good as told us that. She was drunk and she fell. Don't torture yourself imagining it.'

He rubbed at his eyes, his shoulders rising and falling in a sigh.

'Why don't you go and lie down?' she said. 'Just give yourself some time to process it.' It was the kind of thing he'd say to her. 'I'll bring you a cup of tea.'

He nodded then and gave her a weary smile. He'd always expect someone to take care of him, she realised. She shouldn't get annoyed about that: it was a blessing, having a past that allowed you to think that way. Maybe when all this was over, it was a gift he'd pass on to their own children.

She watched him turn and head for the stairs. 'What would I do without you?' he said.

She smiled at his retreating back. 'You'll never have to find out.'

SEVENTEEN

NEW YORK

Now

Maeve is up and about. I think I preferred it when she looked like she was about to faint.

'It's too hot,' she says. She's said the same thing at least six times. The heightened colour I'd told myself meant she was feeling better has developed a hectic quality. Blotches of red stain her face and neck.

'Maybe it would be better to sit down,' I tell her. 'You'll just get hotter moving around.'

She doesn't answer, but she stops pacing. She reaches behind her head and unfastens the silver clip from her hair, placing the end between her lips as she drags her fingers through the honey-coloured strands. The hair at her temples is a shade darker, damp and frizzy with sweat. A few months ago, mine would have been the same. It's too short for that now.

She stabs at the camera with the end of the hair clip. 'Do you think they're watching us?'

I'm not sure whether she means the building maintenance people or the potential terrorists. 'I'm sure they're doing their best to get us moving,' I say, meaning the building people. I'm trying to reassure myself as much as Maeve.

'This is intolerable.' She's pulling her hair about, twisting it viciously into another chignon. 'I've got things to do. And you. Your meeting.' She cranes her neck towards the camera. I can see the tendons standing out beneath the mottled skin. 'Get us out of here!' she shouts.

There is panic in her voice and it startles me. What was it she said earlier? That nothing we could say would make them work any faster. It's being here, the walls too close together. It's getting to her.

I scramble to my feet. Two steps are all it takes to bring me to her side. I place my fingers lightly on her arm. This, I realise with a jolt, is the most human contact I've had for weeks. I pull back my hand.

'We'll be okay,' I tell her, and even as my lips are forming around the words, I know it's the wrong thing to say. She didn't say we wouldn't be, but now the suggestion is out there, the outline of it hanging between us in the heavy air.

She swallows. 'I really don't like small spaces.'

I look around the lift, hoping for inspiration. My eye falls on the crack between the doors. Should we try? Would it help?

'We could try to open the doors,' I say. 'If we can move them a bit, it might let in a draught.'

'What if the lift drops again?'

She's right, of course, it could be dangerous. But the idea of cooler air is irresistible. 'I doubt it would make a lot of difference,' I say. I sound more sure of myself than I am, and I tuck the observation away with a degree of relief: if I can do it with Maeve, I can do it with Leo and Jay.

I cross to the control panel and press the 'open doors' button. I wasn't expecting anything to happen, which is just as well because it doesn't. I step up to the doors and inspect the seam between them. There's a gap of no more than a couple of millimetres. I place my hands flat on either side, the metal cold against my palms. I try to pull my hands apart. Predictably, nothing moves.

I look back at Maeve. 'Give me a hand?' I ask.

She's wearing a doubtful expression, but she comes and stands next to me. I step to one side and stretch out both arms, my fingers pointing towards the gap between the doors. Maeve does the same, her stance a mirror image of mine.

'On three,' I say. Her fingernails are short and neat, I see, unvarnished. Mine are short and ragged, painted bright red in an attempt to cover up the damage. Looking at them now, I can see it was a mistake.

'Three,' says Maeve, and we both pull. I bend my legs and lean into it, but it's impossible to get a grip against the polished metal. My hands slide over the surface, leaving a moist smear in their wake. We reset our positions and try again. This time, it's Maeve who loses her grip. The long sleeves of her linen top ride up a centimetre and I catch a glimpse of silver at her wrist, a bracelet of some kind.

'This isn't going to work,' she says. I know she's right, but I want that air so badly now, I can almost taste it.

'Once more,' I say.

We place our hands against the doors again, our bodies turned sideways. I nod at Maeve. 'Go.'

This time we've both refined our technique. Our hands stay put, and for a brief, glorious moment I allow myself to believe it's working, that the gap between the doors is widening. But the next second, Maeve's hands slip, and as I watch her stumble backwards I lose my grip too. I fall hard, banging my coccyx against the floor.

'Ow!' I let all my frustration out in the cry.

Maeve has sat down as well, her body slumped at a weird

angle against the opposite wall. She looks done in. I shouldn't have asked her to help.

'Sorry,' I say, rubbing my sore back. 'I should have guessed we'd need something to pry it open.'

She exhales and I hear a whistle from her lungs. 'Worth a try,' she says faintly.

Her water bottle is on the floor near me. I pick it up and unscrew the lid, then shuffle over to her on my knees.

'Here, have some of this.'

She looks at the level of the liquid, and I can tell she's worried. Despite the way we've been rationing ourselves, it's going down fast.

'We won't be here much longer,' I say, hoping to God I'm right.

'We'd better not be,' she replies, taking a sip.

She passes the bottle back to me, but I screw on the top again before I'm tempted.

I swivel so I'm sitting next to her, but keep my distance. She doesn't need to feel any more hemmed in than she already is.

'You were cross about what I said before,' she says. I turn to her, not understanding. 'It wasn't any of my business. You and your boyfriend, I mean.'

I bite my lip. I hadn't realised I'd let my annoyance show. That's bad news: I thought I was better at covering up my feelings by now.

I sigh. 'You were probably right. I think he's only back in touch because things have gone south with Elise.'

'Is she the other woman?' She says the words as if they're in quote marks.

'That's the one.' I manage to keep my tone light. 'Sounds like it didn't take her long to get fed up of him.'

'The thing is,' she says, 'you know you can't trust him. You can't come back from that. Take it from someone who knows.'

I study her profile as she talks. There's something about her that's familiar. The line of her nose, the angle of her jaw. I try to put my finger on who she reminds me of but come up blank. Probably it's someone on TV. I watch a lot of that these days.

I say, 'You don't think it's possible to forgive and move on?'

'*Forgive?*' In her mouth it sounds like a curse. 'No, Cerys. Not if you have an ounce of self-respect. And if you think otherwise, you're deluding yourself.'

There's a sudden tension between us and I laugh to try and ease it.

'That sounds like the voice of experience.'

She fixes me with a stare that makes me feel like a butterfly pinned to a piece of felt. 'You could say that.'

EIGHTEEN

BRISTOL

Maeve, fifteen years ago

The black dress lay puddled on the floor. Maeve picked it up and shook it out, forcing the hanger into the shoulders. She'd bought it specially, spending money she didn't have, and for what? For Paul to decide at the final moment that he'd changed his mind.

They'd been about to leave when he'd spun on his heel, one hand held melodramatically to his forehead. 'I can't do this,' he'd said.

She'd thought he'd meant the funeral, but when she tried to tell him he'd be all right, that she'd be there to support him, he shook his head. 'I can't have you there,' he said. 'I'm sorry, Mae, it's just not fair to Anna.'

The hurt had stabbed at her insides, even though part of her was glad not to have to sit through the service. They'd have all been looking daggers at her, the sister and the daughter, everyone blaming her for what they thought had happened.

She'd said as much to Paul in the first place, but that was when he was still hoping for an immediate thaw in relations with Anna. 'But I *need* you there,' he'd said, 'I won't get through it without you.' And worried as she was, she'd felt the warmth of being wanted. Yet apparently, somewhere over the intervening weeks, with his daughter steadfastly refusing to answer his calls, Maeve had become dispensable after all.

She shoved the hanger back into the wardrobe, then picked up the phone from the bedside table. At least she'd have a few hours to compose herself before he got back. Her finger tapped out the number she knew by heart.

Alistair picked up straight away, sounding anxious. 'How did it go?'

'I stayed at home. I decided it was better.'

'Oh,' he said carefully. 'Whatever you think best.' He was handling her with kid gloves since their argument. He hadn't reacted well to the news that Paul was married, convinced she was setting herself up for a fall. She'd had to tell him in no uncertain terms that she was capable of making her own decisions. The subtext, *More capable than you are,* had remained unsaid, but he'd got the gist. They hadn't spoken for a week after that. That was a while ago, but they were both wary of reopening the wounds.

'Paul's still there,' she said.

'Right. How are things with the daughter?'

'Anna,' she reminded him. 'Much the same. I'm hoping it will get easier after today.'

'I expect it will.'

There was a pause. She could almost hear him trying out the words, wondering if there was a way of asking the question that wouldn't sound like an accusation. He'd come close the last time they'd spoken. *Did you ever meet his wife?* he'd asked. *No,* she'd replied. *Why would I?*

'So everything's okay, now?' he said. 'The police haven't been around again?'

'It's fine, Ali. The inquest is over. Accidental death. They wouldn't have released the body if there were any doubts.' He didn't reply, but she could feel his relief down the line. 'Tell me what's going on with you.'

She listened as he updated her on work, the plans to expand his team. He sounded so much happier now, she thought; he'd finally found his fit with this job. Once things had settled down with Paul, perhaps all three of them could meet up, the two men could get to know each other. Their family would finally start to grow instead of shrinking. The thought was like a little ball of sunshine in her chest.

'I need to get out of that bloody flat, though,' he said. 'Kirsten's doing my head in. She had her mates over again last night. Bottles everywhere this morning.'

'Bottles?' The word snapped her back to the present.

'It's fine, honestly. It was just the noise pissed me off.'

'You didn't—' And now it was her turn to pick her words carefully. 'You don't need to socialise with them. You know, if it makes you uncomfortable, perhaps you should talk to Kirsten—'

'I said it's fine.'

She bit her tongue. 'Okay then.'

'I'm going to find somewhere else.' She didn't reply; she'd heard it before. 'I *am* looking, Maeve.'

'I could come and help,' she said. 'Come to viewings with you, if you want a second opinion.'

'Sure. Great. That would be great. Only...' She waited. 'You do know it's expensive down here, right? I won't get anything like your place.'

Her flat. She'd barely set foot there over the last few months. It was silly, really, continuing to pay rent on it when she was here with Paul most of the time. She'd dropped a couple of hints to that effect, but he'd been too wrapped up in trying to make peace with Anna to pick up on them. Everything would be so much easier when he'd accepted his daughter wouldn't be part of his life anymore.

'But you're earning decent money now. We can make a proper budget, work out your disposable income. We'll find you something good. It'll be fun.'

She could feel her own enthusiasm building. It would be nice to spend more time together, doing something productive. Something that showed how far he'd come.

'The thing is, Maeve...'

She heard it then, the note of embarrassment in his voice. It reminded her of their father. 'What is it?' she asked sharply.

'I've got commitments.'

'What kind of commitments?' But there was a sinking feeling in her stomach. She already knew what kind.

'There are these guys...'

She closed her eyes. *Of course* there were. 'How much, Alistair?'

'I'm not asking you for anything. I'll sort it out myself.'

She breathed deep, counting to ten before she said anything she'd regret.

She got it out of him in the end, a figure that made her wince. His gambling had always gone alongside his drinking. She supposed she shouldn't be surprised. Their father had been the same, occasionally dragging Ali with him into the local betting shop, bullying him into picking a horse, a dog, his *lucky boy*, returning smelling of booze and false hope. Then later, the tension as he listened to the radio, the repercussions if his boy hadn't been so lucky after all.

It would never have occurred to her father to take Maeve on those outings. It was yet another way she'd escaped his notice. *It's not Ali's fault*, she reminded herself. The blame lay with their father, but she couldn't let his legacy carry on poisoning their lives – not now, when they both had so much to look forward to.

'We'll work it out,' she'd told him, and despite his protestations of self-sufficiency, she could tell he believed she would make everything all right. Now all she had to do was work out how.

Maeve was sitting at the table going through her budget when the door slammed. She looked up in surprise and checked the time on the laptop. Paul had been gone less than ninety minutes.

She went to meet him in the hallway. He was bent over with his back to her, untying his shoelaces.

'How did it go?'

He kicked off his shoes. One of them slammed into the skirting board and fell back to the floor. She could see a black mark left behind on the wood.

'How do you think?' He turned, shrugged off his jacket. His lips were set in a thin line. 'They all think it's my fault.'

She put her arms around him, but it was like trying to hug an ironing board. After a moment, she stepped away.

'How was Anna?' she said.

He shook his head, swallowed something down. 'She wouldn't even look at me,' he said. She reached for him again, but he pulled away. 'I'm going to lie down.'

She watched him go, his back stooped like an old man. *This is the worst part*, she told herself. *It will all get easier from here.* But she wasn't sure she believed it.

NINETEEN

NEW YORK

Now

'Do you want to talk about it?' She must do. No one says something like 'Take it from someone who knows' without expecting to be asked *how* they know.

Maeve's lips pull down in a little frown. 'You won't like it.'

Despite the sweat on my top lip, my parched mouth, I feel my curiosity rising. 'I won't judge,' I say, meaning it. God knows, I'm in no position to judge anyone.

She smiles as if she doesn't believe me. 'I was the other woman. And he wasn't just engaged. He was married.'

She's right, I don't like it. I'm not a prude; I realise some people find monogamy difficult. But you don't live through what I have without developing strong feelings about men who cheat on their wives. Strong feelings about the women they cheat on them with too.

She turns and catches my expression. Embarrassed, I try to cover it up. 'I know these things aren't simple,' I say, trying to sound worldly. But surely it *is* simple? He was married. She slept with him anyway. Unless... 'Did you know he was married?'

She nods. 'He wore a ring. He didn't try to cover it up. In fact, he talked about his wife the first time we went out. In a strange kind of way, it was what brought us together.'

I don't get it. 'How did you meet?'

A hesitation. 'He was my doctor.'

She looks up at me, and there's something sly in her expression. I feel a flicker of dislike. Is she trying to shock me? 'Right,' I say breezily, pretending she's failed.

'It's not as bad as it sounds.' I don't understand what she means, but she continues before I have a chance to probe. 'We got talking. We had a lot in common – or that's what I thought at the time. And he was good-looking. Older than me, successful. He asked me out and I didn't think twice about saying "yes". I thought it would be fun.'

Fun? I want to ask her. *Was it* fun *for his wife?*

'I was very young, Cerys,' she says. 'And his marriage wasn't in a good place before I came along. His wife – well, she was a troubled woman. I knew what it was like to have someone like that in your life. Someone who depends on you.' Her voice catches. 'I hoped we could depend on each other.'

I feel for her then, in spite of myself. I see how it would have been: a naïve young woman falling for an older man. God knows what he told her about his wife. *Troubled*, indeed. I suppose it's more original than *She doesn't understand me.*

'So what happened?' I ask.

She sighs, and I hear the wheeze at the edge of it again. We'll be out of here soon. I just need to keep her mind on other things until then.

'He left his wife.' She looks up at me and gives a wry smile. 'I know, that's not the way it usually goes, is it? At the time, I thought it was because he realised we had something special.

Now I think it was just easier. He was finding being married too much like hard work. Leaving her became the simpler option.'

'Did he move in with you?'

She shakes her head. 'I asked him, but he said my flat was too small. He rented somewhere close by, though. I spent most nights there. I thought when the divorce came through, we'd get somewhere together.'

I can see her disappointment, even now, after who knows how many years. They shape us, don't they? These failures. These betrayals.

'I was a fool,' she says, 'but I learned my lesson from it. Don't make the same mistakes I did.'

She looks like she feels she's said enough, but I'm caught up in her story. I want to know how it ends. 'Did he go back to his wife?' I ask.

Her fingers pluck at something beneath her sleeve. 'In a manner of speaking,' she says.

TWENTY

LONDON AND BRISTOL

Maeve, fifteen years ago

'At least there's room for a wardrobe in this one.' Alistair turned slowly, his hands on his hips, as he took in the grubby walls and low ceilings of the attic bedroom. 'And there's a view.'

Maeve joined him at the sloping skylight. 'As long as you don't mind standing on a chair to see it.'

He nudged her in the ribs, trying to make light of the unadulterated grimness. 'You speak for yourself, hobbit.'

It was the third flat they'd seen that day, and looking on the bright side was becoming more of a struggle with every passing hour. Broom cupboard kitchens with cabinet doors hanging at jaunty angles, bathrooms with death-trap wiring trailing from beneath the tub, bouncy floors and cardboard walls, smells of boiled cabbage and worse. The thin end of the London property market.

'How much did you say they want?' She turned to the letting agent with a glare.

He managed to keep a straight face as he gave the rental figure. Then, 'It's a ten-minute walk to the Tube. Move fast if you're interested. It'll be gone by the end of the day.'

She snorted, but he was probably right. 'Come on, Ali,' she said. 'Let's get out of here.'

There was a small playground at the end of the road, deserted except for a couple of teenagers smoking on the swings. They took a seat on a bench facing towards the road. Above the peeling railings, a line of grubby windows with yellowing curtains looked back at them.

'That last one wasn't so bad,' he said. 'It would look better after a proper clean.'

Maeve shook her head. 'I can't believe what they're asking. These people should be ashamed.'

'It won't be forever.'

It was what he'd said before. Just a few months, he'd told her, a year at most, and he'd have paid back what he owed. He'd have his salary to spend as he chose then, could put it towards somewhere better. But Maeve knew as well as he did that it didn't necessarily work like that. That the kind of people he was dealing with might decide to increase his repayments at any moment, tell him the interest was rising to reflect their inconvenience in having to wait so long for their money. She hoped she was wrong, but men like that – she'd seen too many of them. She had her father to thank for that.

'There'll be something better,' she said with a confidence she didn't feel. But perhaps she should be encouraging him to take the flat after all. Wouldn't it be better to get him away from Kirsten and her beery mates? Yet the idea of him there, alone between those sad little walls, his salary eaten up by the ridiculous rent on one hand and those crooks on the other – she couldn't bear it.

She linked her arm through his and gave it a squeeze. 'We'll find you something better,' she repeated.

On the train home, she pulled a scrap of paper from her handbag and did the sums again. But it was no good: she couldn't make them add up the way they needed to. The small amount she could afford to lend him wouldn't be enough to make a difference. That's why she knew he wouldn't take it. She'd have been able to persuade him to sacrifice his pride in exchange for getting those bastards off his back; it wouldn't have been easy, but she'd have done it in the end. But not for this. Not when the only hope was shaving a couple of months off the time it would take him to repay them.

Things would be different if she were sharing the rent with Paul. It was madness, carrying on like this. She'd been patient enough. She understood he'd been through a difficult time. And that police officer hadn't helped, dropping by all the time with her questions and hints, just 'double-checking' this, and 'wanting to be sure' that. But Maeve had supported him through it all, even giving him an alibi for the whole period. It had been useful for her too, of course, but they could both see that he was the one DC Laker had in her sights.

Detectives were supposed to have instincts, weren't they? Laker's might have been telling her something wasn't right, but that wasn't enough. She'd been warned off in the end, Maeve suspected, her superiors perhaps feeling she was losing perspective. Either that or her focus had shifted to another case. Whatever the reason, those semi-official visits had stopped. They'd not set eyes on her for weeks. The inquest had concluded, the funeral been and gone. Just some final bits of admin to do, and they could put it all behind them.

Admin. Her pen tapped against the scrap of paper. Bethan's will – or lack of it. It was time to give that more attention.

Maeve placed the flowers in the middle of the table and stood back to admire the effect. Tulips in an array of colours. Nothing too showy, just something to make it look nice. She'd chosen the meal on the same basis: lamb shank with potatoes and vegetables, slow cooked to tenderness. It wouldn't look like she'd spent hours in the kitchen, but it was still several steps up from the microwave ready meals they usually shared.

The aroma of roast lamb filled the flat by the time she heard Paul's key in the front door. She heard the murmur of his voice as she went to greet him: he was on his mobile. He raised a hand to her distractedly and continued his conversation. 'Eleven a.m.,' she heard him say. 'Okay, thank you. See you then.'

She looked up from laying the cutlery as he entered the room. 'Everything okay?'

He nodded, ran one hand through his dark curls. 'I need to see the solicitor tomorrow. Sort out probate.'

She positioned a fork neatly parallel with a plate. 'You're the executor then? I thought perhaps Bethan might have changed that.' Another thing her father had taught her: the administration of death.

He grimaced. 'Bethan hadn't made a will.'

The knife in her hand hovered an inch above the tablecloth. 'But you're still the next of kin. You'll be the one sorting everything out.'

'Yes, yes. I've had Siân on the phone about it all afternoon.'

'What's it got to do with her?' It came out sharper than she'd intended, and she moderated her tone. 'I know she's upset, but she can't keep taking it out on you.'

He puffed out his cheeks. 'Try telling her that.'

'Come and sit down,' she said. 'Dinner's almost ready.'

He dropped a kiss on her cheek. 'I'll get changed first. That smells amazing.'

She listened to him talk about his day as they ate. He didn't ask about hers, she realised; he never did. It wasn't that he was selfish, not really. It was just that whatever he was thinking about absorbed him so completely that he didn't have room for anything else. Not so long ago, it had been Maeve herself who'd commanded every bit of his attention. When all this was over, it would be like that again.

When she was clearing the table, she said, 'How long do you think it will take to get everything sorted?'

'I don't know.' He shrugged. 'A few weeks probably.'

She turned her back to him and piled the plates into the sink. 'Siân isn't going to make trouble, is she?'

He laughed without humour. 'She can try. The solicitor said it's cut and dried. There's an order of priority. Spouse comes before sibling.'

'Well, it's good that it's clear,' she said. She thought she'd done well to disguise the relief in her voice.

'It won't make any difference, anyway. There's no will, so everything comes to me automatically. Because' – his voice cracked suddenly – 'because we were still married,' he finished huskily.

'I see.' She looked at his wobbly lip and couldn't help herself. 'Do the police know that?'

His head jerked up, and he blinked the moisture from his eyes. There. That had put a stop to his slide into sentimentality.

'What do you mean?'

'I was wondering if that's what was bothering DC Laker.' She stared back at him innocently. 'It's just as well I could tell her you were with me the whole time.'

The tears had vanished as soon as they'd appeared. His eyes glittered. 'That was more convenient for you than it was for me.'

Inside her, something sharp-toothed and dangerous opened one sleepy eye. 'How's that exactly?'

'Well, I was actually here the whole time, wasn't I? Which makes one of us.'

'Is that right?' She kept her voice level. 'Because if I wasn't here, Paul, how do I know that you were?'

For a moment, they simply stared at each other. The sharp-toothed thing flicked its tail. *No*, she told it. *Not this time.*

She smiled at Paul. 'Let's not be silly, darling,' she said.

There was a beat before he nodded. 'Sorry,' he said. 'It's been a long day.' But there was something about the way he looked at her that she didn't like.

TWENTY-ONE

NEW YORK

Now

Maeve catches me looking. 'Have a drink,' she says, pointing to the water bottle. It's good of her. Every drop she spares me is one she can't have herself.

'Just a little, then,' I say. 'Thank you.'

It's nearly quarter past one. Two hours and twelve minutes since my meeting with Jay and Leo was supposed to have started. Two hours and thirty-eight minutes since I stepped into the lift. It feels smaller now, even to me. How much worse must it be for Maeve, claustrophobic and breathless? She's handling it well. I admire her for it, even more because I can see what it's costing her to stay in control.

'What should you be doing now?' Maeve asks. 'If we weren't stuck in here, I mean.'

I check my watch, even though it's been only a minute since the last time I did that. 'Lunch break, probably,' I say, 'as long as there wasn't anything kicking off.' My stomach clenches. What if Leo has spoken to Jay after all? What if there *is* something kicking off right now, and I'm stuck in here?

'It's just the technology,' Maeve says, and I realise she thinks I'm worrying about our earlier conversation, the prospect that we're hostages in the midst of some terrorist act.

At least that wouldn't be my fault. The thought shocks me – but it's true. Some ridiculous part of me really would prefer marauding terrorists to that conversation taking place without me there. Because stupid and selfish as it is, at least an act of terrorism would be out of my hands. And because if it goes wrong for Jay like it did for Alistair, if it goes even a fraction as wrong as it did for him, I don't think I'm going to be able to live with myself.

LONDON

Eight months ago

It was a Tuesday when Roberto called me into his office. I remember because it was the day after the regular 'start the week' meeting he'd instituted, one of the myriad new management get-togethers that were apparently a feature of life under Pearl Associates. The former chief executive had retired four months earlier, a decision rumoured to be not entirely voluntary, and Roberto had been installed as the new broom. I didn't dislike him exactly, but I was wary of him. Receiving the summons, I had clicked instantly back to the file I'd opened the previous day, filled with my notes on the various topics on which he'd sought an update, hoping to look suitably switched on and responsive, and like an HR director who very definitely deserved to remain in her job.

I held my tablet in front of me like a shield as I stepped into his office. He was sitting at his desk and didn't stand as I came in, just waved me to the chair opposite.

'Good to see you,' he said. It was his usual opening. I liked it the first time I heard him say it. That was before I'd worked out he used it instead of *How are you?* so he didn't need to pretend to care about an answer. 'I'm afraid I've got a difficult issue to raise with you.'

He didn't smile and I felt my stomach lurch. Had Matt been right after all? Was this where I was given my marching orders in favour of some smooth operator from the New York office? 'Go on,' I said, sounding – I hoped – cool and professional.

'It's about Alistair Douglass.'

I felt my mouth go dry. Alistair had said something after all. My mind raced. Should I try to plead my case? Did I have any leverage? Were they going to offer me anything to go quietly?

'We've had a complaint from a client,' Roberto said.

'What?' I stared at him dumbly. 'About Alistair?'

He sighed. 'Douglass had a meeting with Ted Harvey. You know him?'

I nodded. Harvey and Sons was a development company and one of our longest-standing clients. We didn't have royalty amongst our clientele, but Ted Harvey was about as close to it as it got.

'Ted came to see me afterwards. Said Douglass turned up late and was – what is it you Brits say? "The worse for wear".'

I frowned. 'Is it possible he was mistaken?' I like to think if Alistair had heard that, he'd have realised I tried to stick up for him. The attempt might have been feeble, but I tried.

Roberto gave me a pitying smile. 'Ted said he smelled of alcohol.'

So I'd been called in because Roberto wanted to talk tactics. He was Alistair's line manager, so he'd have to hold a meeting with him, read him the riot act and try to find out what was going on. I felt a glimmer of hope: I could be useful, take the chance to show Alistair I was on his side. If he'd been drunk in front of a client, it would mean a formal warning, there was probably no avoiding that – but I could let him know it was coming, give him time to prepare himself, work out how to handle it for the best. And I could find out what was going on with him, help him to sort it out if I could.

'You've scheduled a meeting?' I asked. I tapped the screen of my tablet, ready to make a note of the date and time.

'I haven't scheduled anything.' I looked up at him in surprise. 'I want you to do it.'

I sat up straighter. 'Right, well, it's usually better coming from the line manager...' I tailed off as I saw his expression. 'I can do it, of course, if that's what you prefer.'

'Good.' He tapped the fingers of one hand lightly on his desk. 'This isn't going to be a problem, is it?'

I frowned. 'In what way?'

'I hear that you and Douglass are friendly.'

I took a moment before replying. 'Not particularly. And in any case, that doesn't come into it. This is a professional matter.'

'I'm glad to hear it. Because I expect him to be given a firm message.'

Then give it to him yourself. But I bit my tongue. 'Of course.'

He smiled then. 'I knew I could rely on you. Our people are our most important asset...' I saw him fumbling to remember my name. 'I don't want to come in and be Mr Bad Guy, but I will if I have to. If there's dead wood here, we need to cut it out. Free up space for new people.'

I gritted my teeth. 'I'll talk to Alistair, make it clear this isn't acceptable. But he's one of our best consultants. I wouldn't want to lose him.'

He hadn't liked that 'but', I could tell. I'd been docked a point in his mental scoring system. I left him already tapping away at his keyboard, ignoring the enquiring gaze of his secretary, Elise, on my way out. It was she, no doubt, who'd told him I was friends with Alistair. I plastered on an expression of supreme indifference, refusing to give her the satisfaction of seeing me rattled.

Back at my desk I considered my strategy. It would be best to get it over with quickly – but should I speak to Alistair in private before I scheduled the meeting? There was a time when I wouldn't have thought twice about that, but things had changed. He might not see that I was trying to help – and besides, I needed to tread carefully. I was under no illusions: as far as Roberto was concerned, this was a test for me as much as it was for Alistair.

I sent him an appointment for the following day. I dithered over the title for a moment before typing simply 'Catch-up' and our initials. Then I dithered some more over the message, eventually deciding on a few sentences saying I understood he was busy – everyone at H&D believed themselves to be relentlessly busy, but in Alistair's case, it was probably true – but that it was a sensitive issue and I hoped he'd prioritise the time. Then I reread it with Roberto's 'firm message' ringing in my ears and deleted 'hope you will' and inserted 'expect you to' instead.

I pressed send and felt immediately queasy. I tried to look at another email, but halfway through reading it realised I hadn't taken in a word. I flicked back to my outbox to see if Alistair had seen my message. '*Unopened*' read the status, and I felt the knot in my spine ease. But when after five minutes and another three checks it hadn't changed, I shuffled uncomfortably on my seat. *Tap, tap, tap* went my pen against the edge of my keyboard. I stood up, then sat down again. I looked at another email. I returned to my outbox.

Unopened.

I got to my feet and swung open the door of my office. The

desks outside were empty. Of course, I remembered now – there was a staff seminar, another of the Pearl Associates innovations. I should be there myself. Roberto was probably noticing my absence at that very moment, another little mark against my name. No wonder Alistair hadn't opened my email. I checked the clock on the wall: still another twenty minutes to go.

I headed for his desk. Empty, as I'd known it would be. I found a Post-it, thought for a moment, then scribbled on it.

I've sent you a meeting request – please give me a shout if you'd like more info. See you tomorrow.

I hoped he'd see it for what it was, a friendly gesture to counterbalance the brusque email.

I took a detour on the way back, skulking outside the glass-walled meeting room where the seminar was taking place. I wasn't about to draw attention to myself by arriving late, but I wanted to catch a glimpse of Alistair, to gauge how he looked. I stood to one side of the glass and scanned the room.

Roberto was sitting at the front, next to an earnest young man in a T-shirt and jacket. On a screen behind them, lines of various colours charted a gentle downwards path. The room was packed with people with enough good sense to know any absence would be noted. But I couldn't see Alistair. A banner on a stand at the back of the room obscured a few seats, and I told myself he must be there; but I felt a prickle of unease as I headed back to my desk.

The rest of the day was busy, meetings and phone calls keeping me away from my emails. At a little after seven, Matt popped his head around the door and asked if I was ready to leave. I took one last look at my outbox.

Unopened.

I shut down the computer and reached for my coat.

TWENTY-TWO

BRISTOL

Maeve, fifteen years ago

Maeve was impatient. Her skin itched with it. It had been weeks now since Paul had met the solicitor, and still he eluded her questions about the will. Whenever she raised it, he changed the subject, or claimed he was too tired or upset to discuss it. And all the time, Alistair was trapped in that flat, a hair's breadth away from temptation.

It was all this crap with Anna that was to blame. She was struggling, Maeve understood that. But that was no excuse for the way she was behaving, her continued refusal to speak to her father. And Maeve could feel what was coming. It was only a matter of time before Anna issued him the ultimatum: Maeve or her. How would he react when the moment came? After everything Maeve had done for him, the answer should have been simple. Somehow, though, it didn't feel simple at all.

She'd been so patient, giving him chance after chance to show he really cared about their relationship, to put her first, just once. Yet every time, he let her down. She looked at him now, his head buried in a book, sitting there while she prepared dinner once again, cooking for them both in the kitchen of his flat, even though she'd worked all day herself. Even though she was tired and anxious and fed up, bored of listening to university students complaining about their course or their accommodation, expecting her to fix everything, treating her like a skivvy. She could do without it at home too. Perhaps it was his age: he thought she was going to slip into the role of little woman. Maybe that's what he'd been used to with Bethan, despite his protestations that he'd been the one looking after her. Well, if that's what he expected, he was in for a rude awakening.

'Paul,' she said.

He pretended not to hear her, and she clenched her fists, feeling her fingernails digging into the soft skin of her palms.

'Paul,' she said again, louder, 'can you put that book down?'

He lowered it slowly, his expression already wary. 'Everything all right?'

'I'm worried about you,' she said. 'You've barely opened your mouth all evening. I know how much you've got on your plate. I want to help, but I feel like you won't let me in.'

That would have been enough once, enough to have him put down that book and pull her onto his lap. Now the book stayed in his hands and the skin between his eyebrows puckered in irritation. 'I'm fine, Mae. I just have to sort out a few things.'

She took the chair next to his and reached for his hands. Did she imagine him recoil, ever so slightly? 'I know you're upset about Anna,' she said. 'I feel responsible. If we'd never met, perhaps none of this would have happened.'

He pushed her hand away, gently but firmly. 'You mustn't think like that.'

It had been the wrong approach. Of course he wouldn't want her to blame herself. Blaming herself meant indirectly blaming him, blaming him for choosing her and leaving Bethan.

If that's what had led to his wife's drinking, to her fall, he was at least as culpable as she was.

She changed tack. 'Still no word from Anna?' He didn't reply and she reached for his hand again, squeezed it gently. 'You're doing everything you can, Paul. She'll see that in the end.'

A nerve pulsed in his cheek. He looked like he might be grinding his teeth. She waited, but he didn't speak. 'I know she's your daughter and you want to protect her.' Her thumb brushed the back of his hand, smoothing the skin. 'But she's a grown woman. She has to make her own choices.'

'I know that.' He looked like he was going to say more, then thought better of it.

'She'll be finishing uni soon, getting a job. Starting out in life.' She tried to make it sound like a good thing, full of possibility. 'I know you want to help her, but you can only do as much as she'll let you.'

He breathed in deep and for a second he closed his eyes. When he opened them again, he was looking straight at her. The effect was disconcerting. 'Are you going to ask me about the will again?'

Her thumb stopped its passage across the back of his hand. 'What do you mean? I'm only trying to help.'

'Are you, Mae? Is that really what you're doing?'

She dropped his hand and pushed back her chair. 'I don't know what you're talking about.'

'Every time we talk these days, it's about the bloody will.'

'You're the one who brought it up! I was talking about Anna.'

'Yes, but we know where that ends, don't we? *Has Anna been in touch?*' He put on a squeaky voice that set her teeth on edge. '*Have you talked to her about the will? What are you going to do about the house?*'

She watched as he got to his feet and began pacing. The

room was too small for it to have the visual impact he was probably hoping for – every few steps he met the wall and had to turn around again.

'I'm only trying to help,' she said again, with infinite patience. 'Things need to be sorted out.'

He spun on his heel and grabbed the edge of the table, his face a few inches from hers. 'Was that what you were doing when you went over there?'

The aggression in his voice made her draw back. 'Over where? What are you talking about?'

'Why were you gone so long, Maeve?'

A distant part of her brain registered the use of her full name with something approaching alarm. 'I don't know what you mean.'

'That Saturday morning when you left the note about seeing Bethan. You were gone for ages.' He was very still now. His eyes burned into hers.

'I told you. She didn't answer the door, so I went for a walk. What are you saying?'

'I want you to tell me the truth.'

'That is the truth!' She noticed with surprise that her eyes were full of tears. 'I know you blame me.' She saw him flinch. 'I know I should have looked through the letter box. Don't you think I know that? If I'd only checked, maybe I'd have seen her lying there. Maybe if they'd found her sooner—'

He looked away. 'I didn't mean that.'

'Don't you think I replay that moment every day?' Her words were coming in sobs now. 'Turning around, going back down that path, when all the time she was lying on the other side of that door? Knowing that if I'd done something different, Bethan might still be alive? Anna might still have her mum?'

His knuckles were white on the edges of the tabletop. And still he didn't reach for her. Still he didn't comfort her.

'I know what it's like to lose your parents young. I know what Anna's going through. I wouldn't wish it on anyone.'

He straightened, turned his back on her. She watched him raise his hands to his scalp, bury his fingers in his hair. His head dropped to his chest.

He wouldn't come to her, she realised, so instead she got to her feet and wrapped her arms around him, pressing the side of her face against his back. 'I'm so sorry, Paul,' she said. 'I'm so sorry for what this has done to you and Anna.'

For a moment, he stood quite still, and she let herself hope he'd apologise. But then he was stepping away from her embrace. 'I need to talk to Siân,' he said.

'What?' She brushed the tears from her cheeks with the back of her hand. 'Why?'

He turned back to her. 'You're right about one thing. Things need to be sorted out.'

He left the room and a second later she heard the bedroom door shutting behind him. For a moment she sat frozen. Then she followed, stopping outside the closed door and pressing her ear to the wood. At first there was silence, then came the rumble of Paul's voice. She'd have known he was talking to Siân from the way he spoke, the mixture of entreaty and wounded dignity that was particular to their conversations. He was speaking softly, and she pressed closer to the door to make out the words.

'I know,' he was saying. 'Of course I know that—' He stopped abruptly, and Maeve imagined the woman on the other end of the line talking over him. He wouldn't like that.

'After her exams, that's what I mean. Will you talk to her?' A pause, then quieter, 'I know I don't, but do it for Anna.' Another pause, longer this time. She imagined that nerve pulsing in his cheek. Then something new, a note of relief: 'Thank you. Thank you, Siân. You don't know – Siân?'

Silence fell abruptly; she'd put the phone down on him. Maeve slipped quietly back down the hall and into the kitchen.

After her exams. What had that meant? Had Siân finally agreed to mediate, to persuade Anna to speak to her father? A meeting after her exams were over, perhaps. That would make sense. The end of June then, July at the latest. A month, two at the most. The delay was unhelpful, but she could be patient.

And then, when everything was settled, Anna would fade into the background. Alistair would be free and Paul would be himself again. Her family would be together. Finally, Maeve could make everything right.

TWENTY-THREE

NEW YORK

Now

The crackle of static over the speaker makes me jump. I leap to my feet. 'Hello? Hello? Can you hear us?'

Maeve stands too, half stumbling as she does so. I rush to her and take her elbow, prop her against the wall. There's another burst of static. 'This woman is ill!' I shout. 'You need to get this thing moving!'

From somewhere above us there's a whirring sound, then a metallic clunk. I grip Maeve harder. Are we going to fall again? But the whirring stops. I twist to look at the camera. 'Can you hear me? Can you hear a word I'm saying?'

Another crackle over the speaker.

'Did you hear that?' Maeve's voice is a croak. I turn to her in confusion.

'Hear what? The static?'

The speaker erupts again and this time I think I catch something at the edge of the white noise. I turn to Maeve.

'There,' she says. 'There's a voice.'

I wait, wanting to hear it again. Nothing. 'Try again!' I shout. 'We can barely hear you!'

We wait. I can hear the air squeezing out of Maeve's lungs. 'Try again! Please!' There's desperation in my voice. But the speaker stays silent.

Maeve bends forwards, her head between her knees. She makes a sound that could be a laugh or a sob. And all of a sudden the force of it hits me: of all days, this had to happen today. Of every moment that I've been in this building, every second that I've been in one of these lifts, this is the time it goes wrong. The one day above every other when I just needed everything to be normal. And who am I stuck here with? Some poor woman with claustrophobia. It's perfect. Just *fucking* perfect.

I want to hit something, scream at the camera. But I can't do that. Maeve is on the edge, that much is clear. I have to stay calm for her.

I take a couple of breaths, force my fists to unclench. When I turn back to her, her head is still bowed, her hair shielding her face. It's possible she's crying.

'This is better, though, right?' I say, desperately trying to force some jollity into my voice. 'At least we heard a voice. The connection must be getting stronger. They must be making progress.'

She nods, but her head stays down. My attempts to reassure her aren't working. I shouldn't be surprised – they're not working for me either.

'It's so hot,' she says. 'I can't breathe.'

I look at her in alarm, but her face is hidden by her hair. What can I do? I'd try the door again, but there's no way I can move it on my own. I pick up my jacket from the floor. 'I could try to fan you,' I say. I flap the hem, careful not to get too close and hit her. But the fabric is wrong, too heavy to generate much breeze. It's just moving warm air around.

'It's all right.' Maeve raises a hand to tell me to stop. Her sleeve falls back, and I catch another glimpse of silver before she lowers her arm again. 'I'm okay.'

But she isn't. 'I suppose it could be worse,' I say.

'How's that?' There's a hint of condescension in her voice, but I ignore it. We're neither of us at our best.

'At least it's just the two of us. All those guys going to that meeting – did you see them at the gates? They're probably all sandwiched in together. If they're stuck in another lift, they must be melting.'

'I suppose.'

'And they're in suits and ties, poor sods,' I say. It's what my mum always told me: no matter how bad things feel, remember there's always someone worse off than you. It never really made me feel better, to be honest, but perhaps it will work for Maeve. 'Can you imagine what that must be like? Having that useless bit of fabric around your throat? I think I'd suffocate on the spot.'

I chuckle – but then I hear a sound from Maeve and when I look over to her my laughter freezes. Her face is distorted and blotchy, her mouth is open. She's panting like a dog, trying to suck in oxygen.

Oh no, no, no.

I throw myself down next to her. 'Maeve. Maeve. You're all right. Breathe, Maeve. Breathe with me.' I try to keep the panic from my voice. 'Try to stay calm.'

Try to stay calm! What am I saying? Is there a better way to make someone the opposite of calm? Maeve's breathing is coming fast and ragged, her chest wheezing like a pair of ancient bellows. Her hands are scrabbling on the floor.

She turns wide eyes on me. 'Bag,' she pants.

It's on the floor, just out of her reach. I lean forward and grab it, pull it towards us by the strap. She grasps it, begins rooting around inside.

'Let me help you,' I say. 'What do you need?'

But she ignores me and continues rifling through the contents. The whistling breaths are louder now, each one ending with a faint squeak.

I try to take the bag from her, but she holds on tight, surprisingly strong. A droplet of sweat has formed on the end of her chin, but still her hands flap at the bag. A pen is dislodged and rolls onto the carpet. A small packet of tissues follows, landing on her lap.

'Is it tablets?' I ask. 'An inhaler?'

She looks up at that and nods, her eyes bulging.

'Let me find it for you.' For a second she holds on – but then the bag is in my hands and I'm groping inside. Matt had asthma, so I know what I'm looking for. I feel a purse, some papers, hear the jangle of keys. This woman is like me; she keeps her life in her handbag.

'Do you have an inside pocket?' I ask; but she's too far gone now to reply, pulling at the neck of her shirt as she gasps for air. I turn the bag upside down and there's a thud as the contents fall onto the floor of the lift.

For a second I freeze, unable to process what I'm seeing. But Maeve's whooping breaths bring me back to life and I reach into the bag once more, this time finding the small pocket in the side. I feel inside and as soon as I touch it, I know. I drag out the inhaler and shake it, press it into her hand.

She puts it to her lips and breathes deep, twice, three times. Then she shakes it again and takes another puff.

Gradually, the wheezing quietens.

I feel like I should touch her, offer her the comfort of human contact – but I can't. My eyes are drawn back to the thing on the floor, the thing that's fallen from her bag. It lies there, the solid reality of it like a punch to the gut. I've never seen one before. Not in real life. Not outside films or TV.

Slowly I turn back to the woman next to me. Some of the colour has returned to her face, though her lips are still parted as she breathes.

She's looking at me, waiting for me to say it.

'Maeve,' I ask her, 'why is there a gun in your bag?'

TWENTY-FOUR

LONDON

Eight months ago

It took two attempts for me to get Alistair to the meeting. He'd accepted my first invitation the day after it had been sent. He'd been in early, apparently, because his response was amongst my emails when I logged in the next morning. I checked the time it had been sent – 7.13 a.m. I wondered if he was making some kind of point, subtly informing me how busy he was. There was no message with the acceptance, no sign that he'd even looked at the Post-it I'd left on his desk, much less acknowledged it as an overture of friendship. At the appointed time, I made myself a mug of tea and headed to the meeting room early, wanting to get settled in before he arrived. He didn't turn up. I waited for fifteen minutes, growing first uneasy and then irritated. Eventually I made my way to his desk, but there was no sign of him, and when I returned to my office, I saw there was an email. Something urgent had come up, he claimed. There was no further explanation and no apology.

Annoyed, I rescheduled the appointment for two o'clock the next day, and the following morning I went straight to his desk. He was sitting hunched in front of his monitor, a mug in one hand and his attention fixed on the screen. When I said good morning, he jumped, and the contents of his mug slopped over the keyboard. He cursed and I smelled coffee. I was relieved it wasn't anything stronger.

I reminded him we were due to meet that afternoon, and he mumbled something noncommittal, refusing to meet my eye. 'It's very important that we talk, Alistair,' I said, and I thought it had come out the right way, one part authoritative, one part concerned. But still he wouldn't look at me. I bent nearer and lowered my voice. 'The sooner we meet, the sooner we can get it over with,' I said; and although his eyes stayed fixed straight ahead, I saw him nod. My hand reached out to touch his arm, but at the last moment I caught myself. I had a job to do. I wasn't there to be his friend.

When the afternoon rolled around, I got to the meeting room early again, feeling a sense of *déjà vu* as I settled into a chair to wait for him. I told myself I'd give him five minutes after the start time, and if he didn't show, I'd track him down wherever he was. He wouldn't escape me again.

But there was no need. He arrived on the dot of two, empty-handed, no pen and paper or tablet to take notes. It threw me: surely he'd realised this would be a formal conversation?

'Please take a seat, Alistair,' I said.

He was already doing so, but I wanted to show I was the one in charge. He pulled the chair away from the table and twisted it to one side, then sank into it with a faint sigh, stretched out his legs and crossed his feet at the ankle, apparently relaxed. Perhaps he'd forgotten that I knew him too well to be fooled. I could see the nerves in the tightness of his jaw, the way his hands were clasped together, trying to prevent his restless fingers from giving him away.

'So what's this about?' His eyes were fixed somewhere over my left ear. 'You said it was sensitive.'

I nodded and got straight to the point. 'I'm afraid there's been a complaint about you. From Ted Harvey.'

He uncrossed his feet then crossed them again. 'Ted? What about?'

But I could hear it in his voice: he already knew. My heart sank. Until that moment I'd been half-hoping it might all yet turn out to be a misunderstanding. But Alistair's expression told a different story. He looked – there was no other word for it – shifty.

'I understand you and he met last week.'

'That's right. I gave him his regular briefing on the Croydon project. Everything was fine.' One index finger had broken ranks and was tapping the back of his hand.

'According to Ted, you arrived late—'

'No more than five minutes. Well, ten perhaps. That's hardly a hanging offence.'

'He said you'd been drinking.'

'What?' He looked at me then, but his eyes slid quickly away again. 'I don't know where he got that from.'

'Are you saying he was wrong?' He didn't reply. 'It would be better for all concerned, Alistair,' I said carefully, 'if we avoid getting into different versions of the truth.'

He didn't respond. I hated it, seeing him sitting there in front of me like a delinquent schoolboy. I wondered if he was remembering when our positions had been reversed.

I tried again. 'Perhaps you'd been out at lunchtime? With a client, maybe?'

He raised his eyes, studied me. He *was* remembering, I was sure of it. 'I had been out, yes.'

'With a client?' I prompted, and he nodded.

'And you'd had a drink? Perhaps at their request?'

I was pushing it now, but I knew Alistair. Whatever was going on with him, he wasn't a piss taker. He wouldn't lie to get himself out of trouble. At least, not without a bit of encouragement.

He nodded slowly. I could tell he was trying to decide what to say. I spoke again before he could get himself into trouble giving details that wouldn't check out. 'But that was it, one drink. You weren't intoxicated when you met Ted?'

'No.' He paused, then, more sure of himself, 'Absolutely not.'

'Right. That's that then.' I sounded as relieved as I felt. It wasn't that I couldn't handle disciplinary discussions; I'd had to deliver my fair share. But this was Alistair, and that made everything different.

'So what happens now?'

'I'll need to talk to Roberto.' I saw a flash of panic cross his face at the mention of his boss. 'I have to, Alistair. He was the one Ted spoke to. But don't worry, I'll explain it was a misunderstanding.'

He bit his lip. 'Should I speak to him too?'

I considered it for a moment. 'Not unless you want to. But you might want to talk to Ted, explain the situation. Apologise...' I left the sentence hanging for a moment. We both knew Alistair had done something to apologise for; Ted Harvey wouldn't have complained otherwise. 'For keeping him waiting,' I finished.

'I'll do that.' He cleared his throat, and there was a catch in his voice when he spoke again. 'Thank you.'

I got to my feet and busied myself gathering my notebook and pen, pretending I hadn't noticed his emotion. 'Don't thank me,' I said. 'Just let's make sure we don't find ourselves here again, okay?'

I'd sounded like a prissy schoolteacher, and I saw him

stiffen. 'Right,' he said, his tone clipped. A moment later the door closed behind him.

As soon as he'd gone, I realised I should have done better. I tried to feel pleased that I'd avoided giving him a formal warning, but I knew I'd screwed up.

It wasn't the practicalities of what would come next that worried me, though heaven knows, they were tricky enough. Whatever had happened with Ted Harvey, it had been more than turning up to a meeting a few minutes late. And Ted was of a generation that wouldn't have batted an eyelid at a lunchtime drink. I'd have to do my best to convince Roberto there was nothing to see here, and hope Alistair could smooth things over with his client. I had some reason for optimism there; the two of them had worked together a long time, and Alistair had delivered enough successful projects for Ted to give him the benefit of the doubt.

No, it wasn't the worry about convincing Roberto that had left a sour taste in my mouth. It was my own failure. I knew I should have asked Alistair what was going on, given him the chance to talk about it. And a complaint about alcohol, of all things – I should have reminded him of the counselling service available to staff, told him he could talk to someone there in confidence.

It was the first time I had a chance to make a difference. The first time I failed him. I should have paid more attention to the guilt I felt in that moment, should have welcomed it as the warning it was. I should have got out of my chair and caught up with Alistair, made him come back and talk to me properly, the way we'd talked to each other when we were friends. Instead I told myself I'd done everything necessary. That our conversation had been the shock to the system he needed. That he'd get back on track, and we could forget all about it.

And I wonder now: was my inaction really just the result of

laziness, a disinclination to do what was difficult? Or was part of me even then considering the alternative? Seeing the opportunities, the benefits that might arise if Alistair were to just – disappear?

It's a question I don't know how to answer.

*

NEW YORK

Maeve, now

The chemicals hit and I feel my airways relax, the thudding in my chest beginning to ease. I breathe deep, once, twice, put the inhaler to my lips and repeat.

I've become so weak. And I know who to blame for that.

But I'm not important. You're the one I'm here for, Ali. And I won't fall apart. Not now. Not when I've come so far.

I need to regain control. Hold on just a little longer. Then I'll be out of here and I can do what needs to be done.

She's watching me, her eyes flicking between me and the gun. I see her anxiety, her questions. But I can handle this. I've handled far worse.

I have to put her at her ease. I'll tell her just enough, and she won't pursue it.

A gun here isn't the same as a gun at home. And she's too polite, too British. She won't want to intrude.

And if I'm wrong about that?
I hope for her sake that I'm not.

TWENTY-FIVE

NEW YORK

Now

Maeve pulls herself upright and reaches for the gun. The effort appears to tire her, and for a moment she weighs it in her hand. It's just a small thing, black and snub-nosed. It doesn't look right lying across her delicate palm, the muzzle brushing the edge of her sleeve. And then she stuffs it back inside her bag and I can breathe again.

'It's for personal security,' she says, as if that explains everything.

'What? I mean, how did you get it?' My brain is caught up on the logistics of it all. I'd been assuming she hadn't been in the States long, but she must have got it here. She'll have had to register it, presumably. Can visitors even buy guns? I don't have a clue how any of it works.

'I bought it.' She raises her eyebrows. 'We're not in Kansas anymore, Toto.'

I swallow. 'But why?'

Her fingers brush the surface of the bag, stroking the place where the gun nestles inside. 'Something happened,' she said. 'I need this now.'

I stare at her, torn between politeness and the urgency of my need to know. But this woman has come into my workplace with a firearm. Courtesy isn't my top priority right now.

'*What* happened?' I prompt. 'Why have you got it with you?'

She looks up at me then, and there is something disconcerting in her gaze, a measure of calculation that touches my skin like a cold blade. I am alone with this woman, I realise. And I have no idea who or what she is.

But then she blinks, and I see the moisture pooling in her eyes. 'I was mugged,' she says, Her voice catches. 'They stole everything from me.'

Too late I see how insensitive I'm being. I shouldn't have asked, should have guessed it would be something like this. I should have minded my own business, but instead I've upset her – now, when she's just had a panic attack. Nice work.

'I'm sorry,' I say, uselessly. 'I didn't mean to pry.'

'It's not your fault.' She takes a breath, still tremulous, touches her fingertips to her eyelids. 'It must have been a shock, seeing the gun. You probably think I'm some kind of headcase.'

'Of course not. It must have been horrific. I don't blame you for wanting to protect yourself.' And I don't, even though I can't imagine ever feeling safer with a gun in my bag. I suppose that makes me lucky.

'Horrific,' she whispers. 'Yes, it was. One minute everything was fine, the next' – one hand forms a fist then opens again – 'there was nothing left.' She raises her eyes. They're dry now, but there's an emptiness in them that pulls at my heart. From nowhere I remember how it felt the moment I heard my mother was dead. Something tells me this was more than a simple theft.

'Did they hurt you?' I ask, choosing my words carefully.

'No – well, not directly. But it was after it happened that all this started.' She points at her chest. 'The claustrophobia, the panic attacks.'

'Have you tried counselling?'

There's a hint of bitterness in her smile. 'I did once. It wasn't for me.'

'Perhaps you could give it another go?' I speak gently, aware that I'm on thin ice. If there's anyone less qualified than me to give advice on mental health... but I'm the only one here. 'I'm seeing a therapist myself, trying to work some things through—'

'Is it working?'

I consider the question. 'I think it's too early to say. But I'm trying to learn how to let go of some stuff. I think – I hope – one day I'll be able to do it. I can see that it might be possible. That's a start, isn't it?'

She smiles again, but the bitterness has gone and she just looks sad. 'That's where you and I are different, Cerys,' she says. 'I don't want to let it go.'

Beneath her fingertips, I see the outline of the gun against her bag.

TWENTY-SIX

BRISTOL

Maeve, fifteen years ago

Maeve checked her watch. She'd been supposed to leave for work five minutes ago, but she'd heard Paul's voice when he answered his phone. She wasn't going anywhere until she knew what was going on.

It was Anna on the other end of the line. She wasn't saying a lot, judging by what Maeve could hear of the conversation from Paul's end. That wasn't much either, to be fair: he'd gone into the bedroom and shut the door when the shrill ring had cut through the flat, though not before she'd seen the look of delight that had lit up his face and told her immediately who was calling. She'd had to press her ear to the door again to make anything out, hating herself even as she did it. Was this what it had come to already? That she had to listen at walls to find out what was going on inside his head? She knew the answer, although she wished she didn't.

She wondered what had finally made Anna pick up the

phone. Siân had spoken to her, presumably. Paul had confirmed his sister-in-law had promised to have a word after Anna's exams were over. He'd looked hopeful as he'd passed on the news – already, Maeve could tell, picturing a reconciliation. Maeve had tried to manage his expectations, not wanting to see his disappointment if Anna kept him at arm's length. But he wouldn't listen to her, even resented her efforts, although all she'd ever done was try to protect him.

She felt something prickle behind her vision and dashed at her eyes with the back of her hand. This wasn't the time to get maudlin. She refocused on the rumble of Paul's voice, straining to make out the words. He was speaking too softly, but something in his register suggested the conversation was coming to a close. She straightened up and hurried noiselessly back to the kitchen.

She was busying herself at the sink when he wandered in a minute later. She turned to look at him and the happiness in his face made her stomach twist. Once, she'd been the one who made him feel that way.

'Was that Anna?' She summoned up a smile. 'I thought I heard your phone.'

He nodded, his eyes glowing. 'We're going to meet.'

'That's brilliant! I knew she'd come around eventually.' Her voice sounded wrong, over-bright, but he didn't seem to notice.

'I have Siân to thank, I suppose.' He wrinkled his nose ungraciously. 'But now Anna's back from uni—'

'She's back?' Maeve blinked at him in surprise. 'Has term finished already?'

'Her exams finished last Wednesday, apparently.' He frowned. 'She obviously wanted to come home straight away.'

He'd stumbled over the word 'home' and an icy fingertip touched Maeve's spine. 'She's not...' Her mouth had gone dry, and she had to lick her lips before she could continue. 'She's staying with Siân, right?' Anna had stayed with her aunt when she'd returned to Bristol for the funeral. Surely, she'd gone back there now.

Paul didn't reply.

'She's not back at the house?' She shuddered. 'Paul, she can't stay there!' She tried to go on, but her mind was sucking her back to that day, the images coming too thick and fast to stop: the broken banister, splinters sharp as teeth; the stained carpet, the smell of copper and urine; the smear down the wall at the bottom of the stairs... Anna would have to walk past that spot to go to bed. She'd have to walk over the carpet where her mother had lain dying...

Maeve screwed her eyes up tight, tried to block out the pictures and the smells. When she opened them again, Paul had taken a seat at the table.

'I can't tell her what to do.' His sigh carried a hint of irritation. If he'd noticed Maeve's distress, he gave no sign. 'At least, they've – you know. It's all been cleaned up.'

'Is she on her own?'

He nodded, his lips pressed together in a line. 'She said it's what she wants. I think she's had enough of Siân fussing over her.'

Fussing over her. In a dim part of her mind, Maeve registered her anger with surprise. But it was natural, she supposed, that she should feel for Anna, this girl not much younger than herself, left without her mum, estranged from her dad. She knew how it felt not to have your parents to turn to. And unlike Maeve, Anna was an only child. How much worse not to have a brother or sister, another to share the same quality of pain.

She took a breath before she spoke. 'So when are you seeing her?'

'This evening. I've said I'll take her to dinner. You don't mind, do you?'

She was surprised that he'd asked. 'No. No, of course not. I'll get a pizza or something.' She paused, weighing the question on the tip of her tongue before deciding to take another tack. 'I'm so pleased Anna's come round,' she said again. 'I know how hard this has been on you. And it'll be good for all of us to get everything sorted at last.'

Something passed over his face, but it was gone before she could work out what it was. 'Yes,' he said, 'it's well past time for that.'

She spent the evening trying to distract herself from thoughts of how Paul and Anna were getting on. He was taking her to The Quayside, he'd said, and she'd tried not to wince at how much a meal at one of Bristol's smartest hotels would be costing. It would be worth it, though. It was the kind of place where it would be possible to have a private conversation, the tables spaced far enough apart that the two of them wouldn't be overheard.

She ate her own dinner of pizza and garlic bread in front of the TV, then called Alistair. The conversation was brief, the dull bass thud of Kirsten's music forming a backdrop that made Alistair testy and Maeve anxious. 'Has she got people over again?' she asked him, and he dodged the question in a way that made her think the answer was 'yes'. They'd be drinking, no doubt, teasing him about not joining them. How many more evenings like that would it take before he slipped?

'You need to find somewhere else,' she said, and then, because she could hear his exasperation down the line, 'I can help. Once Paul's house is sold, everything will be easier. Let me help you get something better.'

'That's nice of you, Maeve, but I'm not taking his money. I can manage on my own.'

He couldn't, though. He never had. 'But Paul and I are together now,' she pressed on. 'He wants to help you just as much as I do.' She heard him snort at that but kept going. 'And it's only temporary. You can pay us back if you really want to.'

There was a pause. Kirsten's music went oompht, oompht, oompht in the background.

'Why not just take a look at what's available?' she said, wanting to inject some momentum. After all, it wouldn't be long now before the money came through. Paul was talking to Anna at this very moment. Perhaps they'd already discussed the timing of the sale. Anna wouldn't want to stay at the house any longer than she had to, surely. And there'd be more than enough from her share for her to find some little flat. That was more than most people her age had. More than Alistair had, despite both their parents being dead, despite how hard he worked.

'I'm not saying look at penthouses in Mayfair.' She laughed lightly, as if none of this really mattered. 'Just check out what you could get with a few hundred extra a month. It could make all the difference.'

Another pause. Then, 'Two hundred a month. A calendar month. I won't look at anything that would cost you more than that.'

His tone was serious, and she knew he was disappointed in himself for giving in. 'That's fine,' she said quickly. 'It doesn't hurt to look, right? At least then we'll know what's out there.'

She ended the call shortly afterwards, inventing a fictitious friend who'd promised to ring her, worried that if they talked much longer, he'd change his mind. Her heart fluttered in her ribcage, but she told herself she had nothing to worry about. Everything she'd said was true. Things *would* be easier when the house was sold. And when Paul had smoothed things over with Anna, Maeve would move in with him properly. Between them, they'd be more than able to spare a couple of hundred pounds a month to get Alistair out of harm's way. Paul wouldn't refuse to help: this was Maeve's brother, after all.

. . .

She was reading when she heard the rattle of Paul's key in the front door. She got up and went to meet him, waiting in the doorway of the living room. 'How did it go?' she asked tentatively.

He jumped and spun round, dropping his keys. She laughed. 'What's up with you? Guilty conscience?'

He bent to pick them up, turning so she couldn't see his face. 'You startled me,' he said from somewhere near the floor.

He straightened and busied himself hanging up his coat. He hadn't answered her question, she realised; perhaps things hadn't gone the way he'd hoped.

'I'll put the kettle on,' she said.

He looked at her then. And from his lips came the words she hadn't known she'd been dreading until that moment. 'Maeve, we need to talk.'

TWENTY-SEVEN

NEW YORK

Now

I've been watching Maeve. And I'm worried.

Because I can see it now – there's an edge to her. Something I hadn't noticed until that gun tumbled out of her bag. A strain that has nothing to do with the rash on her neck – or at least, if the two are connected, the rash is a symptom of the strain and not the other way around. Something inside her is stretched tight, so tight it might snap at any moment. I should have seen it before. After all, it's the same way I feel.

I want to ask her again about the mugging. There's more to it than some chancer grabbing her handbag, I'm sure of that. Was he violent, perhaps? Worse? Is that why she feels she has to carry a gun?

And now part of me is beginning to wonder if that gun has another purpose. If I'm right that she's here without an appointment, maybe she's planning to threaten someone. To do something terrible if she doesn't get what she wants. Perhaps I should try to find some way to warn whoever she's here to see; except that, even if my mobile wasn't useless in the signal desert of this bloody lift, I don't know who that is. I've been guessing, but the truth is I don't know anything about why she's really here.

I should keep my head down. Pissing off an armed woman in a confined space – that's not a risk I want to take. Or then again, perhaps I'm being a coward. Doing the thing that's easy, instead of the thing that's right. Heaven knows, it wouldn't be the first time.

Maeve's head rests against the wall of the lift. Her eyes are closed, and her chest rises and falls slowly. I can't hear her breathing anymore; the inhaler has done its work for now. Her bag is on her lap and her hand rests lightly on top of it. Every so often she stretches out her fingers and gently strokes the leather. Now I know what's underneath, and despite the heat in here it makes me shiver.

I can't make her tell me what's going on, but I can watch her, try to work it out for myself. It's what I told myself I'd do when I came here to Pearl Associates. Less being wrapped up in myself, more looking out for other people.

Across the lift, Maeve stirs. 'You're staring at me,' she says, and I feel the blood rush to my face. 'I'm not going to stop breathing if you look away.'

I try to laugh. 'You're feeling better, then?'

'Hmm.' She sounds sleepy. Perhaps it's the loss of oxygen making her lightheaded. 'Thank you for finding my inhaler. I don't know what I'd have done if you hadn't.'

'You'd have got it in the end,' I say. But I'm not sure that's true.

'You're a good person, Cerys,' she says.

My throat closes up and I can't reply.

LONDON

Eight months ago

'You're a good person.' Roberto swivelled back and forth in his chair. 'You care about people, and that's important. But sometimes you need to use the stick as well as the carrot.'

He smiled at me, all teeth. The man could be in a toothpaste advert.

'I prefer not to think in those terms,' I said stiffly. His smile froze and I knew I had to do better. Whether I liked it or not, this was the new regime: I had to keep Roberto on side. I tried again, injecting what I hoped was a degree more warmth into my tone.

'I'm satisfied with Alistair's explanation. But I've been clear that the situation must be resolved. He's assured me he'll apologise to Mr Harvey.'

'Sure, sure.' Roberto leaned back in his seat, still swinging. A faint squeak emanated from the chrome frame as he moved. 'That's great.' He drew out the word: *graaaayt*. 'But I got to tell you, I'm still concerned.'

I sat up a little straighter. 'Oh?'

'This Douglass guy, his numbers' – he picked up a piece of paper from his desk and inspected it, a frown creasing his forehead – 'they're not what I expect from someone at his level.'

'His numbers...?'

He stared at me as if I'd disappointed him. 'His sales figures are okay. But new business? He's brought in virtually no new clients for over a year.'

I held up my hand. 'Wait a minute. I thought we were talking about a complaint?'

'Oh sure, sure,' he said again, the chair squeaking along like a backing group. 'But we got to look at the bigger picture. It's like we've been saying, we got to get rid of the dead wood.'

We'd been saying that? This was starting to sound like a witch hunt. With an effort, I arranged my face into a look of concern. 'You're right, of course. And I'm just thinking aloud here...' I hated that kind of corporate jargon, but something told me Roberto wouldn't feel the same way. 'We need to make sure we're fair, and seen to be fair.'

He frowned, like a toddler told it was bedtime, but I hurried on. 'Like you say, we should look at the bigger picture. Review our whole performance appraisal system. Make sure there's a clear framework for action where it's needed.'

The chair had stopped swivelling. I wasn't sure whether that was a good sign, but I kept going regardless. At some point, Roberto started to nod and tapped something on his tablet. By the time I got up to leave, I'd promised him a full proposal by the end of the week – but at least Alistair hadn't been mentioned again.

I was halfway out of the door when Roberto called my name. I turned to see him leaning forward, that toothpaste advert smile back in place.

'Just keep an eye on Douglass, won't you?' he said. The chair squeaked one last time as I pulled the door shut behind me.

Matt emailed to say a late meeting had gone into his diary, so I left the office alone that evening and went to the supermarket. After the conversation with Roberto, I didn't have the energy to cook, so I picked up a couple of microwaveable ready meals. I considered waiting for Matt before I ate, but he hadn't said how long he'd be, and in the end, hunger won out. I'd finished my meal and the flat smelled of rogan josh when he came in, calling a greeting from the front door. He bent to where I sat curled on the sofa and kissed me lightly on top of my head. I caught the faint aroma of beer on his breath.

'Just popped out for a couple of drinks with the guys,' he said, moving my feet and flopping down on the other end of the sofa.

I shuffled further up. 'There's a curry in the fridge if you haven't eaten.'

He shook his head. 'I got fish and chips at the pub.'

Just as well I hadn't waited for him then. He pulled my feet onto his lap and started massaging my soles. 'A little bird told me you were in to see Roberto today.'

I stiffened. 'Which little bird was that?'

He laughed, though it wasn't funny. 'It's not a secret, is it?'

I shrugged. 'Just wondered.'

'Was it about Douglass?'

I shifted so I could look at him properly. 'Who told you that?'

He fumbled for the remote control, not looking at me. 'Someone mentioned it at the pub. So what's he been up to now?'

Already, I could feel the evening sliding away with a grim inevitability. I took a breath before replying. 'It was nothing really,' I said, meaning, as he knew full well, *Nothing I can tell you about.*

'I heard he'd upset Ted Harvey,' Matt said. 'Some kind of bust-up.'

I let out an irritated puff. 'Whoever's been gossiping,' I said, 'you can tell them they're way off beam.'

'So what was it then?' He'd turned on the TV, trying to pretend he didn't care.

'Nothing important. Can we leave this, please?'

'Suit yourself.'

He flicked to the news and sat staring at the screen. Then, 'I've been thinking about the wedding.'

The change of topic was a welcome surprise. 'Me too,' I said, pleased. 'I was thinking we should start looking at some venues. Maybe this weekend.'

He started rubbing my feet again. 'Yeah, good idea. We need to start budgeting, don't we?'

I nodded. 'Everyone says the venue's the most expensive bit.'

His fingers rubbed at the arch of my foot. 'I want you to have the best.'

'But that doesn't mean we have to spend a fortune,' I said quickly. 'We agreed we'd keep things small, right?'

'The thing is,' he said, and my heart sank, because although I didn't know yet how he was going to get there, I sensed the destination in the calculation in his voice. 'The thing is, I want to take care of you. I know that's old-fashioned, but it's the way I feel.'

I didn't reply.

'I want you to have the perfect wedding. And I want us to have a wonderful life together.' He kept rubbing my feet, the pressure firmer now, on the edge of discomfort. 'I work hard, you know that.'

I sat in silence, knowing he wasn't really expecting an answer.

'But sometimes I worry it's never going to be enough. Not when there are lifers like Douglass holding on until retirement.'

'Matt, he's practically the same age as us—'

'And I just think, you know, with the Americans coming in, there's a chance to shake things up a bit. Let the cream rise to the top.'

I stared at him. 'I'm not sure what you're saying.'

He clasped his hands around my toes. 'You could help. Help *both* of us. I'm not suggesting you do anything – you know – underhand. I'm just saying, if Douglass has fucked up, if he's on his way out... Well, you don't need to put yourself on the line to rescue him. It will be sad for him, of course, but it could be a great opportunity.'

'A great opportunity for you. To take his job.'

'Like I said, it would be great for both of us.'

My feet were still trapped in his grip, and I pulled them away abruptly. 'Was that what all this was about? All the stuff about the wedding? You just want me to hang Alistair out to dry?'

His expression changed in a flash. The sweetness was gone, the anger back in the lines that bracketed his mouth. 'Alistair,' he sneered. 'What is it with the two of you?'

'Not this again.' But I felt the flush rise to my cheeks.

'It's not fair to *Alistair*. We mustn't upset *Alistair*. Why can't you put *me* first, for a change? What kind of hold has he got on you?'

For a moment I was speechless; but then I remembered that attack was the best form of defence. The conversation went downhill from there.

Matt slept on the sofa that night. I barely closed my eyes myself, running through the argument in my mind. By the time the light began creeping around the edge of the curtains, I'd told myself he hadn't meant what he'd said about Alistair and me. He'd just been lashing out.

I'd started it, after all, jumping to the conclusion that he'd been trying to manipulate me with talk of the wedding. I'd been unfair. A big showy celebration might not matter to me, but that didn't mean it wasn't important to him. And without a promotion, it wouldn't be happening any time soon.

And if there were other reasons for Matt to want Alistair's job, was that so dreadful? Matt was ambitious, but there was no law against that. I knew it bothered him that my position was senior to his. As Alistair's replacement, we'd be peers. Perhaps then he'd be less prickly, stop feeling as if he had something to prove.

As for Alistair, it was his own actions that had put him on Roberto's hit list. Was it really asking so much of me not to let him reap what he'd sown?

At some point, I must have drifted off to sleep, because the alarm jolted me back to consciousness. I shuffled to the kitchen and made Matt a coffee as a peace offering. There was no point sulking like children. We needed to talk, to find a way through this.

I pushed open the door to the living room and blinked in the morning sunshine. The curtains were wide open, a blanket folded neatly on the end of the sofa. And Matt was gone.

TWENTY-EIGHT

BRISTOL

Maeve, fifteen years ago

Maeve sat at her computer, a new email open in front of her. The cursor blinked against the white screen. She could have phoned Alistair, but she didn't trust herself not to give something away if she spoke to him. She pressed her fingers to the keys.

> *Sorry I can't make it tomorrow, something's come up at work and I need to be here.*

'Here.' That was the right word, she thought – nicely non-specific.

> *Don't worry if they can't rearrange the viewing. You can tell me about it afterwards*

She signed off with another apology. Ali would be reluctant

to see the flat without her – since she'd offered to contribute to his rent, he'd been assiduous in sending her details of the places suggested by the letting agent, asking her opinion on price and particulars. She'd suggested he take some photos so they could look through them together before he made any decisions. Perhaps she should have told him to cancel, but she'd have had to explain why, and she didn't have it in her to let him down by email. She felt a stab of pain. She should never have told him she'd be able to help. She'd have to disappoint him now, when he'd got his hopes up, started to imagine how it might feel to live somewhere decent, his own space, away from people who might drag him down.

But it was the least bad option. She'd still be there for him, that was the important thing. And there was no alternative: she'd created this mess, and she had to sort it out. It would cost money too, money she had wanted to put towards Ali's debts – but that couldn't be helped.

She checked the clock in the corner of the screen: a couple of hours yet before she had to meet the man she'd phoned earlier.

He'd sounded keen; most likely he hadn't had much response to his ad. She'd probably be able to talk him into a discount if she tried, but she didn't plan to do that. Keep it short and sweet, unmemorable. Cash in hand, no record of the sale.

She stared at the email on her screen. For a moment, she allowed herself to imagine that there was another way, some other solution that could make everything all right. But she'd already tried to talk to Paul, to make him see sense. He'd refused to do it. And though admitting it finally extinguished the small flame of hope she'd carried inside her, she had to face the truth: he'd never really cared about her. There was no point now in dwelling on what might have been.

She brushed away the moisture that had collected at the corner of her eye and pressed send.

TWENTY-NINE

NEW YORK

Now

Maeve called me a good person. That's not what she'd say if she knew the truth.

'Can I ask you something?' I need to talk, to fill the silence before I get lost in it.

Maeve opens her eyes, a certain wariness mingling with curiosity. 'Go ahead.'

'What you said before – about not wanting to let go of bad stuff that's happened. Do you really think that's the best way? The best way to keep going, I mean.'

She studies me, trying to work out where this is going. 'Are you talking about what happened with your fiancé?' she asks, and I nod, because that's easier. 'I suppose it depends.'

'Depends on what?'

'On whether things are even.' She tilts her head to one side. 'He cheated on you. He let you down. It tips things out of balance. You can't just ignore that. It has to be put right. Then when that's done – if you want to – maybe you can move on.'

I think about what she's said. Perhaps that's where I've been going wrong.

I've been trying to change myself, trying to forget things instead of confronting them. Trying to hide the person I was before, the person who did that terrible thing. A new job, new clothes, new haircut.

Perhaps part of me hopes that if I get it right with Jay, if I manage everything better this time, that will make things even – but it won't. If anything, it's tipping the scales even further out of balance.

Because Alistair can't change his job. He can't move on. You can't do any of those things when you're cold in the ground.

But then there's Maeve, still pale from the panic attack, her hand still resting on that bag with the gun inside it like it's a lifebuoy.

She doesn't look like she's got it together either.

'What if it's not possible to make things even?' I ask.

'It's always possible.'

She sounds so certain, but that can't be right. 'But what about your mugger? Did the police find him?'

She makes a sound somewhere between a snort and a sob. 'The police weren't interested. They didn't even—' She stops short. Whatever she'd been on the verge of saying, she's thought better of it.

'Then what do you do? How do you ever get past something like that if you keep waiting for the world to be fair?' I sound like I'm arguing with her, but I'm not; I just want to know how to do this. How to keep breathing through every day.

'You don't wait,' she says. 'You make it fair yourself.'

It's the kind of thing Matt would have said.

LONDON

Eight months ago

He hadn't left me a note. I checked everywhere, but there was nothing. Maybe, I told myself, Matt thought it best that we stay out of each other's way for a bit, give ourselves time to calm down after our row. Except that I *was* calm – hurt, confused, but calm.

By the time I got into the office I'd decided to find him straight away. I wasn't going to wait and allow things to get even more difficult. We needed to talk, and if we couldn't do that at work, we could at least agree it would happen when we got home. I hung up my coat and stowed my bag under my desk, then went to find him.

Matt didn't have an office of his own. Like Alistair's, his desk was in the open plan. Unlike Alistair's, it wasn't in a prime position in the corner. Instead, he sat next to a walkway. He complained regularly about how distracting it was to have people passing by, speaking at full volume, not paying attention to those who were trying to work. It got to him: he was the kind of person inclined to view thoughtlessness as a deliberate slight.

I braced myself as I neared his desk, not sure what kind of reception I was going to get. But he wasn't there. Perhaps his leaving so early hadn't had anything to do with our argument after all; maybe he'd simply had a meeting scheduled first thing. The office was quiet so I sidled around to his seat and touched his mouse, hoping his calendar would be open so I could check when he was free. But when the screen lit up it showed only the entwined H&D of the corporate screensaver, complete with a request for his password. I stared at it for a second before heading back to my office.

I was at the other end of the corridor when I saw him. He had his back to me, one arm stretched out against the wall. I was about to call out to him when something about his posture pulled me up short. He was leaning forward slightly, his voice low, talking to someone apparently much shorter. He was speaking too quietly for me to make out the words, but then I heard a throaty giggle. I froze. I knew that voice. It was Elise, Roberto's PA.

I doubled back and took the long way around to my office, a route which didn't require me to walk past the pair of them. All I could see was Matt leaning into her, his arm against the wall. It was such a sixth-former-at-the-school-disco pose; but then, Elise had been taken on as part of the graduate programme. She wasn't that long out of sixth form herself.

My heart was racing as I slipped into my office and shut the door behind me, resting my back against it as I waited for my breathing to slow. I could guess what he was doing: having failed to get me to dish the dirt on Alistair, he'd decided to try his luck with Elise. If anyone knew what Roberto was up to, it was the person who managed his diary. And Matt probably thought he was senior enough for Elise to be flattered by his notice. Judging by that giggle, he'd been right.

I tried to put the pair of them out of my mind. Matt had always been a flirt – I shouldn't take it seriously. I only hoped Elise was wise enough to realise the same thing. I had a day full of meetings to distract me, so it wasn't until well into the afternoon that I tapped out a short email to Matt, asking when he'd be finishing. He didn't reply for over an hour, but the time apparently hadn't been spent crafting a response. His message when it came was just two words:

Not sure.

By seven o'clock I was drained and in need of dinner. I went to find him, but his desk was deserted again. Surely he wouldn't still be in meetings? I sank into his chair, intending to wait for him. It took me a moment to realise that his PC was switched off. I pushed the chair back and looked under his desk. His bag had gone.

I don't remember what time it was when he got back to the flat. It was late enough that I'd been dozing on the sofa. I woke when I heard his key in the door and was rubbing my eyes when he appeared in the doorway. 'Hi,' I said, biting down the temptation to ask him where he'd been. 'Have you had anything to eat?'

It wasn't what he'd been expecting, I could tell. He'd been gearing up for a fight and was perhaps disappointed that I hadn't given him an immediate opening.

''S all right,' he said. 'I got a burger on the way back.'

He stood there awkwardly before coming in and slumping into an armchair. 'What a day,' he said, glancing at me to see whether I'd take the bait.

'Busy then?' I was tempted to ask outright if he'd been at the office all this time, but decided against it. If he lied to me directly, I wasn't sure what I'd do.

'Always is,' he said meaninglessly.

I made tea for us both, a second attempt at rapprochement by hot beverage. I brought in a packet of biscuits too, and I could see him start to relax as he munched. The words *About last night* hovered at the tip of my tongue, but I was no longer sure I had the energy. Instead I said, 'I saw you chatting to Elise earlier.'

He stopped chewing for a second, then murmured noncommittally around a mouthful of biscuit.

'The two of you looked as thick as thieves.' He didn't respond. 'What were you talking about?'

I'd hoped to sound playful but hadn't quite brought it off.

He swallowed the remains of his biscuit and shifted to look at me.

'Well now,' he said, 'that would be telling.'

I took a breath and counted to ten – well, five. 'I hope it didn't have anything to do with what you were asking me about last night. About Alistair,' I added, in case he was going to pretend not to know what I meant.

He smiled at me, gleeful as a kid who's got one over on his least favourite teacher. 'Some conversations are private,' he said. 'I'm sure you understand.'

Matt and I settled into an uneasy truce in the weeks leading up to Christmas. If there was no more mention of looking at wedding venues, there was equally no mention of Alistair. Our conversations consisted of practicalities or polite remarks – *Shall I buy loo roll? Thanks for washing up* – and we rarely made the journey to or from the office together. Matt was in early every day: Roberto was an early starter, and I assumed he was hoping to impress him; and when evening rolled around, he often had to work late.

I tried not to let it bother me. We were both under pressure, I told myself. It didn't mean there was anything seriously wrong.

I'd seen little of Alistair, but there'd been no summons from Roberto either. That, I decided, was a good thing. A few times I deliberately walked past Alistair's desk in the hope of striking up a casual conversation, something to gauge how he was doing. But whenever he was there, he was either on the phone or kept his head down. He was aware of my presence, it was clear, but didn't wish to engage. I decided not to push it.

Christmas Day fell on a Tuesday that year, and the corporate Christmas party had been scheduled for the previous week.

It was always a glitzy occasion, the board seeing it as a symbol of Holbrooke and Dean's status and success. That year it was being held in a smart hotel in Mayfair, somewhere upmarket enough to discourage too riotous a celebration, discreet enough to avoid reputational damage should there be any unguarded behaviour at the tail end of the evening. It wasn't the kind of thing I particularly enjoyed and, worse, as a corporate event for staff, it was nominally my responsibility. I looked forward to it in the way I looked forward to a trip to the dentist – after it was over, I could relax in the knowledge I wouldn't have to do it again for another year.

Matt, I observed, had bought a new dinner jacket for the occasion. He'd started going to the gym and his old one had grown tight and the trousers loose. I made an effort too, as was expected, buying a new dress and getting my hair done the day before. It was already past its blow-dried best by the following morning, but I had meetings that afternoon so it was the best I could do. At five o'clock, I locked the door to my office, pulled down the blind and got changed, once again grateful that having my own room meant avoiding the scrum in the ladies' loos.

Matt and I made the journey across town together. It was, I realised, the longest we'd been in each other's company since the evening we'd argued about Alistair. This time we were both on our best behaviour, making courteous small talk until we emerged from the Tube at Piccadilly Circus. It was a five-minute walk from there to the hotel and Matt held my hand the whole way. After the distance there'd been between us, it felt good to be close again. We'd both been stressed with work, I told myself, anxious about the American takeover and feeling as if every move we made was under scrutiny. Matt wanted so much to get on – I couldn't blame him for that.

Tonight was a chance to relax, to remember that we could have fun together.

A waiter handed us each a glass of champagne from a silver tray as we entered the ballroom. It was a grand space, gilt borders around the panels on the walls, ornate plasterwork on the ceilings, extravagantly beautiful chandeliers. The room was filling up fast and we found a seat at one of the tables at the side, a respectable distance from the small dance floor; Matt hated dancing, but I hoped to persuade him up before the night was over. We were soon joined by others, and after a while I excused myself to go to the loo, taking the opportunity to scout for Roberto. I liked knowing where he was, minimising the chance that he'd take me by surprise. I spotted him at another table on the far side of the room, holding forth to an apparently fascinated audience including, I now saw, several members of the board. I was pleased; that would keep him busy for a while. And there was always the chance that if he had a good time tonight, I might benefit from the reflected glory.

When I got back to the table, Matt had disappeared. I scanned the room but couldn't spot him. Perhaps he'd gone to the loo himself, or headed to the bar for a beer. It didn't matter; now that I knew there was little likelihood of being blindsided by Roberto, I allowed myself to relax and begin to enjoy the evening.

I was talking to Simon, one of the consultants, when I became aware of a subtle change in the atmosphere. Simon's gaze travelled over my shoulder and he paused briefly mid-sentence, an expression of part sympathy, part disgust passing over his features. He caught himself and continued talking, fixing his attention on me in a way that suggested he hoped I hadn't noticed. I turned in my chair, curious to see what he'd seen, catching his frown of dismay out of the corner of my eye.

It was Alistair. And one look was all it took to tell me he was spectacularly drunk.

His dinner jacket hung loose on his body, evidence that he'd lost weight since its last outing. He'd either undone his bow tie or hadn't bothered to knot it in the first place: it dangled from his collar like a bedraggled bat. But it wasn't his clothes that concerned me. It was the glazed look in his eyes, his uneven gait as he stumbled towards me like something out of a Japanese horror film.

I leapt to my feet and grabbed his arm. 'Alistair!' I hissed in his ear. 'What the hell do you think you're doing?' I took his arm more firmly and steered him towards the wall, hoping to lean him against it in a way that might pass for casual rather than paralytic.

He started to mumble something, but I couldn't make it out. And it was at that moment that the music which had been tinkling away in the background swelled in fanfare. I looked up, aghast to see Roberto striding to the front of the room. It was time for his speech. People were making their way to their seats, but there wasn't an empty chair that wouldn't require Alistair to stumble into the middle of the room. There was no way Roberto would miss that.

I looked desperately for a nearby exit, but could see only the grand double doors where we'd entered. It was too far – but maybe if we stayed close to the wall...

A waiter swept past us, an empty tray in hand, disappearing through a side door I hadn't noticed. I almost sagged in relief.

'Come on,' I whispered, trying to keep Alistair upright without being too obvious about it. 'Let's get you outside.'

I dragged him towards the door. Our backs were towards Roberto now, and with every step I was convinced his gaze would sweep over us like a searchlight and we'd freeze, exposed in our bid for freedom. The music reached a crescendo and the room erupted in the warm applause of people who've been drinking free champagne courtesy of the person who's about to take the mic.

'Colleagues! Friends...' From behind us, Roberto's voice dipped in fake bonhomie.

Alistair had paused, was beginning to turn in the direction of the podium. In desperation, I tugged hard at his arm and we half-walked, half-fell into the adjoining room. I dragged the door shut behind us.

Everything was in darkness. At the far end of the room, a second door admitted just enough light from the corridor beyond to see that this was another large space, less grand than the ballroom. Chairs and tables were piled up along the walls, the wood veneers and nylon upholstery indicating that the room was used as some kind of conference venue. Tonight, though, it was evidently serving as a route for the waiters to ferry drinks to and from the ballroom. In one corner there was an array of display stands. I pulled Alistair over there and left him propped against the wall as I lifted a couple of chairs from a stack and positioned them behind the screens. Seated there, even a passing waiter wouldn't see us.

'What you doing?' he slurred as I pushed him into a seat.

'Saving your bacon,' I snapped. 'What are you playing at, Alistair? Do you *want* to get fired?'

He rubbed his hands over his face. 'Issa party, isn't it? Iss Christmas.'

'For God's sake...' But there was no point trying to talk to him when he was like this. 'Look, stay here,' I said. 'I'll be back in a minute. Don't move, okay? Just. Don't. Move.'

Out in the corridor I waylaid a waitress and begged for coffee. I waited for it to arrive, ducking back into the room every few minutes to check that Alistair was still there. He hadn't moved. I hoped he'd continue to be as biddable when I'd got the coffee into him.

Finally, it arrived – two disconcertingly small cups, but better than nothing. I thanked the waitress and waited until she'd gone before darting back inside the darkened room and taking my seat behind the screen. I handed a cup to Alistair and he looked at it suspiciously.

'I don't want this,' he said.

'No, but you need it.'

He stared back at me sullenly, but then puffed out an injured sigh and put the cup to his lips.

'There you go,' I murmured, in a way I hoped sounded encouraging. I checked my watch: quarter past eight. Roberto would be finishing his speech by now. Matt wouldn't have missed that. Perhaps he was back at our table, wondering where I was. That thought was immediately followed by the realisation that my phone was still in my evening bag under my chair; I had no way of contacting him without leaving Alistair on his own.

'You don't need to stay with me,' he said, as if he'd read my mind. 'I'll be orright.'

I didn't reply. The more he talked, the slower he'd drink the coffee.

'He'll be wondering where you are.' He lowered the cup and I was pleased to see it was empty. 'Your fyon-say. Matt.'

I passed him the second cup. 'He'll be fine. Just drink up.'

He fell quiet. Then, 'I didn't know...' He stopped, looked away from me.

'What?'

'About your dad. About him dying.'

It took me aback, but then I remembered the conversation Matt had told me about, the one he'd had with Alistair on the train back from Edinburgh. I shrugged, confused. 'It happened a long time ago.'

'You never said.' He held the cup on his lap, his head bowed.

'Do you mean when...?' But of course that was what he meant. I hadn't said anything to him that day, the day we didn't talk about. Perhaps, after all, this really was the reason he'd been avoiding me: he thought I'd deliberately only told him half the story.

'I didn't think it was relevant,' I said. 'It's not like I didn't tell you on purpose. It didn't make a difference to anything, you know – not like with Mum...'

'What happened?' His voice was so soft that even in the hushed darkness I could barely hear him.

'Car accident,' I said briskly. 'Come on, Alistair, finish your coffee.' But the cup stayed where it was. I sighed. 'I'm sorry I didn't tell you,' I said. 'It wasn't...' I groped for the right words. 'I wasn't trying to hide anything.'

Still he didn't speak. 'And I was so – you know how I was.' I felt my voice falter. This was the closest we'd ever come to talking about what I'd done, how he'd responded. Thirteen years, and he'd never mentioned it again. I owed him for that, whatever came next. 'Dad died after my exams. It had nothing to do with...' I tailed off again, unwilling to spell it out.

'After your exams?'

I nodded, relieved that I was getting through. 'That's why I didn't say anything. I wasn't trying to make you feel sorry for me.'

'I know that.'

'I would never have said anything about Mum unless...' I swallowed, embarrassed to find my eyes were filling with tears. 'You were so good to me, Alistair. I know I've never said anything since. But I haven't forgotten what you did. I don't want you to think—'

He stood suddenly. 'I have to go home.'

'Alistair—'

He was already striding back towards the door to the ballroom. I hurried to follow.

'Not that way!'

But he was steadier on his feet now; that coffee must have

been strong. He turned, the cup and saucer still in his hand, and I reached out to take them from him.

'Use the other door,' I said. 'It'll take you into the corridor next to reception. Get the doorman to call you a cab.'

He gave a curt nod, apparently sober now. Perhaps anger with me had driven the alcohol from his bloodstream. I watched him go, a hard knot of anxiety in my stomach. When he got to the door I called *goodnight*, but he didn't answer, just raised a hand and continued on his way.

I brushed the tears from my hot cheeks, pressed the backs of my fingers against my eyes to cool them, and headed back to the ballroom.

I didn't know it then, but the evening was only going to get worse.

THIRTY

LONDON

Eight months ago

The lights had dimmed in the ballroom and the music was louder. Coloured beams flashed and pulsed above the space that served as the dance floor.

I made my way back to the table. Matt had reappeared and was sitting talking to Simon, an empty pint glass in front of him. The other seats were empty, their owners presumably gone to dance or smoke. I placed my hand on Matt's shoulder as I resumed my seat, but he didn't acknowledge me.

Simon smiled at me awkwardly, a flicker of an apology. My heart sank. I could see already how it had gone: Matt returning, asking where I was, Simon relating the story of Alistair's appearance, trying to make light of it but unable to miss his colleague's reaction. He stood up, looking uncomfortable. 'I need to call home,' he said, unconvincingly. 'Check on the sitter.' He hurried off, leaving Matt and me alone together.

'Want to dance?' I asked, hoping to postpone the explosion.

But he folded his arms and stared silently ahead. I sighed. 'I take it that's a no.'

He twisted towards me. A nerve was throbbing at his jaw. 'I'm glad you think this is funny.'

'Actually, Matt, I don't think it's funny at all. Can't we have just one night out together without it ending in an argument?'

'That's up to you.'

He punctuated the 'you' with a stab of his finger on the tabletop, and for a brief, glorious second, I wondered how it would feel to get up and leave him there. He could prod at the table to his heart's content, and I could – well, I could do something, anything, that didn't involve having to watch it.

'Right,' I said instead, assuming my usual role as designated adult. 'I take it you're upset about Alistair.'

'You're doing it again, aren't you?' His expression was thunderous. 'He's pissed out of his head, Simon said, and you're covering for him!'

'He's had a drink, yes. So have I. So have you,' I said, staring meaningfully at his empty pint glass. 'It's Christmas. It's not a big deal.' I was uncomfortably aware that I was parroting Alistair.

'Except that you clearly thought it was, or you wouldn't have bundled him out of here. Wanted to get him out of the way before Roberto spotted him – am I right?'

'This is *my* event, Matt,' I tried to reason with him. 'Alistair causing a scene is hardly going to endear me to Roberto, is it?'

He shook his head. 'Rubbish. You're covering his arse again. After everything we talked about.'

'Now hold on, I never said—'

But he was getting to his feet, pushing back his chair.

'Matt, just sit down,' I snapped. 'You can't strop off every time—'

But apparently he could. I watched him stomp across the room before being swallowed up in a crowd near the doors. I took a gulp of wine and retrieved my bag from the floor, then headed for the ladies, where no one could try to make conversation or ask me what was wrong.

The hotel loos were the kind with thick carpet and soft lighting, and – thankfully – no queue. Beyond the sinks was a separate area with upholstered chairs and a long vanity unit along one wall. Pots of cotton wool and bottles of expensive hand cream dotted the glass-topped surface. Perhaps I'd stay there all night, wait it out until it was late enough to say my goodbyes and slope off home.

I locked the heavy wooden door of the cubicle behind me and settled myself on the closed toilet seat. We couldn't go on like this, I realised. Matt and I barely saw each other these days, and the truth was, things were better that way. Any length of time in each other's company, and we were at each other's throats. How had it come to this?

I tried to remember how it had been at first. We used to have a laugh, used to enjoy each other's company. But somewhere along the line, that had changed. Was that my fault? I wondered. Had I been too focused on my work, guilty as charged of never putting him first?

No, that wasn't fair. Matt was every bit as career-focused as I was. But perhaps, it now occurred to me, he was focused on promotion because he was looking to the future, to raising a family. My spirits lifted at the thought. We'd never really talked about children, but I'd assumed we'd start trying when the time was right. It would explain why he cared so much, why he was so angry at me for trying to shield Alistair.

I heard the creak of a door, a snatch of laughter. Two women had entered the loos together. I rechecked the door was locked and tuned them out.

And there wasn't just Matt to consider, was there? Alistair's drinking, the loss of control – it worried me. People with an alcohol problem couldn't be relied on, I knew that all too well. Our conversation earlier had proved as much. Alistair bringing up things that should have been long since forgotten, things that should never be mentioned again. And doing it while Roberto was in the very next room. What if next time I wasn't around when he started reminiscing? What if he gave me away, not even meaning to do it, just letting something slip when he'd had one too many? There was no denying it – Alistair being gone would have its advantages.

The women had taken a couple of cubicles further down and were continuing their conversation through the partition. I'd sat here long enough. I'd go back in and mingle for a bit, then make my excuses. With any luck, Roberto would be basking in the attention of his admirers and wouldn't even notice I'd left. I stood and reached for the flush for the sake of appearances.

'He should have been out on his ear long ago.'

The voice made my hand freeze over the metal button. Was it who I thought it was?

'I know, right? I can't believe he got away with talking to Harvey like that.'

Harvey. So the news about Alistair had got out. I should have known better than to have expected anything different. I wondered who'd been gossiping, but I didn't have to wonder long.

A flush, the rattle of a lock. 'I suppose it helps having friends in high places.' It was the first woman again, and now I recognised those private school vowels: it was Roberto's secretary, Elise. *No good ever comes from listening at doors*, I told myself. But I stayed where I was all the same. A second flush, another door opening. 'It's a disgrace. The old boys' network covering up for each other.' This voice was lower: one of Elise's friends, presumably, but I couldn't place her.

'Except this time, it's a woman.'

There was a silence, loaded with significance. I felt the blood rush to my cheeks as I realised they were talking about me. My hand was on the door latch, and I was ready to burst in on them and demand they repeat their accusations to my face; but somehow, I didn't move.

There was the sound of running water, then nothing. At any moment, they would leave. If I was going to confront them, I had to do it now.

'Hold on,' Elise said. 'I just need to...' Her voice sounded further away, and I pictured her taking a seat at the vanity unit, digging in her bag for lipstick.

What was the point of going out there? What would I even say? They were right, after all. I *had* been trying to help Alistair. And it wasn't just because I owed him. He'd given years of service to this company; surely he deserved better than to be chucked on the scrap heap the minute things weren't going so well? But these two wouldn't understand that. They were too young to imagine their own stars could ever fade.

'You look gorgeous already, Elle,' the second voice drawled. 'Have you seen him yet?'

'Who?'

'Okay then, have it your way.'

Elise giggled, a sound that set my teeth on edge. 'We might have chatted.' A pause. 'He told me he liked my dress.'

There was a snort. 'I bet he did. Did he manage to keep his eyes on your face as he said it?'

More giggling. I wished they'd get on with it and bugger off. I'd been skulking there for too long to emerge from the cubicle now, and all I wanted was to go home.

'We couldn't talk for long. *She's* here as well, isn't she?'

My ears pricked up. So Elise was flirting with someone else's boyfriend. I found it didn't surprise me. I only hoped it was someone who'd give her holy hell when she found out.

I heard the snap of a bag closing. 'You'd better be careful,

Elle,' said the first woman again. 'She could make things difficult for you if she finds out.'

'She's not going to find out.' I heard the squeak of the door opening. Finally, they were leaving.

Elise's voice grew fainter as they stepped outside. If she'd waited a second longer, I would never have heard what came next. 'Besides,' she said, 'the way things are going, I doubt she'll be the HR director much longer.'

The door closed behind them, and everything fell silent.

THIRTY-ONE

NEW YORK

Now

We're running out of water.

Maeve has been drinking steadily since her panic attack. Every time she lifts the bottle to her lips, I have to stop myself from wincing. She needs it, I realise that. But the clear plastic shows me there's only a couple of inches left at the bottom. And I'm so thirsty my throat feels like sandpaper.

I should go to the speaker and ask for more water, but I don't know if anyone can hear me. I could hold up the bottle to the camera, but I don't know if anyone can see me. And if I do either of those things and it turns out they can't, I'll have drawn Maeve's attention to the problem. I don't want to risk another panic attack.

'You know,' Maeve says quietly, and I force my eyes away from the bottle to look at her, 'I haven't talked to anyone like this for ages.'

I'm about to mutter a platitude, but stop myself. After all, it's the same for me. Since I moved to New York, I've barely spoken to anyone outside work. Keeping my distance has become a way of life. It's better that way. Safer for all concerned.

'I feel like I've been talking too much,' I say, with rare honesty.

She shakes her head. 'You've been trying to keep my mind off this.' She gestures at the walls. 'I appreciate it.'

I make a decision. 'Can I ask you something?' Instantly, she looks wary, so I don't give her a chance to reply. 'Are you here to protest?'

She looks at me blankly, giving nothing away.

'It doesn't matter if you are,' I say. 'People do it sometimes. I don't have a problem with it – no one here does. We understand people care about the projects we work on.'

For a moment, she doesn't say anything. Then she gives a short, sharp nod and looks away.

'So you don't have an appointment?' Her silence is all the reply I need. I remember the fracas at the entry gates, the way she rummaged in her bag as she talked to the security guard. 'Do you even have a pass?'

She bites her lip, and I laugh. 'Well, you've got guts, I'll give you that.'

She doesn't smile. 'It hasn't got me very far, has it?'

I stop laughing. She's right about that.

Should I be worried about what she'll do when we get out of here? She's effectively trespassing after all. Trespassing with a gun in her bag. But she's explained that. And if her intensity makes me a little uncomfortable, something about her makes me feel sorry for her too. That attack, whatever it was, has clearly affected her. And she's here alone, come all this way without any friends to back her up. Trying to do the right thing. To stand up for what she believes in. And now she's finally here, and she's been stuck in a lift for – I check my watch – getting on for four hours.

'Do you want to tell me what project you're here about?' She doesn't respond and belatedly I realise it's better that I don't know. If anyone can hear what we're saying, I don't want to sound like I'm encouraging her. 'Okay, we don't need to talk about it. Just maybe arrange a meeting next time. Whatever it is, I'm sure the team will be happy to discuss your concerns.'

I realise I sound like a company spokesperson. Well, that's what I am, in a way. And it feels good, knowing I still believe the firm I work for is a force for good in the world. That even now, that's something I have left.

'You like working here, don't you?' Maeve says.

'I wouldn't have stayed this long if I didn't.'

'That's good.' She looks thoughtful. 'I've never had that. My jobs have always been something to pay the bills, that's all.'

'There's nothing wrong with that,' I say, and now I'm worried I've given her the wrong impression. 'And it's not always fun here either. There have been times when I've hated it.'

'But not now?' Maeve prompts.

I pause, trying to find the words. 'It hasn't been an easy year.' And there it is, the shadow I've been trying to ignore. My eyes prickle and I bite my lip hard, to stop anything else coming out.

She looks at me with sympathy. 'Do you want to talk about it?' she asks.

I look down at the floor of the lift, and the grey pattern swims in my vision. I press my lips together and shake my head.

For a moment, everything is still. Then I hear the faint slap of water sliding along plastic. Maeve is taking another drink.

THIRTY-TWO

LONDON

Maeve, fifteen years ago

Maeve tried to focus on what Alistair was saying. He'd wired up a small camera to his computer, and displayed on the monitor was a photograph of a nondescript kitchen, plain white cupboards and a grey Formica worktop. Cheap but not ugly. Newish. Clean. Compared to the other places they'd seen, it was a palace.

'There's no washing machine,' he was saying, 'but there's plumbing for one. I thought I could pick up something cheap. And anyway, there's a launderette ten minutes' walk away.'

Maeve murmured. She had to tell him, but her stomach was in knots. The image on the monitor changed to a cream wall with a window in the middle. Light fell onto a plain beige carpet. The arm of a dark brown sofa was just visible on one side. In the opposite corner, the date was printed in orange lozenges.

'He said it can be furnished or unfurnished,' Alistair said.

'The landlord's got loads of flats, apparently, so he just moves things between them.'

She nodded dumbly as he moved on to a photograph of a bedroom, then a shot of a toilet that was presumably as much of the bathroom as the tight space allowed to be captured on camera.

'So what do you think?' Alistair turned to her. He was trying not to give anything away, but she could see the excitement in the way his knee jiggled up and down. She should have told him before, before he'd ever gone to see the bloody flat.

He was waiting for her reaction; she couldn't put it off any longer. 'It's great, Ali,' she said. 'I really like it.' He beamed back at her and was about to reply when she cut him off. 'The thing is, I can't help with the rent anymore.'

She watched his face fall, and her throat tightened. 'Paul and I...' She found it hard to say his name, she realised. How long would that continue? She said it again, experimentally. 'Paul and I have split up.'

His disappointment changed instantly to sympathy. 'Oh, Maeve. What happened?'

She paused before answering, wanting to be sure of picking the right words. 'We haven't been getting on. It's been hard for him, everything with Anna. He won't talk about it. And we've just, sort of, drifted apart.'

He reached out and pulled her into a hug. He'd grown strong, she thought, as his arms closed tightly around her, as strong as their father. But unlike him, Alistair was gentle, kind. She was filled with a fierce love for her brother. He needed her. She had done the right thing.

She drew back from him, eyes dry. She wouldn't let herself cry. 'It's okay, Ali,' she said. 'I'll be fine. But it means I need to keep my flat. I can't afford to help with your rent just now. I'm so sorry.'

'Of course not. I shouldn't have agreed to it in the first

place.' He smiled at her. 'I can't have my big sister sorting everything out for me for the rest of my life. I need to stand on my own two feet.'

She heard the bleakness behind his effort at bravery. *You won't, though,* she thought. *But that's okay. That's why I'll always be here.* Out loud, she said, 'It'll be fine, Ali. We'll find somewhere else. I promise.'

He reached for her hand. She'd thought he was going to take it, but instead his fingers closed around the bracelet he'd given her. She followed his gaze to the silver chain. For a moment, she didn't register the significance of what she was looking at. And then she realised, and the world stopped spinning.

Her brother's voice sounded like it was coming from underwater. 'You've lost your heart,' he said.

THIRTY-THREE

LONDON

Eight months ago

'Sherry, my dear?'

Matt's dad jiggled the bottle at me. I could still taste the sickly sweetness of the glass I'd already forced down. *No thank you*, I went to reply. 'Just a small one, then,' I heard myself say instead. He gave me a stagey wink and filled my proffered glass to the brim.

'Three words. No, four. Are we counting thumbs?'

Matt, standing in the centre of the living room, rolled his eyes at his mother. 'No, Mum! I told you that last time.'

'Oh well, darling, you know I can't remember. Is it a book or a film?'

I watched as Matt drew a square in the air with his hands, and tried to ignore the ache in my stomach that had nothing to do with the gargantuan Christmas lunch we'd devoured an hour ago.

'First word. Straight? Point? Pointer?'

'*Line of Duty*,' I called out.

'Yes!' Matt punched the air.

'Oh. We didn't watch that, did we, Philip?' Eleanor smiled tightly.

I'd done the wrong thing, I realised. I should have let her keep guessing.

'You have my turn, Eleanor,' I said.

'Oh no, dear. Rules are rules!'

I knew better than to argue. I got to my feet, taking the topmost card from the pile on the side table. I felt silly standing there in front of them, trying to think of a way to mime *Unbreakable*. Matt had loved that film, I remembered, but I'd barely stayed awake.

He'd returned to the sofa, next to his mother, and she gathered his arm in hers, relishing the time with her boy. Philip sat on the armchair nearest them, contentment radiating out of every pore. *They're my family now too*, I thought; but I knew it was different. If we split up, Matt's parents might be sad for a moment, but it wouldn't really matter to them, not if Matt was happy. Soon Philip would be offering sherry to another girl, Eleanor checking whether she'd enjoyed the Christmas pudding. Elise's image came into my head and I swallowed. She'd got it all wrong, I told myself, mistaken what Matt thought of as harmless flirting for something more. And she knew nothing about me or my work. If she thought I was someone she could simply brush aside, she'd soon find out she was mistaken.

'What have you done to your hand?' Eleanor's voice was tinged with irritation. 'You're bleeding all over the carpet.'

I looked down in surprise to see blood running down the side of my thumb. I must have been pressing my nail into the skin there without realising it; the tip of my index finger was stained red.

I excused myself to go to the bathroom, and Eleanor

dropped to her knees, dabbing at the carpet with a tissue. When I returned, she was standing in the centre of the room, holding her glasses away from her eyes while she inspected the next card.

'It's a film,' Matt informed me as I took the empty space on the sofa next to Philip. 'Three words!'

She beamed at him, immaculate in her cashmere jumper and sharply pressed trousers. My own mum, I was sure, had never owned a cashmere jumper, and she'd have escaped to the kitchen at the first mention of charades. But she'd smiled at me like that, like I was the most important person in the world. The ache of her absence was like a missing limb.

'Penny for them?' Philip was smiling at me.

'Just enjoying being here with you all.'

'Christmas is a time for family,' he said kindly, and pretended not to notice when I looked away to blink back tears.

For the rest of our stay, I tried hard to immerse myself in the present. So what if things weren't perfect between Matt and me? Surely this was better than another Christmas alone, eating a ready meal and watching *Love, Actually* for the fifty millionth time? Wasn't this what I wanted, had wanted for so long – a family, a home filled with love? I could have those things with Matt. Every relationship had its rough patches, of course it did. Even Philip and Eleanor must have had blazing rows now and again. Sticking with it was what counted, making the effort. That's what I'd do. And when he saw I was really trying, Matt would do the same.

Being on my best behaviour, though, was tiring, and part of me was relieved when it was time to go home. Matt disappeared into the bathroom as soon as we'd unloaded the presents from the car, and I put the kettle on. I wondered if his sudden exit meant he was texting Elise, then chastised myself for being paranoid. That night we made love for the first time in weeks, and as I lay there afterwards, my head against his shoulder, I told myself I should be grateful for what we had. And I'd do whatever it took to keep it.

Despite the cold, grey mornings and the Tube trains full of sniffing commuters, I was pleased to get back to work. It was just after New Year's, and most of the staff hadn't yet returned. I enjoyed having the space to myself, the lights flickering on with the motion sensors as I made my way to my office. Roberto wouldn't be back until the following week, and I'd planned to make the most of my head start and have my proposals for the new appraisal system ready for his return.

Matt had started back the same day, and I'd hoped we'd have lunch together. We'd made a joint New Year's resolution to make more time for each other, and I'd planned to surprise him, persuade him outside to a coffee shop where they'd still have spiced coffee and other festive treats. But when I got to his desk, his monitor was switched off and he wasn't there. Telling myself I was simply stretching my legs, I took a detour past Roberto's office. There was no sign of life here either, but a solitary black coat hung from a coat stand to one side of the cluster of desks outside his door. I approached and peered at the label: Karen Millen. A faint floral fragrance clung to the woollen fabric. It could have belonged to anyone, but somehow I was sure it was Elise's. I stared at it, trying not to let my mind wander to where she might be, who she might be with. I went to the canteen and bought a sandwich to eat at my desk.

The next few days were uneventful. Most people were still on holiday, and it wasn't until the Friday that something happened to shatter the calm.

It was late in the afternoon and I was engrossed in my work. Matt had put his head around the door ten minutes earlier to check what time I'd be ready to leave. I was midway through typing a final email, when I heard a commotion in the corridor outside. I looked up as my door was flung open and Elise burst in, mascara running in streaks down her face.

'That's it! I can't take any more of this!' she shouted, and I stared at her in alarm, suddenly sure that she was about to tell me that she and Matt were together, that he was desperate to leave me and was too afraid to break the news. But instead she said, 'If you don't sort him out, I'm resigning!'

'Sort *who* out?' I asked, bewildered.

She looked at me as if she couldn't believe what she was hearing. 'Douglass, of course! Alistair piss artist Douglass!' My heart sank as she screwed her hands into fists, her chest heaving in indignation. 'He's off his head! I told him to go home, and he said I wasn't his boss.'

I resisted the urge to tell her he was right. But Elise wasn't finished. 'And he said...' She took a quavering breath. 'He said it was none of my business, and he called me, he called me...'

She was puce with rage, and I was torn between wanting to laugh and cry. 'What did he call you, Elise?' I asked, a shameful part of me curious to hear what Alistair had come up with.

She took a deep breath and exhaled. 'A *millennial*,' she choked out.

I spluttered and put my hand to my mouth, turning it into a cough. She glared at me. 'I'm Gen Z!'

'Where is he now?' I asked.

'He was at his desk a minute ago.' She flushed, apparently conscious of a need to explain herself. 'I was on my way back from a meeting and he was just sat there, giggling and stinking of booze.'

I nodded grimly. 'Leave it with me.'

'But aren't you going to do something? He's sitting there out of his mind! Right now!'

I sat back in my seat and folded my hands. I remembered

that conversation in the ladies: *old boys' network*. 'I *said*, leave it with me, Elise,' I repeated icily.

She looked like she was going to argue, but then thought better of it and spun on her heel, stalking out and leaving my door gaping open behind her. I waited until she was out of sight before getting to my feet and making my way to Alistair's desk.

I could hear him muttering to himself as I approached, one finger jabbing at his keyboard. I pulled out the swivel chair from the empty desk next to him and sat down.

'Alistair,' I said, and he jumped and swung around, his eyes wild. There was no question that Elise was right: the smell of alcohol was overpowering. Being in this state at work was a serious offence, but that wasn't what worried me most. It was the look in his eyes. The desperation.

'Oh God,' he groaned. 'Oh God, oh God, oh God.'

'Come on now,' I said, 'you're in no state to be here.'

He looked at me as if he didn't understand what I was saying. 'It's you,' he said. 'It's *really you*.'

I blinked at him. 'Er, yes, it's me. We need to get you home now.'

I reached for his arm, but he scooted backwards, his chair coming to an abrupt halt as it smacked into the wall behind him.

'I didn't know,' he said. 'You have to believe me, I didn't know.'

'Didn't know what?' I said, confused. 'Is this something about what happened with Ted Harvey?'

He covered his face with his hands. 'I thought maybe, yes, when I saw your CV...'

I jerked upright and scanned the office in alarm. The other desks were empty, but who knew how long that would last. 'Shut up, Alistair,' I hissed. 'Just shut up right now.'

'I had my doubts. I always wondered—'

'Okay, that's enough,' I said, getting to my feet. I had to get him out of there before he said anything more. Before someone heard him. I grabbed his arm and pulled him to his feet, terror making me strong. 'Get home right now and sober up. We'll talk about this tomorrow.'

I grabbed his coat from the back of his chair and tugged him down the corridor, gripping his arm like a vice. I bundled him into a lift and frogmarched him to the front door, earning a curious look from the security guard at reception. Alistair was mumbling about being sorry, but I tried not to listen to him. I hailed a cab and made him give the driver his address. 'He'll pay you double,' I said as the cabbie looked at him in dismay. 'Right, Alistair?'

'I can't have him being sick in the cab,' the driver said.

'Then give him a carrier bag,' I snapped, pushing Alistair inside and slamming the door behind him.

The cabbie continued to remonstrate, but his words washed over me as I turned and headed back inside. It was happening, just the way I'd feared. Alistair was coming undone, and the truth was spilling out of him at the seams.

And I'd be the one to face the consequences – unless I stopped him first.

THIRTY-FOUR

BRISTOL

Maeve, fourteen years ago

Maeve tipped back her head and enjoyed the caress of the sunshine on her face. Even now, the last few months fading away, the memory of them lent a sharp joy to moments like this. She was here, in a park, the sun on her skin and the scent of summer in her nostrils. She was free.

'Thanks for coming up,' she said to Alistair. 'You know you didn't need to.'

He stretched out beside her on the grass, watching a group of kids playing football. 'I wanted to. You're always coming to London. Besides,' he said, grimacing, 'the flat still stinks of paint.'

She smiled. Alistair had been throwing himself into redecorating his flat with all the zeal of a first-time homeowner. 'I bet it was worth it, though. Making it your own.'

He grinned back at her. 'It does look good.'

She watched as a boy in a blue T-shirt kicked a ball wildly, narrowly avoiding an old man walking his dog. The man glowered at them and continued on his way. It was strange, the last year felt almost like a dream now. It was hard to remember what a mess everything had been. She'd been afraid of everything then: afraid of Alistair staying in that flat with Kirsten, giving in to temptation and starting to drink again. Afraid that those bastards he owed money to would lose patience and call in a debt he couldn't pay. And then afraid of the mistake she'd made, of putting her trust in someone who didn't deserve it.

She missed Paul sometimes, even now. She remembered returning to the flat that last time, standing there looking down at the bed they would never share again. She'd removed the bracelet Alistair had given her, replaced it with the emerald pendant that had been Paul's gift to her on their first anniversary. ('Emerald is the birthstone for May,' he'd said, smiling at his own cleverness. 'May for my Mae.') She'd looked at her reflection in the mirror as she'd fastened it around her neck, searching for evidence of what she was. But she hadn't cried then. She had saved her tears for when they were needed.

She'd seen less of Alistair for a while after that. She'd lost weight, didn't look well – she didn't want him to worry. He'd had one too many questions before, when she'd told him that Bethan had died. How was the investigation going? Were they sure it was an accident? And all the time his studiously neutral tone was undermined by the anxiety in his eyes. But when she'd told him she'd split up with Paul, he'd respected her need for privacy. He knew, perhaps, more than she'd even acknowledged to herself, how much Paul had meant to her. How their life together had been the hope of something different, something strong and lasting and kind. Something that would in time have incorporated Alistair too, their own small family, always there for each other.

The two of them still spoke regularly on the phone, and despite Maeve's worries it gradually became clear that things were improving for her brother. First there'd been the promotion at work, the new role coming with a significant jump in salary. The extra money had allowed him to pay off his debts – *you see,* she'd told herself, *something always comes along in the end* – and, for now at least, that appeared to be enough for the men he owed. His newfound financial security had brought him fresh confidence, a self-belief she hadn't seen in him before. He'd begun talking about buying his own place, arguing with a self-conscious smile that renting to pay someone else's mortgage made little sense. And finally he'd bought the flat, a ground-floor conversion in a Victorian terrace in Ealing Broadway. He was settled, successful, happy; it was all she'd ever wanted for him.

'So where do they hang out?'

She realised he'd been talking to her and tuned back in. 'Sorry?'

'Your students, Maeve! People who might want to come and work for yours truly.' He nudged her and grinned. 'Have you been listening to a word I've been saying?'

She sat up. 'Course I have. What's this about students again?'

He laughed. 'I told you, for the graduate programme. I want people from outside London, people who don't think the world stops at the M25.' He tapped his bag. 'I've brought flyers. There's a careers office on campus, right? You can take me there. And maybe, I don't know, other studenty places. Cafés or bars, or whatever.'

She wrinkled her nose. 'Just because people live in London now doesn't mean they don't know anything about the rest of the country. Paul's daughter went to uni there, and she was Bristol born and bred.' She noted with satisfaction that she hadn't even paused before saying his name. It reminded her how far she'd come.

But he wasn't deterred, and she followed his lead as he set off for the park gates, brushing the grass from her jeans as they went. They'd taken just a few steps when she felt something hard slam into her back, a stinging pain. She spun around to see a football rolling away from her, the boy in the blue T-shirt smirking, his friends wearing expressions of mingled shock and hilarity.

The fury came from nowhere, a hot red tide that filled her up. 'You little shit,' she snarled, and her clenched fists trembled. 'You *fucking* little shit.'

The boy's grin faltered and he took a step back. He hadn't expected her to stop, thought he could do what he liked to her, just like he had with the man walking his dog. Thought she'd just take it...

She felt a weight on her shoulder, pulling her back. 'Leave it, Maeve.' Alistair's voice was urgent, a sharp edge of panic. 'He's just a kid.'

She shrugged off his hand, her eyes locked on the boy. She held him in her stare, felt the rage rushing through her, wanting him to see how close he'd come. Then she took a breath and felt the tide subside. She turned away. Today was a good day. She wasn't going to let him ruin it.

They crossed the park and headed for the campus. Alistair barely stopped talking, his voice light, making bad jokes. He wanted to take her mind off the boy in the blue T-shirt. Gradually she felt the tight feeling inside her chest loosen and melt away.

Soon they were at the entrance to a brick building with sliding glass doors. Above them a green and white sign read 'Careers Service'. They dropped off a pile of flyers there, then did the same at a couple of cafés at the edge of the campus. 'There's no point in leaving them in bars,' Maeve said firmly. 'They'll just end up as beer mats.'

They were hungry by the time they headed back to her flat, so they called in at an Indian takeaway down the road and bought steaming foil cartons of biryani and dhansak. They were halfway out the door when Alistair stopped and pointed at a notice taped to the inside of the window.

10% OFF FOR STUDENTS WITH NUS CARD

He turned and pulled the last few flyers from his bag. 'Can I leave these here, mate?'

The man behind the counter raised a hand distractedly, his attention already on his next customer.

'Honestly, Ali. A takeaway?'

He shrugged. 'Why not? Anyone who likes a curry is all right by me.'

Her flat was just around the corner, and the cartons of food were still steaming as Maeve dished them onto plates. Alistair was already laying the small table with cutlery. He had settled into domesticity quickly, she thought, imagining him doing the same in his own home. Maybe he'd find someone to share it with soon. It would be difficult, probably, seeing another woman take her place as his first confidante, but she would cope with it when it happened. He deserved someone to share his life with, someone who'd see how special he was. She thought she'd found that with Paul, but she'd been wrong. She wanted better for Alistair.

He looked up, sensing her eyes on him. 'Everything okay?' he said.

She nodded, feeling a lightness in her chest. 'Yes, it is. Everything's just as it should be.'

*

NEW YORK

Maeve, now

You were happy once, weren't you? I've tried to hold on to that, to help me get through the days. To keep going until I could find what I needed.

You loved your job then. I never really understood what you did, though you tried to explain it to me often enough. But I could see the satisfaction it gave you, the sense of purpose. That was good enough for me.

Maybe you'd have transferred here if things had been different. Got some smart New York apartment, showed me the sights when I came to visit. You might have been in this lift instead of me – joking with Cerys, probably, making her laugh.

But it all changed, didn't it? And I tried to ignore it, tried to pretend everything was all right. I should have acted, but I didn't.

I won't make the same mistake again.

THIRTY-FIVE

LONDON

Maeve, eight months ago

It was the first Christmas he hadn't decorated the house.

Maeve could tell as soon as she glanced at the front door as she drove past, searching for a parking space. In other years, there'd have been an extravagant wreath, something involving berries and fairy lights and big velvet ribbons. The Christmases of their childhood had never had anything like that. It didn't bother Maeve one way or the other, but since Alistair had upgraded his flat to a house, he'd made more of an effort with every passing year. It had become tradition for him to walk to the local cemetery and cut long boughs of holly and strands of ivy from the overgrown hedges, threading them around candlesticks and heaping them on the mantelpiece in his living room. There'd been spiced candles and jars of baubles, strings of lights and a tree festooned in white and silver. One year had even seen a reindeer made of woven willow branches grazing indifferently in the tiny front garden. But today the front door was bare and the window dark.

She parked at the nearest spot, a few doors away, and bundled her case and the bag of presents from the back seat. *He's been busy*, she told herself as she locked the car and walked to the front door. *That's all it is.*

She'd called from the motorway services to update him on her arrival time, but it was still a long minute after she rang the bell that she heard his footsteps in the hallway. When the door opened, the sight of him made her catch her breath; but she recovered quickly, dropping her case and leaning into him for an awkward hug. His shoulder blades were sharp beneath her hands. She tried not to breathe too deeply, wanting to preserve the fiction that he hadn't lapsed.

He ushered her in, taking her case in one hand. There was a nervous energy about him. He offered her a drink and she asked for tea, hoping he'd follow her lead. She kicked off her shoes and followed him to the kitchen, chattering about the traffic as he boiled the kettle. There was already a half-empty glass of wine on the worktop. He finished and refilled it as she talked.

'What happened to the reindeer?' she asked, hoping to make light of it. 'Is Rudolph on strike?' He frowned, as if he didn't understand. 'You had it in the garden before,' she persisted. 'The reindeer made of willow.'

'I wasn't in the mood this year.'

'Oh. Right.' Silence between them as the kettle burbled and hummed. Then, 'So where shall I put the presents?'

He pulled open a jar and placed a teabag in a mug. 'I haven't bought much,' he said. 'I hope you don't mind. I've been... My mind has been on other things.'

She tutted. 'You know I don't care about presents. But you've been working too hard again. I can tell. You haven't been taking care of yourself.'

He said something too low for her to hear.

'What was that?'

He cleared his throat. 'Don't, Maeve. Just don't.'

She thought about arguing, but something stopped her. He was having a difficult time at work, that much was clear. Those Americans, probably, the ones who'd bought the firm. He'd brushed away her concerns about the takeover at the time, saying he wasn't worried about job cuts – but somewhere along the line, that had obviously changed. She'd tackle him about it later, get to the bottom of what was going on. For now, she was content to let it lie; it was Christmas, after all.

They settled in the living room and Alistair switched on a table lamp, the light casting a rosy glow over the furnishings. Maeve piled his presents on a corner table and lowered herself onto the sofa, folding her legs beneath her and nursing her mug of tea, holding the comforting warmth to her chest. 'This is nice,' she said. 'I've always loved this room.' And even bare of decorations, it was true. She loved the high ceilings, the beautiful plasterwork. Alistair had added thick rugs and comfy chairs, and the alcoves next to the fireplace were filled with bookshelves. But more than the elegance of the surroundings, she loved being here with him, even if he was on edge. She'd get him to open up in time, talk it through, make everything better.

'Do you remember those flats we looked at? Back when I was trying to get out of that place with Kirsten?' he said.

'God' – she laughed – 'we saw some real dives, didn't we? Do you remember that loft conversion? You could only stand up in it in the middle!'

He looked into the distance, took another gulp of wine. 'They weren't all like that. That one I saw on my own was okay.'

'Which one—?'

'You were going to come with me, but you had to cancel. You told me to take photos. We looked at them together afterwards.'

Maeve placed her cup carefully on the floor. 'Did we?'

He reached onto the bookshelf next to him and lifted something down. 'I found them the other day,' he said. 'Do you want to take a look?'

He held out a pile of photographs, the surfaces glossy. It was a long time, she realised, since she'd looked at a photo that wasn't on someone's phone. 'How long ago was this?' She smiled at him. 'I can't believe you kept these.'

'You know me,' he said. 'I don't throw things out.'

She stared at the image. It showed a room with cream walls, a square of light reflected from the window onto a beige carpet. To one side it was just possible to make out something brown. It looked like the arm of a sofa. Her eyes fastened on something in the corner, and for a moment she couldn't breathe. Her fingers tightened on the photograph and the image trembled gently in her hands. She rested her elbows on her knees to make it stop.

'It was fourteen years ago,' he said. 'Can you believe it?'

She nodded, mute. The evidence was there in front of her. The date in orange digits in the bottom right-hand corner.

'The twenty-fifth of June,' he said, and he was watching her now. She could almost feel him looking into her mind, watching the memory of that day playing back like a film.

'I remember feeling guilty,' he continued. 'All the travelling back and forth you were doing. And when you had so much going on too.'

'Did I? I don't remember.' Her voice sounded strange in her ears.

'You were with that guy at the time, the psychologist. What was his name?'

'I don't remember,' she said again. She had to change the subject, but her brain had stopped working.

'Paul, that was it. He was older than you, a lot older. It's all coming back to me now.'

She forced a laugh, but it sounded jagged, like something

shattering. 'You have a better memory for my old boyfriends than I do.'

He stared at her. 'Do I?' She didn't reply. 'I kept thinking it wasn't fair to you, to keep you coming up and down to London like that. But then I thought, *You know what? It's only right that Maeve sees the flats.* Because you'd said you were going to help with the rent. It was only fair you saw what you'd be paying towards.' Maeve tried to speak, but her mouth was dry. 'And then you couldn't come that day, so I went on my own and took the photos. Do you remember why that was? Why you had to cancel?'

'God, I've no idea.' Maeve finally found her voice. 'Work probably. It was all so long ago. And it worked out for the best in the end. You found somewhere a million times better.'

'You split up with him not long after that, didn't you?'

'Paul?' She shook her head. 'I honestly don't recall.'

'But you did.' He sat forward in his chair. 'That's why you couldn't help with the rent in the end. You'd been going to move in with him properly, get rid of your place. And then you split up and had to keep your flat. Not that I minded about the money. I felt bad for saying I'd accept it in the first place. I was always doing stuff like that, wasn't I? Always making a mess and expecting you to clear it up.'

The self-loathing in his voice shook her. She looked across at him, hunched over in his chair. When had he last eaten a decent meal?

'No, Ali,' she said. 'No. It wasn't like that.'

'Do you miss him?' he said suddenly.

'What?'

'Paul. Were you sorry it ended?'

She swallowed. 'It had run its course. We both knew that.'

'You'd been arguing?'

'Yes, I mean – no. We'd just reached the end of the line.' With an effort, she straightened the pile of photographs and held them out to him. 'Why are you so interested in Paul Morgan all of a sudden?'

He took the photographs. He didn't return them to the bookshelf, instead raising himself from the chair and tucking them into his back pocket. 'No reason,' he said.

THIRTY-SIX

NEW YORK

Now

I check my watch. It's been four hours and thirty-eight minutes.

My throat is parched and although it's so hot in here the air is like treacle, my skin is no longer damp. Is it possible that I'm dehydrating so soon? I don't know, but thoughts of water fill my head, and there is none to be had. Maeve offered me the last of it ten minutes ago, and though I should have known better, I didn't have it in me to refuse. I drained every drop.

I held the empty bottle upside down in front of the camera. There's no point trying not to stress Maeve out about the gravity of our situation any longer. She knows it as well as I do. A moment afterwards there was a crackle of static on the intercom. Maeve thinks it means someone saw me, that they're trying to tell us they're going to get to us soon. At least, that's what she said. We're both trying to reassure each other, to keep our spirits up.

I keep reminding myself that we're in an office block in the middle of Manhattan. That we're only feet away from other people, people with access to tools and equipment, people who'll get us out of here soon. But I'm finding it hard to think, and when I try to imagine them on the other side of the lift shaft, those firefighters with their harnesses and jackhammers and circular saws, the only faces I see are Jay's and Leo's, the two of them sitting in an office together. 'I'm afraid I have to tell you something you may find disappointing,' Leo is saying. And then I watch as Jay's face crumples in shock.

It wasn't like that with Alistair. He buried his feelings deep down, even that final time, even when he was at his lowest. He was cryptic too. He'd say things I thought I understood, and then later I'd realise I hadn't understood them at all. That our wires were permanently crossed in a way I couldn't begin to untangle. I could say that I tried, but does that really matter when all's said and done? It doesn't matter to Alistair.

LONDON

Eight months ago

I got into the office early and went straight to Alistair's desk. I didn't expect to see him there after the horror show of the previous day, but I wasn't prepared to take any chances. His monitor was switched on, but the screen had gone to sleep. I hadn't returned to shut it down after hauling him out of the building. I did so now, double-checking there was no sign of his coat or belongings before making my way to reception. I waited there for ten minutes, trying to look nonchalant as I returned my colleagues' greetings. It occurred to me that I could have asked IT to disable Alistair's pass, asked reception to inform me when he complained it had stopped working; but there was a strict protocol for such requests. Besides, the news would have leaked out and added to the rumours already swirling about the building. Fool that I was, I still hoped it might be possible to sort it all out quietly.

Eventually, I could bear the waiting no longer. I returned to my desk, logged in and brought up Alistair's personal file. I picked up the phone and dialled his mobile. It went straight to voicemail and I wondered if that meant it had run out of charge while he was sleeping off what surely had to be the mother of all hangovers. There was a landline number too, and I was partway through dialling it when I thought again. I replaced the receiver, scribbled some details on a Post-it, and closed down my computer. There was a better way of doing this.

I swung past Alistair's desk a final time on my way out, but it remained deserted. Out on the street I considered hailing a cab before remembering that it was still rush hour. I punched the postcode into my phone, then headed for the Tube instead.

Alistair's address was a few minutes' walk from the station, a well-kept row of Victorian terraces. A count of the wheelie bins at the front suggested that most of them had escaped being converted into flats, at least for now. The woodwork was freshly painted, front doors in trendy shades of sage and dove grey, window boxes stuffed with festive foliage and fairy lights draped through skeletal trees. It was a million miles from the flat Matt and I shared, and I felt a stab of envy.

At first sight, Alistair's house was as smart as the rest. It wasn't until I was walking up the front path that I became aware of a faint air of shabbiness, a sort of dispirited look about the place. Bare twigs that had once presumably been flowers protruded from the soil of the window boxes. Here and there, straggly blades of grass crept up through the gravel that covered the small front garden. An old crisp packet had taken refuge in the far corner beneath the bay window. And although the paint on the front door was smooth, a thick layer of dust had accumulated on the ledges below the stained-glass panels.

There was a push button doorbell to one side and I pressed it, wondering if it would work; but I heard it ringing in the space beyond. Too late it occurred to me that Alistair might simply ignore it, but almost as soon as the thought had entered my head, I heard footsteps and the jangle of a latch, and the door was opening.

'Alistair,' I said. I was relieved to see that he was not only up but dressed. Better still, the baggy jumper and worn jeans suggested he had no plans to come to the office.

His eyes were wide with shock. 'What are you doing here?'

'I would have thought that was obvious,' I said, aiming to project more confidence than I felt. 'We need to talk about what happened yesterday. At work,' I added, feeling the need to remind us both that I had a professional reason for being there.

He stared at me, a muscle working in his jaw.

'So can I come in?' I asked, taking a half-step forward in anticipation. But he moved to bar my way, pulling the door tight against his shoulder. I looked up at him in confusion. 'We need to talk about what's going on.'

'It's not convenient.' He glanced back over his shoulder. 'And I don't appreciate you turning up here unannounced.'

The sharpness of his tone took me aback. 'I'm sorry,' I stuttered. 'I did try to call. There was no reply.'

'So you just decided to come to my house? This is harassment.'

'Now wait a minute—'

'Who is it, Ali?'

A woman's voice drifted down the hallway. Instinctively, I tried to peer over his shoulder, but he shifted to block my view.

'Just a survey,' he called back.

He leaned towards me, lowered his voice. 'As I've told you, this isn't convenient. I'm not feeling well, but I expect to be back at work tomorrow. If you have anything to say to me, Anna, you can say it then.'

I opened my mouth to reply, but the door was already closed.

THIRTY-SEVEN

LONDON

Maeve, eight months ago

Maeve balanced the tray on her hip as she knocked on the bedroom door. Alistair didn't answer, but she went in anyway, placing the tray on the floor while she crossed to the window and opened the curtains. He grumbled then and turned over in bed, shielding his eyes from the light with the back of one hand.

She said, 'I've brought you breakfast.' He grunted like a recalcitrant teenager. 'Are you going into work today?'

He didn't stir, and she bit down a sudden wave of irritation. 'Alistair,' she said more sharply, 'are you going to work?'

The hand moved from his eyes and made a kind of waving sign that she took to mean 'no'. She nodded, relieved. It was for the best. She wanted to spend the day with him, force him to tell her what was wrong. 'Eat your toast then,' she said, 'and get dressed. I'll see you downstairs in half an hour.'

She left him to it, closing the door behind her. He'd do as she asked; he might be losing his grip, but she was still his older sister, the closest thing he'd had to a mother since he was a small boy. Even now, he would look to her to make things right.

Sure enough, when thirty minutes had passed, he appeared in the doorway of the kitchen. He'd dressed in an old pair of jeans and a tatty jumper. He'd left the tray in his room, she realised; she made a mental note to retrieve it later. He sidled onto a stool at the island, avoiding her eyes.

'You're drinking again,' she said, without preamble. 'What's wrong?'

'Nothing.' He wouldn't look at her. 'I just wanted a drink.'

'Is it work?' No reply. 'Alistair? Is it work?'

'I told you, it's nothing.'

She studied him, her teeth gnawing at her bottom lip. She'd seen him worse than this, and yet – there was something different about him this time. He still wouldn't look at her, she realised; maybe that was it.

'You can tell me, Ali.' She softened her voice. 'We've always been able to talk to each other, haven't we? We've always been there for each other.'

His head dropped lower. 'Why do you do it?'

'What?'

'Why do you always try to protect me?'

'You're my little brother,' she said. 'It's my job.' He didn't reply. 'Whatever's bothering you, it's not worth all this. You know that.'

His fingers knitted together and unknitted again. She waited. If she gave him time, he'd talk to her in the end. The seconds ticked past and twice she saw him shift, lift his head as if about to speak. Finally, he clasped his hands together. 'I have to ask you something,' he said.

And then a shrill ring cut through the silence. *The bloody doorbell.*

'I'll get it,' she said, but he was already on his feet, scuttling off to the front door as if his life depended on it.

She raised her eyes to the ceiling in frustration. The latch clicked and she heard a murmur of voices from the end of the hallway. She tried to tune in to the conversation, but it was a shade too quiet to hear; but then Alistair's voice was raised, an edge of anger. Had she heard the word 'harassment'?

Fear stabbed at her insides. Was this why he'd started drinking again? Some gambling debt he couldn't pay? And if whoever he owed money to was coming to his house...

'Who is it, Ali?' she called, wanting to show them he wasn't alone.

'Just a survey,' he called back.

It was exactly the kind of thing he'd say. No wonder he was embarrassed about telling her. No wonder he was harking back to that time she'd offered to help pay his rent. All those years ago, but it was the last time he'd been in debt, pissing off people he shouldn't have pissed off. He must be worried about her finding out, worried about asking for her help. Of course, things were different now – he had a good job, was making good money. But if there was trouble at work, if those Americans were talking about cuts...

It was suddenly all so clear. That's what he'd been about to ask her. He'd been plucking up the courage to ask if he could borrow money. That's why he'd bought hardly any Christmas presents, why there had barely been food in the house when she arrived. She could kick herself for not having guessed before.

The front door slammed and she made her way to the hallway. Alistair was leaning with his hand braced against the door, as if afraid that the person on the other side would try to break it down.

'Everything all right?' she asked.

'Fine, fine,' he mumbled, straightening up. But she could see it was a lie.

'Come back and sit down. I'll make us some coffee.'

'I can't. I need...' He was turning away, reaching for his coat.

'You wanted to ask me something. Please, Ali. Whatever it is, you can ask me. You know I'll help you if I can.'

He looked at her then, and she was shocked to see tears in his eyes. 'I know that,' he said. 'God help me, I know.' And then he opened the door again and was gone.

THIRTY-EIGHT

NEW YORK

Now

I can hear something. It's in the lift shaft above us. A buzzing, rasping sound like stone against a blade. I look at Maeve and she looks back at me. 'Is that...?' she says. I don't know what to say, so I pull a face I intend to look hopeful without counting any chickens. It sounded like cutting equipment, but I'm not sure how much that's because I so desperately want it to be.

There's a sudden shriek of metal against metal. Maeve and I grab at the walls of the lift, brace ourselves for another fall. But nothing happens. The buzzing stops and we stare at each other again. I swallow. 'I think they're coming for us,' I say.

The relief lasts about ten seconds. Then I feel it hit me again: the wave of anxiety. Perhaps I really will get out of here. I will drink water and feel fresh air on my face. I will go home and shower and dress in clothes that aren't infused with sweat. And then I will have to come back to this place and do what comes next.

'What's wrong?' Maeve asks. 'Are you worried you'll miss me?'

I should laugh, but I can't. 'It'll sound silly.'

'Try me.'

'It's just – it's been awful being stuck in here.' I hesitate, struggling to put together the words to explain what I mean. 'But I was on my way to do something awful too. And not being able to get there – it almost feels like being let off the hook.'

'And now you're having to think about it again,' Maeve says.

I nod; she's understood exactly what I mean. It occurs to me that it might be the same for her. She's probably nervous about the reason she's really here, too.

'Was it your meeting? The one with Leo?' she asks. I look up, too surprised to reply immediately. She shrugs. 'It was obvious it was bothering you. Are you worried it will have happened without you? Or that it won't?'

It's a good question. I wanted to be there, to control how it all went, the words that were used, the tone of the conversation. But maybe I've been fooling myself. Maybe I'm no better qualified to handle this now than I was before. Perhaps they'd both be better off without me there.

'Tell me about it,' Maeve says. 'What does it matter? We'll be out of here soon, and you'll never see me again.'

There's something oddly final about her words, and I feel an unexpected sadness. But she's right, of course. Of all the people I've met in this city, she's the one person I could share this with. She'll be gone soon, back to Britain, and she won't care about any of it.

'You never know,' she says, 'it might even make you feel better.'

I take a breath. 'Leo is one of the consultants here,' I say.

She nods encouragingly. 'And the two of you were going to talk to someone else? You said you wanted Leo to cancel the meeting if you couldn't make it.'

She's got a good memory. I'd thought she was barely paying attention when I was talking into the microphone. 'That's right,' I say, 'Jay. He works for Leo. At least, he does for now.'

She raises an eyebrow. 'And that's what you're talking to him about,' she says slowly. 'Because you work in HR.'

I nod. 'We're going to let him go.'

'Sack him, you mean?'

'Well, not technically. Jay is still on probation. We're just not going to make him permanent.' I see that her second eyebrow has risen to join the first, and I stop trying to split hairs. 'But yes, it amounts to the same thing. He'll finish the month and then he'll be gone.'

'What has he done?'

I swallow, force my voice to stay even. 'Nothing, really. But Leo says he's just not making the grade. We took on a bunch of new starters at the same time, and he thinks Jay's not as sharp as the rest.' I look down at the floor, my fingers tracing the geometric patterns on the carpet. 'He's within his rights to make that call. That's why we have a probationary period.'

I try to sound matter of fact, as if this is no big deal. But I know what it can mean if this goes badly. And he's so quiet, Jay. The sort of person who might have all kinds of things going on beneath the surface. Who might feel this too deeply. Who might need help but not ask for it. That's why I have to do better than I did last time.

I wait for Maeve to tell me I'm being stupid, that this isn't the sort of thing an experienced HR professional should be worried about. But instead her voice is full of sympathy. 'And you're the one who gets to pass on the good news.'

'Them's the breaks,' I say, trying to make light of it. 'Leo will be there too, but I'll take the lead. Make sure it's all done properly.'

'But you're worried about it.' It's a statement, not a question. 'You shouldn't be.'

I don't reply. If she knew what I'm responsible for, she wouldn't say that.

'I mean it, Cerys. If this Jay person isn't up to the job, it's just as well he hears that now. He can cut his losses and go somewhere he'll have a better chance of getting on.' She waits for me to reply. Then, 'There's something else, isn't there?'

'It just doesn't seem fair,' I say. 'It feels like there isn't room for anyone to be less than perfect anymore. And we're none of us perfect, are we? Doesn't everyone deserve a second chance?'

Maeve is watching me, her eyes gimlet sharp. It's like she can look right into my mind and see what I'm thinking. Or maybe it's just my guilty conscience that makes it feel that way.

'Someone did that for me once,' I say, and my voice is trembling. 'They gave me a second chance, and I've never forgotten it.' *Even though I was too weak to do the same.*

'But you said you'd only ever worked for Holbrooke and Dean. You said it was your first job after university.'

I laugh in spite of myself. 'God, you remember everything, don't you? That's right. It was when I first started. I did something stupid...' I fast forward; she doesn't need the details. 'My boss could have sacked me, but he gave me the benefit of the doubt.'

'Okay,' Maeve says, frowning, 'but that was his choice. He obviously saw something in you that made him think you were a good bet. That doesn't mean you have to do the same for this Jay person.'

I'm only half-listening to her. Something has dawned on me that I've never realised before. 'I think that's why I changed jobs,' I tell her. 'Why I moved away from consulting. I never really felt I was there on merit. Transferring to HR felt like a fresh start somehow.'

'There you are, then.' Maeve nods as if I've proved her point. 'You found your own way to move on, even if you were still at the same firm. You'll be doing this guy a favour. He's never going to get on somewhere people think he's not quite good enough.'

I savour it for a moment, the feeling that maybe she's right. Perhaps, after all, Jay's just not the right fit for Pearl Associates. Maybe we're not the right fit for him either. And maybe he'll just shrug this off and find something new, go to the pub and get pissed with his mates, laugh about how this was a shit job anyway.

I'm on the verge of believing it, and I can almost feel how it would be not to carry this weight on my shoulders. But then I remember the exchange at the end of our last review meeting, the one that's been bothering me.

'Glad to hear it's all going well,' I'd said, the bland remark that signalled we were done, he could be on his way.

Jay nodded, shuffled on his seat. 'I really like the team,' he said. I could see a faint flush above the collar of his shirt. 'This company, everything.'

'That's good to hear,' I said. It was clear he was leading up to something.

'My dad wanted me to be a doctor.'

I smiled. 'Parents, right?' Though mine had never been that way, never tried to mould me into the life they'd wanted for themselves.

'He's proud of me now, I think. A friend of his told him how tough it was to get a job here.' He grinned, but I could see the shadow behind it. His own word, his own wishes, had never been enough. He got to his feet then, surprised me by reaching out to shake my hand.

'Thanks,' he said. He must have read the puzzlement on my face. 'I mean, for giving me a shot. I know you must have turned down lots of good people. I want you to know you made the right decision.'

He was so young, so earnest. I imagined him rehearsing the words, trying to find the moment to say them. I said something inconsequential in reply, I don't remember what. But I thought about him after he'd gone.

I worry about it now, about what this job means to him. And I know: this idea that letting him go will be the best thing for him? That's just a story I'm using to try to make myself feel better.

Alistair didn't try to fool himself like that. He could have pretended that sacking me would be for my own good, that it would teach me a valuable lesson. He could have told himself that I could never repair the trust I'd destroyed, that it would be better for me to start afresh somewhere new. But he didn't do that. He saw how broken I was, and he helped me. And suddenly I'm there in that room again, watching him get up from his seat across the desk, his hand reaching out, gentle on my trembling shoulder. I hear the compassion in his voice: *we all deserve a second chance.*

Something touches my arm. I look down in surprise and see that Maeve is holding out a tissue. It's only then that I realise I'm crying.

THIRTY-NINE

BRISTOL

Fourteen years ago

My parents are dead, as I've said. I don't talk about them often; Matt never understood why. He didn't say it, but I could tell he thought there was something wrong with me, some kind of emotional miswiring that left the connections that should have made me sad they were gone failing to fire. He didn't know what it was like. I'd learned quickly that crying brought no comfort. The grief I carried around inside was a deep, cold well. It didn't matter how many tears I shed, I never came close to emptying it. So instead I tried my best to cover it over and forget it was there.

My mum died first, three months before my finals. I sat my exams in a haze, hardly knowing where I was. My friends told me I should talk to the welfare department at the university, ask for some kind of dispensation. I couldn't face it. I knew they'd want me to explain what happened, and even if I'd tried to gloss over the details, they would read between the lines. Mum had been a drinker, you see. She'd been at home alone and she'd fallen down the stairs and broken her neck. I was ashamed, for her and for myself. And I wanted to protect her, to keep her secrets, even though it was too late, even though I'd let her down when she needed me most.

We'd been on our own by then, just the two of us, and I'd gone back to university after the summer vacation despite knowing she wouldn't cope. I'd tried to pretend that a daily phone call home was enough, that she was okay, even when I could tell from the slur in her voice that she'd been drinking again. I'd put myself first and I'd failed her. It only seemed fair that the balance be redressed.

When the time came, I flunked my exams in spectacular fashion. I scraped a third only because the first two years of the course counted towards my results. I didn't care. I left my student halls in London as soon as the last exam was over and returned home to Bristol. At first, I stayed with my aunt, my mum's sister. She did her best, but her kindness was suffocating. Soon after the funeral, I moved back to what had been our family home. There, the days bled into each other. I barely ate. I slept on the sofa, washed – when I washed – in the sink in the downstairs loo. I couldn't face climbing the stairs that had taken my mother from me.

And then my father died too. He'd left us for another woman the year before – a girl, more accurately, or so I had gathered from the screaming rows between my parents. The same sad old tale of male middle-age. I'd been embarrassed for him. But after he walked out, Mum's drinking got worse, and then I began to hate him too. After she died, I couldn't bear to speak to him. I'd seen him at the funeral, his head bowed, unable to look anyone in the eye. It filled me with such disgust that for a moment it drove away the pain. So I held on to that feeling, nursed it, refused to have anything to do with him.

Things went on like that for months. I wouldn't answer his

calls, pretended I wasn't there when he came to the house. Eventually my aunt persuaded me to talk to him. There were things we needed to discuss, she said. My parents had still been married when Mum died, and she hadn't left a will. The house I lived in was now my father's, and there were practicalities to resolve. I'd seen him once after that, a painful affair in which I accused him of unrepeatable things. He called me the following day, claiming there was something he needed to tell me. I grudgingly agreed to see him again, dictating the time and place – later than he wanted, neutral ground. He'd just left his flat to make his way there when he was mown down by a hit-and-run driver.

So in a way I was responsible for his death too. If I'd spoken to him earlier, if I'd agreed to meet that morning, like he'd wanted, if I hadn't been so desperate to show him I was in charge – if I'd done any of those things differently, he would never have been there when that car came speeding down the road. I have to live with that. It's why I never resort to the kind of euphemisms Matt deploys. My parents are dead: not passed away, not 'no longer with us'. And though over time I've started to accept that I'm not responsible for everything that happened, I know too that I played a part. If I'd been a better person, they might still be alive. I can't hide from that truth in gentler words.

I was in a dark place after my father died. The house was mine, and it was quickly sold. I authorised the executors to accept the first offer they received. Most of the furniture went too, and I bought a characterless flat on the edge of town. My aunt came by now and again, and I forced myself to let her in and pretend everything was fine, knowing it was the best way to get rid of her as quickly as possible. Most of my friends were in London and got in touch by phone, allowing me to invent imminent outings or distant doorbells to get them off the line at the first decent opportunity. Gradually they got the message and the phone calls dried up.

But I couldn't stay a recluse forever. My parents' house had been mortgaged, and by the time I'd bought and furnished my own little shoebox, the proceeds had dwindled in a way that caused a knot of anxiety to form in the pit of my stomach on the rare occasions I made myself look at my bank balance. I knew the numbers couldn't keep going in only one direction indefinitely. I had to find a job.

I picked up some bar work at the student union, but it wasn't enough. Every so often, my aunt would gently encourage me to apply for what she called a 'proper job', reminding me how proud Mum had been when I went to university, telling me she'd want to see me 'getting on' with my life. She wasn't to know I'd already applied for every research assistant job I'd seen. I hadn't heard back from any of them.

I found myself dwelling on the past, tracing the threads back to where it had all gone wrong. At the end of my second year, I'd been on track for a 2:1, possibly even a first. I should have been able to walk into an interview for those jobs. But then Dad had left, and everything had changed.

Back then, I had determinedly avoided thinking about the woman he'd chosen above his family, but now she was constantly in my thoughts. Her name was May, but that was pretty much all I knew. I'd thought I would see her at the funeral, and had been half-dreading, half-anticipating our encounter; but she hadn't come, afraid, I suppose, that she wouldn't be welcome. I began to believe that she held all the answers. If I could see her, talk to her, I'd be able to get some peace. I'd know who she was, this person who had taken my father from us. I'd understand how it had all happened, what made her so much better than my mum and me. I'd ask her how they'd met, whether they'd been happy together.

It became an obsession. I began to believe I would only be able to move on if I met her. My aunt had, I knew, been in touch with her over the arrangements for my father's rented flat – as I understood it, she'd been as good as living with him – and I called her to ask for contact details.

'You're best staying away,' Siân had told me. 'How do you think it will help? What if she shuts the door in your face? How will you feel then?'

'I don't care,' I'd said. 'I just need to see her.'

In the end she gave in. She tried to persuade me to let her come with me, but I refused. I told her it was none of her business. I'm ashamed of that too – she'd lost her sister, and yet she'd had to put that to one side, to behave like the adult I believed myself to be and wasn't. But it worked – I hurt her, and she let me have my way.

For the first time in weeks, I showered and washed my hair. I found a clean pair of jeans and a top that didn't look too creased when I pulled it on. And then I left my flat and headed to the address Siân had given me, knowing that if I left it too long there was a chance she might think better of her promise not to warn May I was coming.

It was on the other side of the city centre, a bus ride and a walk away. I tucked myself into the corner of the seat as the bus meandered along the streets, my eyes glued to the windows to make sure I didn't miss my stop. The traffic was bad that day, the inside of the bus like an oven. I cracked open the window, but the air that entered was no cooler and I felt my T-shirt grow sticky against my back. The journey seemed as if it would never end, and my resolve began to falter. Was it possible, after all, that this woman would refuse to talk to me? What if she was angry that I was there? Would I back down and leave? Or would I insist she owed me her time after everything that had happened?

I was still turning those questions over in my mind when

the bus pulled up at the stop nearest to her address. I'd been so intent on not missing it that I got to my feet automatically, and a moment later I was standing on the pavement. Not having any other plan in mind, I began to walk.

May's flat was a couple of streets away, and I found my steps slowing as I got nearer. I scanned my surroundings as I went, checking the faces of everyone I passed. I'd never seen a photo of her, but I knew from my mother's disparaging remarks that she was just a few years older than I was. Somehow I was sure that if I saw her, I would *know*. But no one fitted my mental picture, and a few minutes later I found myself turning a corner and looking up at a nondescript block of flats.

The building was set back a couple of feet from the road, a thin strip of grass skirting the perimeter. Small, white-framed squares of glass punctuated the brown brick walls, and a dark green panel sat beneath alternate windows on the ground floor. There was something sad about it, an air of disappointment and neglect. It wasn't what I'd expected.

As I stood there staring at it, an old man holding a carrier bag emerged from a passageway to one side and eyed me with suspicion. I nodded to him and tried to smile, but he shifted his bag to his other hand and gave me a wide berth as he passed.

I turned my attention back to the building. May's flat, Siân had told me, was on the first floor and I scanned the windows, wondering which one belonged to her. Net curtains in varying shades of cream hung at most of them, no doubt to keep out prying eyes from the flats opposite. There was an occasional slatted blind too. Her window would have one of those, no doubt.

'Who you looking for?'

The old man had stopped a few steps down the road.

'I'm just visiting a friend,' I said.

He stared at me balefully, his chin jutting out. He looked about to question me further, so I started down the passageway before he had the chance. To the left stood a wide green door with a glass square at the top and a metal kick plate at the bottom. On the wall next to it was a metal panel, two long columns of buttons, each with a number printed above it. May's flat was number 14. I took a breath and raised my finger.

A movement in the periphery of my vision caught my attention – but there was no one there. It must have been my own reflection in the glass of the door. It was bright out here, so bright that the glass showed me nothing of the hallway inside, just my own face staring back at me. The sight made me catch my breath.

My cheeks were sunken and there were shadows under my eyes. My T-shirt hung from bony shoulders. But it was the fervid gleam in my eyes, the twitchiness around my mouth, that stopped me in my tracks. And all of a sudden, I could see it. I could see what Siân saw when she gave me those worried looks of hers. I could see what the old man had seen when he'd kept his distance as he passed by, when he'd asked me what I was doing there. I was glad, then, that I hadn't allowed my friends to visit. They wouldn't have recognised this person I'd become. I didn't want her to be me.

I let my hand fall. What was I doing here? What did I think May could tell me that would make any of it better? I'd imagined her as some kind of enchantress who'd stolen my father away, but that wasn't true. He'd had a choice, and he'd made it. And what had it mattered, in the end? We'd both lost him now.

I took a step back from the door, then another. Then I turned and made my way slowly back to the road. There was no sign of the old man. It felt like a reprieve, and my step was lighter as I headed back towards the bus stop. I became aware that I was hungry, and for the first time in weeks the prospect of food was appealing. There'd been an Indian takeaway near the bus stop, I remembered; I'd caught the aroma of spices as I passed. My stomach rumbled. I'd get samosas and find a wall or bench to eat them on before I headed home.

There was no one at the counter – perhaps they weren't expecting customers in the middle of a blazing hot day. I looked idly around the space as I waited – lots of white tiles and a glass-topped counter that made me wonder whether it had been a chippy in a recent life. A small cardboard box sat on the countertop, a sheaf of takeaway menus propped upright inside it. Beside it was a stack of other paper, flyers or some such.

There was no sign of a bell. I toyed with calling out but decided against it. I was in no rush to get anywhere. I picked up one of the sheets of paper from the pile, expecting to see details of a special offer. But something inside me quickened as I read the words at the top. I lifted the paper closer, read them again, feeling the rightness and the wrongness of it all at once. For here, on the counter of an Indian takeaway on the other side of town, was an advert for my perfect job.

FORTY

BRISTOL

Fourteen years ago

I sat in front of my PC, staring at the document for what felt like the fiftieth time. I'd sent off this CV so many times before, and it had got me nowhere. This time it had to be different.

I scanned the notes I'd made from my phone call with the HR person. I'd been sick with nerves when I'd rung her, but Elizabeth Fraine obviously had a script for such occasions. She'd promised to send me an application pack and advised me to look at the website of the company, Holbrooke and Dean.

It was a two-year placement, she confirmed, followed – if all went well – by a permanent role. I could rent out my flat in Bristol, or better still, sell up; there was nothing keeping me here. A move to London would be a fresh start, but in a city I already knew. It was almost too perfect. By the time I hung up, I was convinced of it: those other rejections, that ill-considered trip to see May – they'd all been leading up to this. It was Fate that had made me walk into that Indian takeaway that day. This job had to be mine.

I read through my CV again, then worked on it for another hour, drafting and redrafting every sentence until I was satisfied. I was about to press print when my eye snagged on the one thing I'd been resolutely avoiding thinking about.

> *University College London, BSc Chemistry – dissertation topic 'Use of CO_2 in Enhanced Oil Recovery', III.*

The three black lines of the Roman numerals stared back at me. I chewed on my lip. The job pack had been clear. There it was, the first item on the list of essential criteria, '2:1 bachelor's degree in chemistry or related subject'. Elizabeth had mentioned it too, passing over it lightly as if there was no question that I'd have the required qualification.

But I *was* qualified, I told myself. The only thing that degree reflected was that I'd been in no state to sit my exams. That wasn't my fault. Why should I have to keep on being punished for it? It wasn't fair.

I positioned the cursor at the end of the line. Three backspaces and it was gone.

There. I would simply not mention it. I'd get to the interview and make it clear how much I wanted this job and how hard I'd work. I'd impress them so much they wouldn't care about the number on a piece of paper. They'd see I was the right person. And if it came to it and I had no choice, I'd swallow my pride and explain. I wouldn't go into details. I'd simply say that my parents had died around the time of my exams. They would understand.

I printed everything off, stapled together the sheets of my CV and placed it in an envelope. I was about to seal it shut when something occurred to me and I checked the time: I'd already missed the afternoon collection. Perhaps that was a good thing. The deadline was still two days away. I'd give myself a chance to sleep on it, take a final look in the morning.

I slept badly that night. For the first time in over a year, I had something to be excited about. I was unused to the feeling. It was true I could have moved to London without already having found a job. There'd have been more opportunities there than in Bristol, and I'd have found something sooner or later. But somehow this job, moving house, a fresh start – it had all fused together, a bright shining star of possibility. I couldn't, wouldn't, let it fade away.

But then, in the midst of picturing buying cutlery or a desk lamp, of leaning across a pub table, wine glass in hand, laughing as I caught up with the old uni friends who'd be so pleased to see me back, I heard that little voice. *What are you thinking?* it whispered. *You know it's not going to happen. They won't want you. Just like none of the others wanted you.* And my mind would drift back to those three vertical lines disappearing from my CV. I'd been fooling myself. No one simply forgot to mention their degree classification. They'd see right through it. I'd never even get that interview.

In the morning I was up early. My head felt like it was stuffed with cotton wool, the sound of my feet on the laminate floor of the hallway muffled in my ears. In the single room that served as lounge, study and dining room, the envelope I'd addressed so neatly the night before sat innocently on the desk. The sight brought a sour taste to my mouth. Thank God I'd never sent it. At least now I could spare myself the humiliation. I snatched it up, meaning to throw it in the bin, but as my fingers closed around the paper something stopped me. I could hear Siân's words echo in my mind: *your mum was so proud of you.* My vision blurred and I sank into the chair. What was there for her to be proud of now?

I found myself opening the envelope, removing the paper inside. I'd been so different before, so sure everything in my future was rosy. I'd won a prize in my first year, the award for the student with the highest marks in the end of year exams. I'd gone on to do work experience with a pharmaceutical company, gaining the place in the face of stiff competition. By then I could see on my visits home that things weren't right between my parents – the stilted conversations, Dad's regular unexplained absences. But I did my best to push it from my mind, and to a large extent I'd succeeded. I was doing okay.

It didn't last, though, did it? said the familiar voice. *And this is where your selfishness has got you.*

'Shut up,' I said aloud, then pressed my fingers to my mouth. Was this what it had come to? Talking to the voices in my head? Was this what Dad's patients did? Did they go over and over the same things in their minds, digging themselves ever deeper into a hole of their own making, until they had no choice but to rely on someone else to try and pull them out? I didn't want that to be me. I had to make a change.

I switched on the computer again and opened the file with my CV. The cursor hovered over the line: *October 2001 to July 2004, University College London.* I typed 'First Class', just to see how it looked, then deleted it and typed '2:1'. *It would have been at least that,* I told myself. *The very least, if everything had been different.*

I saw the cursor hovering over the print icon – and then, somehow, the printer was whirring and a sheet of paper was edging out, line by line. I didn't look at it, but printed off the second sheet too, stapling them together and inserting them into the envelope in place of the previous version. Then I stuck down the seal and headed back to the bedroom to get dressed.

It was still early, but the sun was already beating down, the heat radiating from the pavement. I tipped my face briefly to the sky as I walked, trying to concentrate on the feel of it on my skin, blocking out the thoughts running through my head. I found my pace slowing as the post box came closer. *It's a beautiful day,* I told myself. *Enjoy it while it lasts.*

And then I was there, the paper white against the dark chasm of the letter box. The envelope was in my hand and then it was gone, swallowed up. The skin on the back of my neck prickled.

There was no going back now.

*

NEW YORK

Maeve, now

They are coming. I can hear them above us in the lift shaft.

I need to consider the logistics of what happens next. I worry that Cerys and I have been stuck here too long – they might want to check we're okay. Take us away for some kind of medical assessment.

Don't worry, Ali – I won't let them do that. I'll get to the 26th floor if I have to crawl every step on my hands and knees.

Cerys is crying. She's upset about something at work, overwrought after all this time in this lift. She has a kind soul, like you. It makes her vulnerable. Some day she'll learn that.

But tears won't help. I don't want them thinking the pair of us are traumatised, that some kind of intervention is required. All I need is to be allowed to go on my way. To keep the promise I made to you.

Cerys sniffs, and I want to tell her to pull herself together. I offer her a tissue instead.

FORTY-ONE

NEW YORK

Now

From somewhere Maeve has produced a tissue. I take it from her and dab my eyes. My cheeks are flaming, but I'm angry with myself as well as embarrassed. I may be stuck in this useless lift, but I'm still at work. I'm supposed to be behaving like a professional. Perhaps the sounds coming from overhead, the scraping and drilling, mean we're going to get out of here soon. Perhaps they don't. But whatever happens, I won't break down again. This time, I'm determined to keep my dignity.

Out loud I say, 'I'm sorry,' annoyed at my faltering voice.

Maeve doesn't say anything. She has picked up on my embarrassment and turned away, trying to give me time to pull myself together.

'It's not this thing with Jay,' I say, needing her to know I'm not an HR director who can't sack someone – except that perhaps that's exactly what I am. 'It's just – it's been a difficult time. Just, one thing and another.'

I'm aware my words are meaningless, but she's kind enough not to point it out. 'There's no need to apologise,' she says. 'Sometimes it all gets too much. I know that.'

I nod, keeping my eyes on the floor. I want to talk about something, anything else. But then I look at Maeve and I see that something in the line of her jaw again, and all of a sudden, I know. I know who she reminds me of.

The air catches in my throat, and now there's no stopping it: the memories are coming at me like tidal waves. I can't catch my breath before another one rolls in. The weight of them is on my chest, crushing my lungs, squeezing my heart.

The pictures I've seen in my dreams are flooding back. The imagined horror of that day. His eyes stare at me. *I kept your secret,* he says.

'Just breathe, Cerys,' says a voice from a thousand miles away.

And another voice, one that sounds like mine except that it's cracked with tears, says, 'That's not my name.'

FORTY-TWO

LONDON

Eight months ago

The morning after I'd been to Alistair's I woke with stomach cramp. I got out of bed with a sour taste in my mouth, careful not to disturb Matt, and headed for the bathroom. I bent over the sink, splashing cold water on my face and slurping it from my cupped hand. I felt lightheaded too, but after I'd gone to the kitchen and made myself a slice of toast, I couldn't eat it.

On the train, I checked my emails. I'd done the same thing on my return from Alistair's, but there was still nothing from Roberto. Was it possible that I'd misjudged Elise? She'd been angry with Alistair, it was true, but it was hardly fair to blame her for that (though I remembered how appalled she'd looked as she'd repeated 'millennial', and to my shame, had to stop myself from smiling). She was right, it had been inexcusable for him to turn up drunk to the office. Maybe, after all, she'd leave it to me to deal with it.

I had just enough time to hang up my coat and turn on my

PC before I had to leave for the first meeting of the day. When I returned to my desk, I saw it straight away. There in my email inbox, a red exclamation mark beside it. There was no message, just the subject heading next to Roberto's name:

My office, 11.30 please

I stared at the screen, trying to read something positive into the 'please'. But Roberto was always scrupulously polite. Like a dentist who asks if you're sitting comfortably before sinking a needle into your gum.

I checked the time, and to my horror saw it was almost half past. I grabbed my notebook and pen. He'd want to talk to me about Alistair again, I was sure of that. What I still wasn't sure about was how I was going to respond.

Elise was stationed at her desk outside Roberto's room, pretending to be engrossed in her computer monitor. I swept past her, rapping on the door and sticking my head around it. I took a grim satisfaction at hearing her spluttering in the background.

Roberto was on the phone. His brows drew together in an automatic frown when he saw me, but he waved for me to enter and take a seat.

'Preee-cisely,' he said to the person on the phone. 'So let's circle back to that next week.'

I gritted my teeth and forced my face into what I hoped was an expression of expectant calm. God, it was hot in here. The whole building was supposed to be temperature controlled, but maybe he had some kind of heater hidden away somewhere. I ran my finger beneath the neckline of my blouse.

His eyes flicked to the clock on the wall, just as the long hand clicked to the six. 'Ciao,' he said, as he hung up. I'd never believed people who spoke English as a first language really said that.

He swivelled towards me, but this time there was no toothpaste advert smile. 'Good to see you,' he said insincerely. 'I'm afraid we need a serious conversation.'

'I've been trying to catch you—' I lied.

'Alistair Douglass,' he said, cutting me off. 'I need him gone.'

I swallowed, aware of the unpleasant taste in my mouth. 'I'll need to give him a formal warning.'

'No, you won't. *One*' – he held up a finger – 'that should have happened after that business with Ted Harvey.'

'We discussed—'

'*Two*' – another finger – 'he's abused another member of staff. That's grounds for immediate dismissal. I've checked.'

He held up a printout. *Disciplinary policy and procedures*, I read at the top. A paragraph had been neatly highlighted with yellow fluorescent pen. I was pretty sure who'd done the highlighting.

'I understand that Elise is upset,' I said, with an effort at keeping my voice even. 'I'm not sure that I'd characterise what she described to me as abuse.'

'I want him gone,' he said. 'Today.'

The chair swivelled back, dismissing me. This was all happening too fast. I couldn't think straight, so I played for time.

'I'm concerned that unless we're clear about the grounds—'

'For God's sake, the guy was blind drunk in the office! Twice! What does it take round here to fire someone?'

'I just think—'

'What is it with you? I don't listen to gossip, but I'm starting to wonder.'

For a moment I wasn't sure I'd heard him properly, but that half-raised eyebrow banished any doubts. 'Wonder what?'

'You and Douglass. I mean, I know you've both been here a long time.'

My stomach had started to churn. I put my hand to my forehead and it came away damp. With a supreme effort, I tried to focus on the conversation. 'I'm not sure I understand what you're saying.'

'You're colleagues.' The way he said it made me think he meant something else. 'But we can't give out special treatment. You understand that, right?'

I opened my mouth to reply, but another wave of queasiness washed over me. How could he bear this heat?

'Because you know, I can't have an HR director who doesn't get that.'

I stared at him. 'I get it.'

'Good. Then he'll be gone today.'

He turned back to his computer, and I didn't have it in me to argue further. Perhaps, after all, this was for the best. Alistair had made his bed, now he'd have to lie in it. I made for the door, desperate for cool air, feeling Elise's eyes on me as I passed. I didn't have time to see whether she looked as pleased with herself as I expected. I had to get to the bathroom.

I hurried down the corridor and burst into the ladies, slamming open the door of the nearest cubicle. I just managed to pull the lock across before I was bent over the bowl, heaving. I hoped to God there was no one else there to hear me. When it was over, I wiped my mouth with a tissue, then flushed the loo and sank onto the seat, resting my head against the wall. I tried to breathe slow and deep, waiting for the last tentacles of nausea to uncoil from around my stomach.

It wasn't the first time I'd felt sick recently, but this was the worst. I'd have to get to a doctor, see if they could give me something to clear it up. But that wasn't what I had to focus on right now.

I closed my eyes. Poor Alistair. But Matt would be happy, at least. I couldn't deny my life would be less stressful too. There'd be no one at Holbrooke and Dean who'd know what I'd done. It would be like wiping the slate clean. And when it came down to it, firing Alistair was Roberto's decision, not mine. Alistair would understand that. He wouldn't try to take me down with him, no matter how angry he was. He wasn't that kind of person. I was certain – almost certain – of that.

My stomach felt easier now and I got to my feet, flushing the loo a second time before opening the door. But there was no one else there. I dabbed water on my forehead and cheeks, then pinched them so I wouldn't look like I'd just stepped off the set of *Shaun of the Dead*. I'd get a glass of water, then go and find Alistair. Best to do it now, before I had time to dwell on how much I owed him.

I stood waggling my fingers under the dryer. There was a tampon and sanitary towel dispenser on the wall above. The contents were free, a 'perk' at Holbrooke and Dean. They weren't a brand I liked, though. I preferred to get my own, included once a month in my regular online order.

Once a month. I stopped moving as I stared at the white box on the wall.

Oh God. Once a month.

And suddenly the nausea made a horrible sense. I swayed on my feet and had to grab the dryer to steady myself. I might not need a doctor just yet. But I sure as hell needed a chemist.

FORTY-THREE

NEW YORK

Now

'What did you say?'

Maeve has pulled away from me, and I feel so brittle and alone. If she touches me again, I will shatter into a thousand pieces.

I say again, 'That's not my name.' There's no way back now. But this is better, surely? Surely it's better to tell Maeve, this woman I'll never see again after today? I'll tell her and then I'll be able to go back to being Cerys, and no one else here will ever have to know.

She says, 'What are you talking about?' Her voice is sharp.

'I lied,' I say, and a crazy little laugh hiccups out after the words. 'Or no – at least, I'm Cerys here. I want to be Cerys here. In New York.'

There is silence. Above us, the drilling and scraping has stopped. I don't know what that means.

'You changed your name.'

I look up at her in surprise. She's so smart, this woman. Remembers everything. Sees everything. She wouldn't have missed things the way I did. I realise she's expecting a reply and I nod.

'Why did you do that?'

She sounds on the verge of anger. We've only been together a few hours, but she must feel like I've lied to her. How much worse would it be for the others, the people I've been working with for months?

'Something happened. Before I left London. It was – upsetting. I needed to get away.'

'You said you split up with Matt.'

'No.' I shake my head. 'I mean yes, I did, but that wasn't it. Matt and I – we split up after it happened. I wasn't coping. He couldn't help me. I was better off on my own.'

For a moment she doesn't say anything. I imagine she is retracing the lines of our conversation, remembering the things I've told her, identifying the ones that aren't true. 'So this thing that happened – was it why you came to New York?'

'Yes. My boss at the time, she tried to help. She fixed me up with the job here. I didn't want people to know who I was, so I changed my name.'

I lift my eyes from the carpet, wanting to see how she's taking this. But her face is blank. I guess she doesn't want to upset me by appearing judgemental, but I think I would prefer a frown or even a sneer. There is something unsettling about the way she's looking at me.

'So your boss – she knew what happened?'

I nod again. 'It was a work thing.' I sound deliberately evasive, I know. But I've carried this for too long. Even now, standing on the cliff edge of revelation, the habit of concealment is like a hand pulling me backwards.

Her eyes don't leave my face. 'Tell me everything,' she says.

FORTY-FOUR

LONDON

Eight months ago

I was shaking as I made my way back to my office. My bag was there, my coat too. I'd collect them and then get out of there. I couldn't wait. I needed to get to a pharmacy and buy a test.

My mind was full of numbers, days, weeks, trying to work out the possibilities, trying at the same time to tell myself it couldn't be, it just couldn't. I was careful. Though perhaps, it was true, not quite so careful recently. Forgetting the occasional pill hadn't felt like a big deal when Matt and I were barely speaking, far less having sex. And yet, there had been times...

I wouldn't think about it. There was no point thinking about it until I knew for sure. I pushed open the door to my office and stopped short. A man stood at the window, his back to the room. My heart sank.

'Alistair,' I said, 'we need to speak, but now's not a good time—'

He turned to face me. He was dressed in a suit and tie and

his shirt looked freshly pressed. But his cheeks were sunken and his eyes – the word came into my head unbidden: *haunted.*

It would be best for both of us to get it over with. 'Take a seat,' I said.

We manoeuvred around each other in the small space. I caught an undertow of something sweet as I passed him, but it was faint. He hadn't, I thought, been drinking today. But had *I* been drinking? If the sickness was what I feared, had I been drinking while—

'I've tried to do the right thing,' he said, cutting into my thoughts. His fingers drummed against his knee.

It wasn't the opening I'd expected. 'The right thing?' I echoed, closing my mouth before the words *Like turning up pissed to the office?* made their bid for freedom. Doing the right thing, indeed – wasn't that what we all tried to do? Wasn't that what I was doing right now, about to have one of the most God-awful conversations of my career, when all I wanted to be doing was peeing on a stick?

'I tried to help you, Anna,' he said.

I stiffened. 'This isn't about me—'

'You know that, don't you?' A pause, then, 'I'm so sorry about your parents.'

I stared at him in disbelief. Was this really where he was going? My hands had started to shake, I realised. I clasped them together to make them stop.

'Are you threatening me, Alistair?'

He looked appalled, began to rise from his seat, then subsided again. 'I would never… How could you think that?'

I allowed myself to breathe again. 'Then what's all this about?'

'Do you remember that day? When you first started here? You'd only been here a week, and I called you in.'

I checked over his shoulder to make sure the door was closed. 'That was a long time ago.'

'You were so young. When you told me about your mum... I think I knew, even then. I tried to tell myself it was a coincidence – your name, the Bristol connection.'

He must have been drinking after all. I didn't have time for this; I needed to be at the pharmacy. 'Alistair,' I said sharply, 'I really need to explain the position.'

'I just thought, if I could help... I knew I could never make it up to you...'

'Okay, I need you to stop talking now and listen.'

His head had dropped to his hands. Oh God, I couldn't do this. I had to do it.

'I've spoken to Roberto this morning.'

'Your dad.' He looked up again. 'It was a hit and run.'

The conversation was like quicksilver. 'Alistair, please, you need to listen to me.'

'Did they find out who did it?'

'What? No.' I'm so surprised that I answer in spite of myself. 'It was a woman, that's all they knew.'

His knee jiggled up and down and he ran his hands through his hair, leaving tufty bits on the crown. He licked his lips. Was he on something, something stronger than alcohol? Should I be calling a doctor?

'Someone saw her?' he asked. 'What did she look like?'

I answered, though there wasn't much to tell. It would be the quickest way to get it over with, I thought. But he kept at it. Was that all they'd said? Was I sure there was nothing else? He was manic one minute, dazed the next. Could it really be drugs?

After a while he fell silent and I said, 'I don't know what this is all about. I told you I was sorry I hadn't said anything about Dad. But really, it had nothing to do with anything.'

He stared ahead. His knee had stopped jiggling and he sat perfectly still. Closed door or not, I lowered my voice. 'I was upset, yes. I wanted a new start. I felt like I needed... well, you know all about that. And I'm grateful to you – really, I am. But I've got a job to do. I hope you understand.'

He turned to me then, blinked slowly as if he was waking from a dream. 'You're firing me,' he said.

'You'll be paid until the end of the month...' I'd been going to say, *as a gesture of goodwill*, but found I couldn't form the words. 'I'm afraid you need to leave immediately.'

He placed his hands on his knees and leaned forward to pull himself upright, as if all the strength had gone from his muscles. At the door he paused, one hand on the doorknob. 'I'm sorry,' he said, his back to me. 'I'm so sorry for everything.'

Then he was gone. I pressed the palms of my hands to my eyes and sat there, breathing deep. After a minute or so, I pulled my keyboard towards me and brought up a new email. I added Roberto's name, then shifted the cursor to the subject line.

It's done

I pressed send and put on my coat.

FORTY-FIVE

NEW YORK

Now

There is a blast of static from the speaker and I feel a burst of panic. Suddenly, I don't want the lift to move. I need more time. Time to get this stuff out of my head, to vomit it into this fetid air. To leave it behind when I walk out the doors.

'I was pregnant,' I say.

There is silence as Maeve digests the past tense. Then, 'Was it Matt's?'

I look at her in surprise. But of course; she had an affair with a married man. She is not a stranger to infidelity as I am. And then I catch myself and almost laugh – even now, after all I've done, I have it in me to pass judgement on someone else.

'Yes,' I reply.

'But you lost the baby?' I don't answer and I hear her take a heavy breath. 'That must have been devastating.'

I shake my head. If I am going to admit the worst of it, I may as well start here. 'It was a shock, yes, but part of me was relieved. It was all but over between Matt and me. I didn't want him staying with me because I was pregnant.'

Above us I hear the muffled scream of some kind of equipment. It sounds like it is cutting something, a diminuendo that dips in pitch as it fades away. Are they going to slice open the top of the lift? But it is too far away for that, somewhere higher up the shaft.

Maeve says, 'But I don't understand. You said something happened at work?'

I am telling this all wrong. My thoughts are wound around each other like wet wool. I can't find the ends.

'I did something,' I say. 'Something terrible.'

LONDON

Eight months ago

I sat on the edge of the bath, staring at the bit of white plastic in my hand. The window showed a jaunty little line drawing of a stork carrying a baby in a cloth suspended from its beak. A headache pounded at my temples.

There was already a similar plastic gadget in the drawer of my bedside cabinet. I'd left it there the previous day, hidden away where there was no chance of Matt stumbling across it, until I could repeat the procedure the following morning. The leaflet in the box said that would be more accurate – higher levels of hormones, apparently. I needed to be sure.

I'd intended to take the first test at work, but when I'd got back to the office, I found I couldn't face it. My mind was full of Alistair, the shadows under his eyes, the hollows of his cheeks. The way he'd fidgeted as we talked, then sat still as marble. The way he'd said, *I'm so sorry.*

How would he cope without his job, the reason it gave him to get up in the mornings? I was still no wiser about what had brought him to this. I hadn't asked, hadn't given him a chance to explain. I'd seen the evidence of his drinking, wondered whether he was taking drugs – yet I hadn't offered him help. Even with Roberto's clear instruction to show him the door, I could have offered him counselling – we had a contract for such things, and I had the authority to extend it to an ex-employee if I chose. I hadn't even suggested Alcohol Concern. I had just wanted it over with as soon as possible so I could get to the chemist.

Well, I'd got my answer now.

'Can you hurry up in there?'

I jumped at Matt's voice and shoved the test into the pocket of my bathrobe. How could I tell him? Should I do it now? But no, I needed time to think.

'I'm going to be late!'

I unlocked the door and he brushed past me. I was half out of the bathroom when some instinct told me to look back, make one final check. And that's when I saw it.

Oh God, no.

My heart leapt into my throat. Matt had his back to me, fiddling with the shower settings. I kept my eyes fixed on him as I backed up to the sink. If I watched him, I told myself, he wouldn't turn around. If I just kept my eyes glued to him, everything would be all right.

I stretched out my hand.

'Don't know why you have to have it so bloody hot.'

I snatched up the cardboard box with its giveaway branding and stuffed it into my pocket with the test. I allowed myself to breathe. 'I don't know why you insist on showering in icy water,' I replied, because that's what I always said.

Back in the bedroom, I stowed away the box and the test, then dressed in a daze. I sat on the bed to put on my tights and paused, entranced by my stomach. There, below the skin, another life was growing. It didn't seem possible, hadn't been planned and yet – I couldn't deny what I was feeling. A spark of something. A stir of anticipation.

Sure, Matt and I hadn't been getting on. But couples had their ups and downs, everyone knew that. And with Alistair gone, Matt would be well placed to fill the vacancy. He'd been working hard; Roberto had to have noticed that. And with a promotion under his belt, he'd be happier, more secure. I could make more of an effort too. It had been so long since I'd had a family of my own. It was so close now. Me, Matt and a baby. Could it really be possible?

Matt hurried back into the room, followed by steam and the scent of lemon. 'Have you seen my white shirt? The Charles Tyrwhitt one?' he asked. 'Have you moved it?'

The spark sputtered. 'Why would I do that?'

A clatter of coat hangers. He mumbled something. I caught the words 'fucking late'. I had no meetings that morning, so I took my time getting dressed, waving him on when he said he had to go. 'I'll see you tonight,' I said, his nose bumping against my cheek in a goodbye kiss that was one part affection, ninety-nine parts routine. The door slammed and the flat seemed to exhale around me.

On the train, I gave up my seat for a woman with a 'baby on board' badge. I found myself staring at the front of her dress, the bump faintly visible beneath the fabric. She placed her bag on her lap and I forced myself to look away. When I turned to go, she caught my eye and smiled. I smiled back.

Most people were already there when I got to the office. There was a hum as I walked down the corridor. The official rule, I knew, was that I had to tell my line manager as soon as I knew I was pregnant. What would Roberto make of it? I wondered. But I was getting ahead of myself. I couldn't do anything until I'd told Matt.

I passed a couple of people on the way to my desk, and I had to force myself not to cover my stomach with my hands. They smiled in the tentative way some people do with senior colleagues, but their eyes didn't travel to my abdomen, didn't widen in surprise. I felt an irrational relief.

The morning went by in a blur. I answered phone calls, read emails, accepted a handful of meeting requests. I took out my phone and googled 'how big is an embryo at seven weeks?' Ten millimetres, apparently. The size of a blueberry.

When one o'clock rolled around, I went out for lunch. Matt, his electronic diary informed me, was in a meeting. I considered waiting for him, buying sandwiches and salad and eating together in the public gardens along the road. Telling him about the blueberry as we were surrounded by roses, pigeons pecking at the crumbs around our feet and traffic humming in the background. But I couldn't hold on for that long. I needed to get out, feel the air on my face.

There was a small supermarket on the corner, and I bought water and one of those packs of apple slices where the cut edges stay unnaturally crisp. For once I didn't head straight back to my desk but went to the gardens alone. All the benches were taken, and I wondered if someone would get up for me if I told them I was pregnant. I hovered at the periphery instead, waiting until a couple of French tourists in backpacks went on their way.

When I next looked at my watch, I realised half an hour had slipped past without my noticing it, without checking my phone for emails or worrying about my next meeting. Was this what it would be like, I wondered, to have a different set of priorities? For work to no longer be the first demand on my time? Juggling everything would be hard, but Matt's parents would want to help. And maybe motherhood would finally help Eleanor and me to bond. For a moment I gave in to the fantasy of telling my own mother, of the way her eyes would have widened, how she'd have squealed in excitement and enveloped me in one of her enormous hugs. My throat tightened then, and I swallowed back the sudden tears.

Back at the office, the afternoon was taken up with a meeting on performance management. I was chairing, but let my mind wander as the discussion flowed, nodding now and again to look as if I was paying attention.

I tried to imagine how Matt would react to the news. Would he put a stop to whatever was going on with Elise? It's true that we'd never talked seriously about children, but he'd made vague remarks that I'd assumed meant he wanted them someday. All that talk of wanting to provide for us – surely that had to be part of his thinking. Even so, I admitted to myself, the reality of a baby *now* might be a different matter. And a child wasn't always enough to keep a couple together – I, of all people, knew that.

Gradually, I became aware of people looking at their watches and realised the meeting had overrun. I brought things to a close and checked my phone as the others made for the door with indecent haste. There was a text from Matt.

Gone for a couple of drinks with Simon. Join us when you finish?

He hadn't told me which pub, I noted, so there was no chance of my turning up without notice. Presumably he really was with Simon, or he wouldn't have risked being caught in a lie. Or then again, perhaps he thought the chances of my saying yes were low enough not to worry. I typed out, *Which pub?* then deleted it and tried again.

Feeling a bit tired. Enjoy yourselves xx

He replied a minute later, just a couple of kisses. I shut down my PC and went to wash up my mug. The office was mostly empty, so it was hardly surprising that Elise had left for the day too. *Not surprising at all*, I thought, and tried to believe it.

The weekend passed and still I didn't tell Matt. I tried rehearsing the words, but nothing seemed right. Once, I got as far as opening the drawer of the bedside cabinet, looking at the picture of the baby-toting stork. I considered simply handing the test to him, waiting for the realisation to dawn. But it smacked of melodrama and I closed the drawer again.

When night came, I found it difficult to sleep. But this time, it had nothing to do with the blueberry. Whenever I closed my eyes, I was back in that room with Alistair. He'd been all over the place – all that fidgety nervous energy, then just as suddenly so still, so quiet. And all those questions about what had happened to Dad. What was all that about? Was it reminding him of his own father, in some way? Both his parents, I'd picked up from things he'd said in passing, had died young. Or was he just fixating on a detail in my life because he couldn't face thinking about what was happening in his own?

I should have done better by him, I realised, made an appointment with a counsellor. I couldn't have made him go, but at least he'd have had to decide not to turn up. I would phone him on Monday, I told myself. Check in on him, encourage him to get some help. He might not want to talk to me, but at least I'd have tried. And maybe in time he'd realise that in spite of it all, I could still be his friend if he'd let me.

And somewhere along that road paved with good intentions, I fell into a dreamless sleep.

FORTY-SIX

NEW YORK

Now

'There was someone at work. A colleague.'

My voice is trembling, and I no longer feel the heat in here. It's as if the blood has stopped moving around my body. Maeve hasn't spoken for ages, but I don't want to look at her. If I do, if I have to see the judgement in her eyes, I may never be able to tell her what comes next.

'I had to fire him, but I was worried about him. About how he'd cope. I tried calling him afterwards.' I hear the attempt to justify myself in my words. I hate myself for it.

'It was just a few days later,' I continue, 'just the other side of the weekend. I'd have done it earlier, but I didn't have his number at home. There was no reply, so I left him a message. I don't know if he got it. I don't know when...' I have to stop, catch my breath.

Still Maeve doesn't speak.

I start again. 'I was in my office a few days later and my

phone rang. It was Roberto, my boss. He sounded – strange. Not like himself. He told me he needed me to come to his office. I told him…'

LONDON

Eight months ago

'I have a meeting,' I said, checking my watch automatically. 'I can be with you at eleven.'

'Now,' he said, and put down the phone. I stared at the receiver, irritated. It was unlike him to be so rude, and at any other time it would have made me anxious. But not that day. I had done everything he had asked of me. I had toed the party line. He should be thanking me, not snapping out a summons.

I took my time moving, wanting to remind him that he might be the boss, but I was a senior member of staff too. He couldn't just click his fingers and expect me to come running. I considered taking my mug of freshly brewed tea with me, but decided that would be a bridge too far. Instead I collected my usual props, my notebook and pen, and strolled down the corridor to his office, determinedly unhurried.

I felt it as soon as I reached the open-plan area outside Roberto's office. There was a stillness, as if the handful of people at their desks were holding their collective breath. Elise looked up, then immediately away again. She was pale, her lipstick a slash of colour over bloodless skin. Something in her expression brought me up short, and I stopped mid-stride, my notepad against my stomach. 'What is it?' I said. 'What's happened?'

I swung around as Roberto appeared in his doorway. He

didn't speak, just stood back to let me into his office. I stared at him quizzically as I passed, but he wouldn't meet my eye.

The door closed behind me. 'Take a seat,' he said, the words clipped. A moment's hesitation, then, 'Please.'

I watched him return to his chair. He dropped into it, shuffled forwards so he was leaning over the desk. He picked up a pen and jabbed at the button on top. The nib clicked in and out.

'What's going on?' I'd never spoken to him like that. It was the strangeness of it all, twanging at my nerves. But he barely seemed to notice.

'You spoke to Alistair,' he said. I wasn't sure if it was a question or not.

'You told me to. I did it.'

'When?'

'What?'

His lips were pinched, the words squeezed out between them hard as pebbles. 'When did you speak to him?'

'I told you. I emailed you afterwards.' He was still staring at me. Something cold made its way up my spine. 'Thursday. Thursday morning.'

'And the next day?'

'What do you mean?'

'Did you see him on Friday?'

'No, of course I didn't.' It was rude, but his mood was infecting me, the anxiety cutting through my usual careful phrasing. 'You were clear you wanted him gone straight away.'

'Whoa, now.' He raised his hands to me, palms out. 'That's not what I said.'

Wasn't it? I cast my mind back, but so much had happened since that conversation. Perhaps I'd misremembered. 'It wouldn't matter, anyway,' I said. 'It's company policy not to have someone on the premises after they've been dismissed.'

Surely he should know this. But he was already moving on.

'What did you say to him?'

'What you'd expect! I told him we were terminating his contract and asked him to leave.'

'What else?'

'Nothing! There was nothing else to say.'

'Did you offer him support? Access to counselling?'

It was the way he said it. I felt myself go very still. 'What's happened?'

His voice was level, but the words were so slow it was clear the effort it cost him. 'Did you remind him about the counselling service?'

'I rang him on Monday. I told him to get in touch if there was anything he needed. Please, Roberto. Just tell me what's going on.'

He rested his elbows on the desk, buried his head in his hands. 'We're both completely fucked,' he said, raising his eyes to me again. 'Alistair's dead. He's hanged himself.'

The floor slipped sideways. Roberto was saying something else, but there was a loud ringing in my ears and I couldn't make out the words.

I got to my feet. I said, 'I'm sorry, I'm pregnant.' And then I vomited all over the carpet.

FORTY-SEVEN

LONDON

Maeve, eight months ago

The echo was the first thing. Something in its quality. A hard-edged hollowness.

Maeve heard it through the door, the buzzer reverberating through the hallway beyond. Her stomach clenched, but she told herself it was dread of the conversation to come. It was early, but that wouldn't matter. Alistair hadn't been answering her calls and she knew what that meant. Whatever the time, he'd be drinking. Or blacked out. Or coming to, still drunk.

She pushed her key into the lock, feeling like a trespasser, calling his name as she stepped inside. The smell hit her immediately. The sour tang of alcohol.

Her voice fell flat into the emptiness of the house, and that was the second thing. Her mouth went dry, and she had to take a breath and lick her lips before she could call him again.

In the kitchen, bottles on the counter, most upright, some

horizontal. Three more in the sink. An open box of cereal surrounded by cornflakes. No bowl.

A flash of another house, another time. But no – this was different. She turned her back on the mess and headed for the stairs.

Bathroom first. She gagged and flushed the loo, averting her eyes from the pan. Towels all over the floor. She'd have to wash them. Clean the kitchen too.

The door to his bedroom was open, the curtains wide. She blinked in the light.

His bed was unmade, one pillow sideways as if he'd clutched it in his sleep. The wardrobe door gaped at her. On the floor beneath lay a coat hanger, the kind with thick plastic to hold the shoulders of a suit jacket, a bar underneath for trousers.

For a moment, she let herself believe he'd gone to work.

The door to the spare room – her room, he called it – stood ajar. She pushed it open. She'd changed the sheets before she'd left after Christmas, and the duvet was still crisp and smooth, the pillows propped up the way she liked them. In front of each one, a rectangular cushion sat neatly aligned.

Heaviness in her limbs, as if the absence her mind refused to acknowledge had seeped into her muscles instead. Her feet dragged as she went downstairs, gripping the stair rail like an old woman.

Lovely high ceilings, she'd said when he'd moved in, and he'd laughed at her, pretending he didn't care. But he'd bought a mask and goggles and overalls, and applied poisonous-smelling paste to the beautiful old ceiling rose, stripping it back layer by layer, until the anonymous lumps and bumps were transformed into apples and cherries.

She pushed open the door of the living room and that was the third thing. The darkness that clung to the shape in the middle of the room.

She already knew what it was. Knew even as she flicked the switch. Knew that the blinds had been drawn for a reason.

But as the shape in the centre of the room rotated gently in the draught from the hall, the tie knotted tight around the light fitting, she saw his face and the knowing didn't matter.

She opened her mouth and screamed.

Four months passed before she brought herself to return.

Standing there in the hallway the silence wrapped itself around her, stuffed itself down her nose and throat. If she didn't move, it would smother her. Perhaps that would be for the best. She could just lie down and wait for it to end, there in the place that had seen him take his final breath. Would he come for her if she did? Would she see him again, his hand outstretched to her like the small boy he'd once been? He had trusted her then, and she had kept him safe. But she'd failed him in the end, and how could she go on like this, day after day, the knowledge of it her first thought every morning, the recurring motif of every night's restless dreams?

Gradually she became aware of the plastic bag cutting grooves into her fingers. She shuffled forward, staring straight ahead, ignoring the blackness seeping from the doorway on her left. The blinds were still drawn in there. She couldn't process that now.

In the kitchen, she set the carrier bag on the worktop, pushing it into a space between the empty bottles. Glass clinked together and she flinched at the noise.

She reached inside and removed a roll of black plastic bags, unwinding it carefully, pulling as she did so they'd come apart at the first perforation. She scrunched the plastic in her hand, rubbing the layers together to find the seams, then shook it open. She stood there, holding the empty bin bag, surveying the wine bottles and the open cereal box and the pile of dirty crockery and the sheer cold absence of it all. Then her legs gave way and there was stone beneath her cheek and salty wetness running down her face and into her mouth.

She realised that the afternoon was wearing on when she found herself holding the bills towards the window to read them. She rose from the desk, her knees stiff, and flicked the light switch. The bulb didn't respond. How long had it been that way? she wondered. How long since Alistair had done any of those trivial tasks that keep a home ticking over – changing a light bulb, reading the meter, opening the post? The latter, at least, she had a better idea of now. The gas bill from November had been in the file marked 'utilities', opened and stuffed back into its envelope, 'PAID' underlined twice in Alistair's writing. She had placed her fingers on the indentations on the paper, touching the mark he had made with his own hand, a living, breathing man. The bill for the following month had been amongst the detritus on the top of the desk, the envelope still sealed.

She had seen for herself how it was at Christmas. Barely any food in the house, let alone decorations or presents. She'd known he was in trouble, yet she'd let him brush her off instead of forcing him to tell her what was going on. But she'd put two and two together herself, known he was in debt again, worried about whatever loan sharks he was in hock to this time. One of them had even turned up when she was there, and still she hadn't sorted it out. She had his bank details. She could have transferred money at any time. But she hadn't. She'd told herself she'd get to the bottom of it, find out how much he owed, that they'd come up with a plan together. She'd been deluding herself and now he was gone.

Somehow she found herself standing before the door to the living room. Her breathing was faster now, the tightness in her chest that had visited her for the first time that day, the day she'd found him, making its presence felt. She could feel the hard cylinder of the inhaler in her pocket, but she didn't use it. Instead she watched as her hand pushed the door further open, the darkness beckoning her forward.

She groped her way inside, refusing to try the overhead light and fumbling instead for the table lamp she knew was there. It took a moment before she found it; she could hear the air rasping in her lungs. The dark turned pale yellow, the light incongruously warm. But whatever had once been cosy about this room had fled.

There was the mantelpiece on which he'd left the note. *So sorry*, he'd said. And there in front of the fireplace, the chair. Her mouth filled with saliva and she swallowed, breathed deep, forced herself to hold her ground.

It lay on its side, wooden legs pointing towards the window. Had she left it there? She couldn't remember. It was as if her brain had shut down the moment she'd seen Alistair, her mind refusing to acknowledge it and somehow at the same time knowing instantly, without a shadow of a doubt, that he had left her. She had screamed, apparently. A neighbour had heard, had called the police. They had radioed for the ambulance, though they too must have known that Alistair was beyond the reach of medicine. She had a vague memory of fluorescent jackets, someone speaking to her, unable to make sense of their words.

The chair, then. One of the last things he'd touched. It belonged in the kitchen. She should take it back there, but she couldn't bear to touch it. She was panting now, her skin clammy. She reached into her pocket for the inhaler, shook it, raised it to her lips. Water. She needed water. She switched off the lamp.

It was as she turned to go that she saw the green light blinking in the corner. Alistair's landline. The light, she knew, meant there was a message, perhaps more than one. Probably it had been left months ago, the caller knowing by now that Alistair would never reply. But still: she would have to check. It might be important, some part of officialdom she'd missed in the rounds of forms and phone calls.

She leaned across the armchair – Alistair's chair; she would never sit in it – and pressed the button on the base of the phone. *You have one message.* She pressed again. *Monday 28th of January at 11.25 a.m.* A pause, then a female voice.

'*Hi. Alistair. It's Anna. Anna Morgan. From work – er, Holbrooke and Dean. I was hoping to talk to you.*' A longer pause, as if she suspected he was there and was hoping this might bring him to the phone. '*Well, right. I wanted to say – I should have said – if you'd find it helpful to talk to someone, we have the counselling service, as you know. And if you wanted to, we could make you an appointment. They could signpost you to other services for – well, whatever you need. I'm sorry, I should have said all this on Thursday.*' The voice went quiet. Then a sigh. '*I'm sorry, Alistair. I'm sorry it's been this way. If I can help, please let me know. You've got my number. Bye then. Bye.*'

Silence. The green light was steady now, satisfied it had done its job. Maeve stared at it. Then she pressed the button again. '*Hi. Alistair. It's Anna. Anna Morgan...*' She listened until the end, then reached out a shaking finger, pressed down once more. '*Hi. Alistair. It's Anna...*'

The darkness crept closer as she listened. And when she finally turned to leave, every word of the message burned into her memory, the night was upon her and there was no light left at all.

FORTY-EIGHT

LONDON

Four months ago

The woman behind the desk that used to be Roberto's was beautiful, elegant, intimidating. Her hair was cut close to her scalp, showing the curve of her skull. I wondered how she felt about being dragged halfway across the globe to sort out our shit.

She had stood to welcome me, and she was taller than I was, slimmer too. Immaculately dressed. Was this what everyone looked like in the New York office? If I'd understood her correctly, it was possible I might soon find out.

'I realise this is a lot to take in,' she was saying, 'but I hope you'll consider it seriously. It's not at director level, but it's a good team and it's growing. There'd be lots of scope for you to shape the role.'

I nodded, trying to appear calm. She had no idea what it was taking for me just to sit there, in the same room where Roberto had told me what had happened to Alistair. It was as much as I could do to keep my attention on her, to listen to what she was saying instead of replaying his words that day, the panic in his voice.

My eyes travelled down to where I'd been sick. There was no shadow of a stain. Perhaps they'd replaced the carpet along with Roberto. The first I'd heard of his departure was the call from the woman opposite me – Grace, she was called. It had been over a month since I'd been signed off on sick leave, Roberto practically bundling me out of the door. A month since I'd woken in the night to discover a wetness between my legs that told me I no longer had to worry about how Matt would react to me being pregnant. I was too numb to grieve then, but I knew: I didn't deserve a baby after what I'd done.

I suspected there might have been more difficult discussions at work if that hadn't happened, the forces which had led to Roberto's removal circling me too. But when Tamsin, my deputy, had phoned a few days later, ostensibly to ask how I was, her tone had changed markedly when I told her I'd miscarried. I could almost hear the words 'work-related stress' running through her brain. They'd been handling me with kid gloves since then, knowing I understood the system, doubtless imagining an expensive tribunal if they put a foot wrong. They needn't have worried. If they'd sacked me, I wouldn't have had the energy to challenge it. I wouldn't have had the energy to collect the pot plant from my desk.

But it was probably that concern that lay behind Grace phoning me herself, instead of leaving it with Tamsin, asking me to come for a meeting to discuss what she called my 'future'. I didn't have one, I wanted to tell her, but that wasn't the kind of thing you said at work. So I had showered, washed my hair, brushed my teeth – things I hadn't done regularly since the day I'd heard about Alistair. Matt had moved out, so there was no one to nag me about it. On the whole, it was a relief. I hadn't found the moment to tell him about the baby, and then there was nothing to tell. He'd tried to be supportive, he said, his suitcase at the front door like a scene in a film, but I'd shut him out. Maybe he was right about that – but I'd see something tighten in his expression whenever I tried to utter Alistair's name. Part of him still thought we'd been having an affair, I think. Perhaps it was his own guilty conscience. I'd heard he'd moved in with Elise, which didn't surprise me. He wasn't the kind of person to leave one bed without having another to get into.

I'd been worried about returning to the office, worried I might run into him – but presumably Elise had warned him to steer clear. Her desk was empty too as Grace ushered me in, though there was a half-drunk cup of coffee next to the mouse mat. A well-timed trip to the ladies, I imagined.

'It could be a great opportunity,' Grace was saying. 'A new city, new colleagues.'

'Is there – anyone there I know?' We both knew I meant Roberto. The circumstances of his departure had been left vague.

She shook her head, put down the silver pen she'd been fiddling with. 'I can't imagine how it's been for you,' she said, and to my horror I felt my eyes fill with tears. From somewhere she produced a box of tissues and pushed it across the desk. 'Here, have one of these. I know Roberto – let's just say I can guess you didn't get a lot of support.'

I blinked rapidly and took a tissue. I wanted to argue, to let her know that I was professional enough to take responsibility for my own failures. I knew it was my fault, but I was afraid. If I sat there and said the words I knew to be true – that my inaction, my failure to support Alistair, as a member of staff and, worse, as a friend, had killed him – what happened to me then?

She said, 'I've heard good things about you, Anna. We don't want to lose you.'

I found my voice. 'Thank you. I appreciate what you're trying to do—'

She cut me off. 'We lease apartments near the office. You could move straight in. We'd help you with moving expenses, take care of all the practical arrangements.'

They'd done it for others, I recalled, staff moving to the New York headquarters to help what had been two companies feel more like one. It seemed to have gone smoothly enough.

'It could be a fresh start. Get some distance, focus on something new.'

She meant it, I could see. The offer was calculated, but there was kindness there too. I felt a lump in my chest. What, after all, did I have left for me here?

I cleared my throat. 'Could you tell me about the team?'

We talked for almost an hour, Grace taking me efficiently through the structure, the staff I'd be responsible for, the tasks to be delivered. I began to imagine it, walking into a different office, a new city, New York no less. I'd been there only once before, a long weekend with Matt involving hours following him around gleaming department stores while he exclaimed at the prices of the designer labels and bemoaned our meagre luggage allowance. This would be different – no Matt, no one I knew. No one who knew what I'd done.

Except that – perhaps they would. I'd had some dealings with the New York office from time to time, mainly, thanks to the time difference, in the form of emails. But there were people there who would know my name, know that I'd been the HR director in London. People who would perhaps have heard about what had happened to Alistair, despite all the attempts I was certain would have been made to keep it quiet. I couldn't face that – the whispering behind hands, conversations that stopped when I entered the room. I couldn't travel three thousand miles and find I'd brought it all with me.

Grace was winding down. 'There's no need to decide now. Take your time, think it over. I'll call you in a few days and we can talk again.'

I shook my head. 'I don't need time. I'd like to accept.'

She smiled, and I saw the relief there. 'Well, that's just wonderful—'

'But there's one thing I need. And I'm afraid if it won't be possible, I can't go.'

She listened patiently as I explained. And when I was done, she nodded briskly. 'We'll find a way to make it work,' she said.

FORTY-NINE

LONDON

Maeve, two months ago

Maeve's hands were trembling as she followed the woman who'd met her at reception – a girl, really, below the carefully applied make-up. She'd introduced herself, but Maeve had forgotten the name immediately. She wasn't the person she was interested in seeing.

They came to the end of a corridor and an office opened in front of them, a cluster of desks in front of a glass-walled cubicle. The latter, presumably, belonged to the CEO, Grace Reffell. Maeve's eyes roved systematically over the occupants of the desks. Four of them were men; one desk presumably belonged to the girl now walking in front of her, raising her hand to tap on the door of the glass box. The others were occupied by women. Was it possible that one of them was *her*? But one looked too young for the voice on the answerphone, one too old. One somehow subtly not right.

It wasn't logical, but she felt the truth of it in her bones: if she saw Anna Morgan, she would know her. She would feel the pull of the thread that bound them together, smell her poison.

'Ms Douglass, please come in.'

An elegant black woman had come to the door of the cubicle, an arm outstretched in invitation. The girl who'd shown her in was scuttling back to a nearby desk. Maeve straightened her shoulders and went inside.

'Firstly, let me express my heartfelt condolences for the loss of your brother.'

Maeve nodded curtly, noting the American accent. 'Thank you.'

'I'm sorry I never met him, but I know he is much missed by his colleagues.'

'*Former* colleagues.' She saw Grace stiffen at the icy tone. 'After all, he had been sacked. Just a few days before his death.'

Death. She was pleased she could say the word with such apparent ease. She was glad she had practised it.

'That is sadly true. There were a series of disciplinary issues, I'm afraid.'

'Do you know how long my brother worked here?'

'I understand that he made a very valuable contribution over a number of years.'

'*Seventeen* years. Seventeen years of loyal service, and your company just threw him on the scrap heap.'

'Ms Douglass—'

'Who is Anna Morgan?'

There was a pause as the other woman studied her. Then, 'I'm afraid I can't discuss other members of staff with you.'

Maeve felt the blood rush to her cheeks. She took a breath, struggled to remain calm. 'She was the one who did it, wasn't she? She fired him?'

'I understand this is very upsetting for you.' Grace looked as if she meant it, those brown eyes full of empathy. 'I can assure you that the termination of your brother's employment with us was undertaken in accordance with our policies and procedures.'

'That's not what she said.'

'I'm afraid I don't understand.'

'She called him. Anna Morgan. Left a message. Do you want to hear it?' She pulled her phone from her bag.

Grace held up a hand. 'I can assure you, Ms Douglass, that I have personally looked carefully at everything that happened in relation to this tragic affair. I am saddened that your brother's time with us came to an end, and of course, deeply saddened to hear of his death. But I am entirely satisfied that the proper procedures were followed throughout.'

She was a politician, this one. Maeve should have guessed as much. 'You need to listen to this,' she said, fumbling with her phone, trying to find the recording.

Grace shifted in her seat, probably debating whether to ask her to leave now, whether it would be better to humour her. But there it was, the red button on her phone screen. She touched it, listened as the voice filled the room. *'Hi. Alistair. It's Anna. Anna Morgan.'*

She watched Grace as the voice continued, as it confessed its failings. But her expression didn't flicker. The recording finished.

'You see? She said she should have talked to him about counselling, but she didn't.'

Grace dipped her head. For a moment, Maeve thought she was nodding. 'I appreciate it must have been difficult to hear that.' Grace met her eyes again, held her in her steady gaze. 'It sounds as if the caller—'

'Anna Morgan.'

'As if she was concerned about your brother, and seeking to provide additional support.'

'Additional—?'

'Our counselling service is for current members of staff. It wouldn't be normal practice to offer it in those circumstances.'

'But she admitted she should have done it when she fired him! On Thursday, she said. That's when she did it, wasn't it? And she left that message on the Monday afterwards. Do you understand what I'm saying?'

'I understand that you're upset—'

'Stop saying that! Are you even listening to me? If she'd done her job properly, Alistair might still be alive!'

She saw the shutters come down then. Grace folded her arms. 'I don't think it's productive to continue this conversation. Perhaps we should—'

'Where is she?' Maeve got to her feet. What had she been doing, thinking she could talk to this woman? She should have simply told the receptionist she was here to see Anna Morgan, made up some story to get inside. Cut through all this bullshit. This was what you got for trying to do things properly.

'Ms Douglass, please—'

'I said, where is she? Anna Morgan. I want to talk to her.'

She was halfway to the door when Grace replied. 'She's not here. Anna Morgan no longer works here.'

Something in her voice told Maeve it was the truth. She turned back to her. 'You fired her too?'

'I'm afraid that's confidential.' But she detected something, the ghost of a nod. The woman wasn't able to tell her outright; no doubt that would be breaking 'policies and procedures'. But she was giving her a hint, letting her know that something had been done.

'I need to talk to her,' she said again. 'Please.'

Her voice cracked on the last word, and she saw the other woman's eyes cloud with pity. It was too much. She couldn't stand it.

'I'm sorry,' Grace said. 'I can't give out personal information. It's for the best, Ms Douglass – Maeve.' She was picking up a card, holding something out to her. For a wild moment Maeve let herself believe that it was Anna Morgan's contact details, that perhaps there was some kind of surveillance device in the office, some hidden listener Grace was appeasing with her words while surreptitiously passing her the information she needed. But then she took the card and read what it said: *Crest Counselling and Mediation Services.*

'I'm so sorry we weren't able to help Alistair,' Grace said. 'But if you'd find it valuable, I'd be more than happy to extend the same offer to you.'

Maeve stared at her, feeling the red wave rising within her, knowing she must leave before it took over. She turned and pulled open the door, her stride almost breaking into a run, needing to get outside, away from these people. Dimly she was aware of the girl who had shown her in rising from her seat, perhaps intending to escort her out. She waved her away and made for the corridor, the walls shimmering around her, into the stairwell, clattering down the stairs, her breath coming hard, her chest aching.

Outside, she leant against the wall of the building, her head between her knees, waiting for the wheezing to stop. Bitterness stabbed at her insides.

Counselling. What good had it ever done her? It would have been better for her if she'd never walked into Paul's office that day. Better for him too. But then maybe for Alistair it might have been different. If nothing else, it would have given him something to do, an appointment to make and keep, some practical task to tether him to the world. To keep him there until she could reach him, promise him she'd make it right as she had so many times before. *Oh God, Ali!* He should have believed in her. Should have trusted her.

She straightened up, holding her hands to her aching ribs. It wasn't his fault. He had been let down. It didn't matter what that American woman said. Maeve knew who was to blame.

Anna Morgan had said so herself. *Sorry*, she'd said, more than once. But sorry wasn't good enough. Sorry wouldn't bring Alistair back. And she'd made a promise to Alistair as she'd listened to that message: she'd make that woman pay for what she'd done.

And now Anna Morgan had gone, lost her job. It was a start. But it wasn't enough, not by a long way. Maeve breathed deep, ran her fingers through her hair, smoothing it back into place. She couldn't afford to fall apart. She had to think.

The door beside her opened again, ready for someone else to exit the building. But there was no point in going back in there. The American wasn't going to tell her anything. She'd have to find another way.

'Excuse me?'

She looked up at the figure who'd emerged behind her.

'I have something I think you need to hear.'

FIFTY

NEW YORK

Now

I've done it. It's hard to believe, but it's out there now, the whole sorry story. Did I expect telling someone to make me feel better? It hasn't worked yet. Perhaps it's because I've been keeping my eyes on the floor, tracing the pattern of the carpet back and forth, seeing where the pale grey becomes darker, then darker again, almost black. I haven't looked at Maeve. I haven't seen how she's reacting.

'You left your job to come here,' she says. 'You weren't sacked.'

Her words suggest she thinks I should have been. I shake my head. 'It was because of the baby, I think. They were worried I might sue. Roberto was... the way he told me what had happened to Alistair... it was abrupt. But I don't blame him. There's no good way to break news like that. I think he was in shock himself.'

A buzz of machinery cuts me off. The sound is closer now.

Perhaps soon there'll be feet on top of the car. It reminds me that this conversation might not be private. We may be hearing only static from the speaker on the wall, but someone in a control room could have been listening to every word I said. I find to my surprise that it doesn't bother me as much as I would have expected.

'I wasn't sure I should come here,' I say when it's quiet again. 'To New York, I mean. I was worried that people would find out, that I'd lose their confidence before I'd even started.'

'But you did it anyway. You ran away.'

It hurts, hearing it put so baldly, but she's right. 'Yes. That's exactly what I did.'

I hesitate, but there's no point stopping there. If anyone at Pearl Associates hears what I've said already, it will take them approximately five seconds to work out who I am.

'It's why I changed my name,' I say; and finally, I know that I've done the right thing. It's like I've put down a heavy weight. 'Cerys is my middle name really.'

There's a sound. A kind of choke.

I look up to see Maeve staggering to her feet, scrabbling in her bag.

'Are you okay?' I ask. 'Do you need your inhaler again?'

But then I catch sight of her face. Her skin is bloodless, her eyes wide and staring, blazing with emotion. She drops her bag to the floor and there is something in her hand. Something metal that glitters in the beam of the spotlights.

'You're her,' she says. 'You're Anna Morgan.'

FIFTY-ONE

NEW YORK

Now

Oh God. How could I not have seen it? It's so obvious now. That small bump on the bridge of her nose. The angle of her jaw. The grey-blue eyes. Alistair. They are all of them Alistair.

And in an instant it all makes sense. I am the reason she's here. She's not an activist, hasn't travelled three thousand miles to protest about some patch of greenbelt. She has come to get vengeance for her brother. She has come for me.

'You killed him,' she says. 'You killed Alistair.'

I thought I'd understood the horror of what I'd done. Looking at Maeve now, at her white face, the lines of grief etched into her skin, I know that I was wrong. Her pain is so raw it burns. And it's all my fault.

'I'm so, so sorry,' I say, but my words sound hollow. They *are* hollow. What good can they do her? 'I know that doesn't matter, but I am. I think of him every day. He never leaves me.'

'It's not about you!' she screams, and I flinch.

'You're right. I'm sorry.'

I stare at the black hole that is the barrel of a gun. When I first heard about Alistair, I asked myself whether I deserved to live. Considered whether I should follow his example. Once, I counted out the sleeping tablets I'd been prescribed, wondering if it could be that simple, if I could just go to sleep and not wake up.

And in this moment, the gun inches from my face, the irony of it strikes me with the force of a slap. Now, when judgement is here at last, I realise I want to live.

Maeve takes a step forward then back again. The hatred crackles off her like electricity. 'You didn't even try to help him! Everything he did for that place. All those years of his life he put into that fucking company. None of it counted for you, did it? None of it was good enough!'

'I tried,' I say, though she is saying only what I've told myself a thousand times. 'I should have done more—'

'Yes, you fucking should!'

The shame should bow my head, but I can't take my eyes off her. Can't stop staring down that black tunnel. 'You're right,' I say.

She bends, one hand wrapped around her waist, as if she's trying to hold herself together. The other arm stays outstretched, the barrel of the gun trembling. She straightens, then throws her head back in a howl. The noise is like nothing I've ever heard. The anguish it carries is like a knife, sharp enough to cut me open.

I deserve this. God knows, I deserve it. But this will to live – I've never felt anything so powerful. Now, at the end, I want to hold on to it all. The smelly, sour air of the lift. The smooth, solid wall against my back. The buzz of power tools above my head. I love them all. I want to stay.

Power tools. The sound is getting louder. They will be here soon; I must believe that. All I have to do is keep her talking. 'Please, Maeve,' I say. 'Please put down the gun.'

*

NEW YORK

Maeve, now

It's as if I'm right there again. I see your swollen tongue, your distended neck. Your eyes, normally the same colour as mine, but not that day.

I screw my own eyes shut, try to block out the pictures. The pressure builds inside, and I open my mouth to release it. The sound shatters around me, bounces against the walls of this dead box, falls at my feet.

The woman who is Anna Morgan is saying something. I don't want to hear it. All I have to do is move my finger and it will be over. It's all I can do for you now.

'He wouldn't want this.'

The voice slices into my thoughts. I try to ignore it, try to focus my aim. I won't miss, not at this distance. No matter how much my hands tremble. But it's never been this way before. I've never had to look them in the face.

'Please, Maeve. Alistair wouldn't want this.'

I grip my wrist to steady my aim. As if she knew you! As if she knew anything about you.

'He was my friend.'

'Your friend?' I would laugh, but it's so been long I've forgotten how. 'That's how you treat your friends, is it?'

'He was my friend,' she says again. 'I told you about my boss, didn't I?' She is talking softly, as if that will calm me. As if lowering her voice will make me forget what she's done. 'I told you he'd given me a second chance. That was Alistair.'

The trigger is firm against my finger. Just one small movement and this will end. I won't have to listen to this anymore. Yet – were you really her friend? I want to know. To find out something more about you, about the part of your life I didn't see. A new memory of you is precious. It's all I have left.

'He was a good man, Alistair. He was kind to me, kinder than I deserved.'

My arm is aching. I could lower it, just for a minute. Just until I hear this story. One last reminder to bring you close before the end.

'Tell me, then,' I say. 'Tell me what he did.'

FIFTY-TWO

LONDON

Fourteen years ago

Have you ever had that feeling when you know, just know, you're in the perfect place, doing the perfect thing? That everything is exactly how it should be? That's how it felt the moment I walked through the sliding glass doors into the offices of Holbrooke and Dean.

I'd got there early, leaving plenty of extra time in case of problems on the Tube. But it hadn't been necessary. Trains ran frequently, my connection went smoothly. I'd even got a seat on the final stretch. I emerged into sunlight, found my way straight to the address on the letter. When I got to reception, the woman who asked for my name looked just like my friend Saima from university. She smiled as she asked me to take a seat, and I could already imagine how it would feel to walk in there every day, say hi to her and ask about her weekend plans, just raise a hand in greeting if she was busy. It was mid-morning and the place was buzzing, people striding in and out as if they had somewhere to be, something important to do.

I'd been there for only a few minutes when I saw a man jog down a flight of stairs at the far end of the reception area. He was tall and wiry, and as he jumped down the final step, he fixed his eyes on me and smiled, already holding out his hand as he closed the distance between us. I liked him immediately.

'Alistair Douglass,' he said, his hand taking mine in a firm shake. 'And you're Anna Morgan, am I right?'

He led me back up the stairs and into a bright, airy room with a window looking out onto the street. A well-built woman I judged to be somewhere in her fifties, greying hair in a smooth bob, stood as we entered. 'Elizabeth Fraine,' she said, offering her hand. 'I run the HR department.'

Alistair pointed me to a chair, poured me a glass of water. 'For you, Elizabeth?' he asked, gesturing at the half-full glass on the desk in front of her, and I was pleased that he'd offered, hadn't left it to the woman to take charge of the refreshments.

They were skilled interviewers, although I was too inexperienced to see it at the time – even though Alistair, surely, couldn't have conducted many at that stage in his career. They put me at my ease, asked me about my journey, Alistair telling me he'd followed the same route many times himself. He had family in Bristol, apparently.

'Morgan,' he said. 'That's a Welsh name, isn't it?'

'Dad was English, but Mum always said he must have had Welsh ancestors somewhere. She was Welsh, though. I think she only said it to wind up her in-laws.'

I wondered if I was babbling, but Alistair laughed so I carried on. 'Dad's always lived in Bristol. He set up his business there. He's a counsellor.' I realised as I said it that I'd got the tense wrong, but ignored the jolt in my stomach. 'A therapist,' I clarified.

There was a brief pause and I saw Elizabeth dart a glance at

Alistair, expecting him to ask another question. But he was studying his notepad, apparently finished for the moment. She picked up the conversation, asking how I'd heard about the job, what had made me apply.

'I saw a flyer,' I said, 'in an Indian takeaway of all places!'

Alistair looked up at that. 'The Rose of Bengal,' he said with a smile. 'I know it well.'

Elizabeth gave him a look of surprise. 'I rather thought the university careers office might have had something to do with it.'

'That too, of course, Elizabeth.' He smiled at me as he said it.

I'd sat up a little straighter at the mention of university, conscious that we were nearing dangerous ground. But when we moved on to my degree, it was Alistair who asked the questions, focusing on the modules I'd covered, the topic of my dissertation. As we talked, I remembered that I loved my subject, that I'd been good at it. I felt myself begin to relax.

Eventually, Elizabeth brought things to a close, thanking me for coming in. 'We'll be seeing other candidates today and tomorrow, but we'll let you know the outcome by the weekend,' she said.

My face must have fallen at the mention of the competition because Alistair said, 'I'm so pleased you've applied, Anna. It's always good to meet a fellow curry lover.'

For a moment I didn't understand what he meant, but then I remembered the flyer in the takeaway. I smiled back at him, thinking about the day I'd found it, the state I'd been in, my stupid idea of visiting my father's girlfriend. And I thought, *It's Fate. I was always supposed to come here.* And for the first time in a very long time, I felt it was possible that everything might, after all, come out all right.

It was just a day later that I got the call. I was watching daytime TV and eating a cheese toastie. I picked up the phone, expecting it to be Siân asking how it had all gone, mumbling 'Hello,' around my mouthful of half-chewed cheddar.

'It's Alistair Douglass,' he said, 'from Holbrooke and Dean.'

I jerked upright on the sofa, nearly choking on crumbs of toast. 'Hello, Mr Douglass, Alistair, I mean.'

'It was lovely to meet you yesterday, Anna. I very much enjoyed our conversation, and both Elizabeth and I feel that you would be a real asset to the team.'

His next words faded away as I tried to process what it meant. I'd got the job. *I'd got the job!* At some point I must have made an appropriate response because he was suggesting a start date, explaining that they'd send me a form for my bank details, a pack about the pension scheme. (*Pension scheme*, I remember thinking in disbelief, *I'm going to have a bloody pension!*) I was already imagining ringing Siân, telling her the good news as he said he was looking forward to seeing me again.

'Oh, nearly forgot,' he said. 'Could you send us a copy of your degree certificate? Elizabeth needs it for your file.'

There was no alternative. The words tripped off my tongue. 'Of course,' I said. 'I'll send it right over.'

My first week was busy and terrifying and exciting, and best of all, *new*. I was introduced to different people every day, given organograms, copies of policies, checklists to sign, taken to meetings with people whose work I apparently needed to know about. They all seemed impossibly competent, even the youngest, only a year or two older than me, self-assured in a way I aspired to be. None of them knew what had happened to my parents. None of them looked at me with pity.

I had found a flat share forty minutes' journey from the office, and when I finished for the day my time was filled with sorting out my belongings, making polite small talk with whichever of my flatmates was around. Every day was full, and being constantly on my best behaviour left me exhausted, so that by the time my head touched the pillow at night it was easy to ignore the fleeting worry that I was living on borrowed time. *It will be fine*, I told myself. *They'll forget all about it.*

It was Friday morning and I was reading a site report given to me by one of the consultants when a shadow fell across my desk. I looked up to see Alistair and smiled automatically. He didn't smile back.

'Could you come to my office, please, Anna,' he said. 'Right away.'

I knew immediately what it was. A lead weight fell into the pit of my stomach, and I wanted to run to the bathroom. But Alistair was already turning away, and I had no choice but to get up and follow him.

He didn't say another word until we were in his office, the door closed behind us. The walls were glass, as they all were at Holbrooke and Dean. I took the seat he pointed me towards, glad that it would keep my back to them. I didn't want anyone else seeing my face when I heard what was coming.

'I won't beat around the bush,' he said, taking his own seat opposite me. 'I know about your degree. You received a third, not a 2:1. Do you want to explain to me why you lied?'

I could feel the tremor starting somewhere near the base of my spine, spreading through my body. I clasped my hands together to stop them from shaking, tried to form my mouth into the shape required to make words. 'I—' I said, and swallowed, tried again. 'I knew my degree wasn't good enough.' I heard the crack in my voice and stopped. I would not cry. I would *not*.

I was aware of Alistair shifting in his seat, but I couldn't look at him.

'The advert was very clear that we required candidates to have a minimum of a 2:1,' he said. 'I told you when I offered you the job that we'd need your degree certificate. You said that wouldn't be a problem.' I could hear his exasperation. 'How did you imagine this was going to pan out?'

I didn't reply. What was there to say? I just wanted the humiliation to be over.

'That degree requirement was there for a reason. We need to be confident the people who work for us have the right level of technical proficiency for the job. It won't do us or you any favours to keep you in a role where you'll struggle.'

I kept my head down, shame burning my cheeks. For a moment there was silence. I wondered if this was it, whether this was the moment I could get up and leave.

Alistair sighed. 'What were you thinking, Anna? You were so impressive at the interview. We had a good conversation, didn't we?' He sounded perplexed, sad almost. 'I enjoyed talking to you. But you weren't honest with me. I can't work with someone who isn't honest.'

The words stabbed at me, the unfairness of it. Yes, I'd lied about my results, but they weren't the truth. They didn't represent who I was, what I could do. 'I'm sorry,' I said, meeting his eyes for the first time, 'but if I'd told you my real results, you'd never have interviewed me. And I'm better than they make me look. If things had been different—'

I came to a stop. Did I want to go there? Did I have a choice?

'Go on,' said Alistair.

He wanted to know, I could see that. And surely that meant he was prepared to give me another chance? And was it so hard, really, to tell him what had happened and leave him to make his choice?

I took a breath. 'It was my mum,' I said.

FIFTY-THREE

NEW YORK

Now

Maeve has slid down the wall and is resting on her haunches, the hand with the gun resting on her knees, the muzzle never shifting from its target – me.

'I don't believe you,' she says.

I fight down a rising tide of panic. 'What? It's true. Alistair helped me. He let me keep my job.'

'But you lied.' Her lip curls. 'He hated liars.'

I shake my head. 'He was kind. He understood. I told him what had happened, why I'd done so badly in my exams.'

'You made excuses, you mean.'

'No, it was true. My mum died before my exams. I wasn't – I couldn't concentrate on anything else.'

Maeve pulls a face. 'So why not resit them? Why lie about it instead?'

Even now, even with a gun pointed at my chest, some small spark of resistance, the desire to protect, wants me to tell her it's none of her business. But I am scared and weak, and I have already told Mum's secret once. She'd want me to do this, wouldn't she? If it's the difference between keeping Maeve talking and her pulling that trigger?

'I didn't want to tell anyone. I was ashamed.'

'What? That doesn't make any sense.' She waves the gun impatiently and for a moment I can't breathe, watching that dark circle fly around the space. 'Your mum died. That's nothing to be ashamed of.'

I wait until her hand is still again and I can form a coherent thought. I have to do this, I tell myself.

'It was the way she died,' I say. 'Mum had a hard time.'

Maeve gives a humourless laugh. 'Welcome to the club.' But at least she's listening.

'My dad walked out on us. He'd been seeing someone else. Mum found out and she – she just couldn't take it.'

Too late I remember Maeve's own affair; Mum will get no sympathy here. 'Poor her,' she sneers predictably. 'So what happened?'

'She started drinking. Or no – not started. She used to drink sometimes before, but not like that. She tried to hide it from me, but I knew. I should have done something, should have made her get help.'

I see something flash across Maeve's face, a flicker of understanding. But she doesn't speak, and I press on.

'I was away when it happened. I left her on her own, even though I knew how much she needed me.' I hear the strain in my voice. I've never said this stuff out loud. 'I was at uni, having a laugh with my friends, and Mum was there with no one.'

'She was the parent, not you,' Maeve says, surprising me. 'You can't stop someone drinking. They have to want to stop.'

It's what the books say, but I know it's not as simple as that. 'I should have been there. It would never have happened if I'd been with her. But I was too selfish. There's no point pretending anything different. It was my fault. She died and I have to live with that.'

I feel the change instantly, a charge in the air. I look at Maeve and her eyes are blazing.

'But you can't say the same about Alistair?' She leaps to her feet, towers above me, the gun pointing down.

I cover my head with my hands, as if they can stop a bullet.

'You sacked him, and he killed himself!' Her voice is shrill. 'You're to blame! My brother's dead, and that's your fault. But you can't say it, can you? You can take the blame for your mother, but not for him!'

Something hard jabs against my skull and my stomach turns to liquid. It is the barrel of the gun.

'Say it!' She's screaming now. 'Say it's your fault!'

My head is on the floor, pain at the side of my skull. Maeve is pressing down so hard the bone must surely fracture soon. My vision wavers, darkens at the edges.

'You took him from me!'

My lips are moving, but all I can hear is Maeve.

'Say it!' she screams over and over.

I cannot raise my head. The carpet scratches at my mouth. And suddenly there's silence, and my words fall into it soft as snow.

'Yes,' I say, 'it was all my fault.'

FIFTY-FOUR

NEW YORK

Now

It is over. This is how it ends.

No scenes from my life flash before my eyes. All I see is Maeve. She stands above me, suspended with me here in this moment.

The terror has gone. I realise now I have been waiting for this, perhaps for my entire life. That an unacknowledged part of my brain has always wondered how it will be for me. It was sudden for Mum and Dad. Different circumstances, but in both of them speed, momentum, substances harder than bone shattering their bodies. And now it's my turn. A bullet to my head. I'd never expected that.

I close my eyes.

I feel the breath travelling through my body. Someone is sobbing. The last sounds I'll hear.

Another breath. Another. Gradually, I become aware that something has changed. The pressure against my head has gone.

I feel the carpet damp beneath my cheek. I open my eyes and see the grey pattern stretching away from me.

I turn my head. Maeve is leaning against the wall of the elevator, looking at me. Her arms hang at her sides. The gun is still clutched in one hand. The muzzle points at the floor.

A feeling floods through me – hope, and with it fear. I do, after all, have something left to lose.

I am lying on the floor, my legs curled against my body. Slowly, I unwind, my eyes never leaving Maeve's. There are tear tracks on her cheeks, but her expression is blank. Why did she stop? I have no idea.

I pull my body upright, my legs straight out in front of me. I slide backwards, trying to move slowly, not wanting to startle her from her trance. My fingertips brush metal and I stop as the wall of the lift hits my spine. It's all the distance I can put between us.

It isn't enough.

Above us, something clanks and squeals. I look up, but there is nothing to see, only the nine spotlights gleaming steadily down. When I look back at Maeve, she hasn't moved. She no longer seems to care what's happening out there. But I am still alive, and those noises are my salvation. If I can just hold on long enough for whoever is making them to reach us. If I can just find a way to keep her talking...

'It won't work,' she says. 'We're not getting out of here.'

Her voice is flat. I try to reply, but my throat doesn't work.

'It's good you've admitted it, but it doesn't change anything. Ali's gone and you're here. I can't allow that.'

I stare at her. I can't believe what she's saying. She had the gun against my head but she didn't pull the trigger. That has to mean something. That has to mean I have a chance. I just have to find some way to reach her.

'You loved him,' I say. There is a tremor in my voice, as if I have been crying. I put my fingers to my cheeks and realise I have.

'He was my brother,' she says simply. 'He was all I had.'

My brain is racing now, making connections like a super-computer, desperately trying to keep me alive. I remember what she said about being attacked, the reason she carries a gun. *They took everything from me.*

'That was what happened to you,' I say. 'The reason for the panic attacks. You found him.'

She doesn't reply and I know I'm right. Oh God, what that must have been like! How many times have I seen Alistair in my dreams? My imagination was bad enough. How did you live with the reality of seeing something like that? Her own brother.

I swallow. 'You came to find me. How did you know I was here?'

'You're stalling,' she says, with the ghost of a smile. 'You think I've bottled it once, I'll do it again. You think if you keep me talking, someone's going to burst into this lift and save you.'

'No, I—'

'I understand. Even when we know it's the end, we want just another minute. Just another story.' She bends her knees, crouches down so her eyes are almost level with mine. 'It won't hurt,' she whispers. 'It's so fast. I've read about it. There isn't time for your brain to register the bullet.'

My stomach turns and I taste vomit.

'It will be better for us than it was for Alistair.'

Us. I stare at her in horror. Of course she can't live with what she's seen. She has no intention of trying.

Another noise from the lift shaft – an echo of something. Voices? *Oh dear God, please, let them be coming.*

Maeve looks up, returns her gaze to me. 'You won't feel it. I promise.' She folds her legs beneath her, makes herself comfortable. 'We've still got some time. Why don't you talk to me about Alistair? He was kind to you, wasn't he?'

She sounds calm, dreamy almost. All traces of the woman who pushed the gun against my head have gone. It should be reassuring, but it's the opposite: the tranquillity of someone who has accepted that what comes next is inevitable.

She's waiting for an answer. It takes every ounce of my will to summon my voice.

'Yes,' I say. 'He was very understanding. He tried to make me feel better about Mum. Tried to tell me it was an accident, that no one was to blame.'

'An accident?'

Her voice is sharp, and I flinch. Perhaps she thinks I'm making excuses, trying to hint that sometimes people die and it's no one's fault. I hasten to soothe her. 'The way she died – it wasn't like Alistair. She'd been drinking and she must have been unsteady on her feet. She fell down the stairs.'

There is a long silence, as if she is pondering what I've said. I sneak a glance upwards, towards the camera. Perhaps someone is watching us right now, someone who can see the gun and knows I'm in danger. Perhaps at this very minute they're screaming over a radio, telling the people in the lift shaft to hurry. But that glass dome is giving nothing away.

I turn back to Maeve. For a moment I can't decipher her expression; it's so different from what I expected that at first I can't put a name to it. But then I realise – it's pure horror.

*

NEW YORK

Maeve, now

Anna Morgan.

Morgan.

Morgan.

How could I have been so blind?

I would never have recognised her – but then, why would I? It was years ago, the girl in the photos I saw just a child. She was wearing school uniform. Had long curly hair, not this short crop. But yes, there it is – something in the shape of her eyes. Now that I look for it, it's unmistakable. This is Paul's daughter.

Some people would say this is karma, that it always comes for you in the end. But I know better. There are no divine forces making sure everything balances out. If you want justice, you have to take it for yourself. So it doesn't matter who this woman is. All that matters is that she's responsible for your death.

Yet a thought is worming its way into my head. I know it

can't be true. You'd have told me, wouldn't you, Ali? You wouldn't have hidden that from me. And yet the thought is there, and I can't let it go.

I have to know for sure.

FIFTY-FIVE

NEW YORK

Now

'You told Alistair your mother fell downstairs.'

For the first time, there's a note of uncertainty in Maeve's voice. Something I've said has thrown her and I struggle to understand it, to pinpoint the relevance of that conversation with Alistair. If I know what it is, perhaps I can use it, find some way to convince her to let me live.

She says, 'I need to know exactly what he said.' She taps the gun against the floor, her knuckles white. It reminds me I don't have the luxury of keeping her waiting while I choose my words.

I swallow, try to pull myself together. 'He told me I shouldn't blame myself.'

She shakes her head. 'You said before he told you it was an accident, that no one was to blame. Which was it?'

I stare at her in confusion. 'I don't know. Both, maybe. He was just trying to make me feel better.'

Silence. The gun taps against the floor. The barrel is at an angle. If she hits the trigger by accident, the bullet will strike the door. Would it ricochet? I don't have the first idea.

'How did you find me?' I ask for a second time, hoping to stop the tapping. 'How did you know I was here?'

The gun stills and I feel the band around my chest loosen infinitesimally. 'You need to be nicer to people, *Anna*,' she says, grimacing as she speaks my name. 'There are some people in London who really don't like you at all.'

Perhaps that's true – but only a handful of people knew about the transfer. I'd not said a word to my former colleagues, deleted my social media accounts. The official line was that I was taking a career break, and Grace had assured me she'd handle the liaison with New York herself. I couldn't see her going to all that trouble only to out me to Maeve. Besides, it was in her interests to draw a line under events. So if not Grace...

'Matt?'

She smiles at me sadly. 'You're really not a very good judge of character, are you?' There's a pause, as if she's not sure I deserve to know. Then, 'I'm not sure who it was. She didn't give her name. But after what you've told me, I can guess.'

It takes a moment before the penny drops. 'Elise.'

'I'd gone to see your boss – Grace, wasn't it? I told her you'd admitted you'd done everything wrong. I even played her your answerphone message.'

So Maeve has heard my message. The knowledge is like a stone in my chest. How will I convince her it wasn't my fault when she's heard me apologising to Alistair? Admitting I should have referred him for counselling? How will I convince her when I know as well as she does that it *was* my fault?

'She was no help, though,' Maeve continues. 'Just covering her back. Even though I told her when you'd phoned. That Ali might still be alive if you'd done your job properly.'

My mind catches on something, the emphasis of her words. But Maeve is still talking and I'm carried onwards.

'I would have found you eventually. I would have found a way. But that woman followed me out, the one who'd come to meet me at reception. I was standing outside, trying to decide what to do next. She said I deserved to know.'

Of course. With Roberto gone, Elise would have become Grace's PA. She'd have had access to Grace's email. Nothing would be off-limits to her.

'She was young,' she says, a glint of malice in her eyes. 'Very pretty.'

If she wants to wound me, she's barking up the wrong tree. I've long since stopped caring about how I measure up to Elise.

'She didn't tell me about your name change, though.' She frowns, and I find myself thinking it's best for Elise that things have turned out this way. An unsuccessful visit to New York, and Maeve's opinion of her might have taken a decided turn for the worse. I wonder if she was protecting me in spite of herself? More likely, the detail had simply slipped her mind.

That's not what's bothering me, though. Something about what Maeve said is still scratching away in a corner of my brain. I am scared to interrupt her, scared that anything I say will provoke her further. But I have to know.

'You said you told Grace when I phoned. I don't understand. Why did that matter?'

She stares at me, watching me struggle to catch up. 'Don't you know?' she says. And all of a sudden, I wish I hadn't asked, sense the shape of what is coming. I want to tell her to stop, to put my hands over my ears before it's too late. But it's already too late. Everything is too late.

Maeve leans forward, her eyes blazing. 'When you left that message, my brother was already dead.'

FIFTY-SIX

NEW YORK

Now

I experience it as if I'm asleep and dreaming, but I'm awake and I know I'll never escape it. Alistair, blood cold in his veins, the silence broken by a ring, a beep. My voice, my pathetic apologies. Telling him I'm there if he needs me. And all the time the sound echoing, echoing.

Maeve is still talking but I can't listen to her. I can't breathe. I feel like I'm falling—

Maeve screams. The sound rips through the air and my eyes snap open. It's not my mind that has created the drop in my stomach. The lift is plummeting.

The lights flicker, and I see Maeve's face through a strobe, her eyes wide with fear. There's a sudden metallic pop, pop, pop, a shriek of steel against steel. An impact jolts my body upwards and for a brief moment I'm suspended in air. Then I feel the breath leave my body as I'm slammed against the floor. A crash. A groan. Everything is still.

I raise my head, barely daring to breathe. And I see it. There in the middle of the floor, as close to me as it is to Maeve. The gun.

I look up at her. She looks back. A thin streak of blood trickles from her temple. I notice it even as I spring forwards, arm outstretched.

I think I'm going to get it. In my mind, my fingers are already closing around the metal. But then Maeve's foot strikes out and the gun is sliding away from my grasp, clattering into the corner of the lift. I lunge for it on hands and knees, but pain shoots through me. I curl back instinctively, one hand clutching the other, holding it against my body. Needles of fire streak through my fingers.

She's stamped on my hand.

I try to blot out the agony as I reach forward again – but it's too late. Maeve is on her feet, swooping down, her arm swinging forward. There's a clatter as she scoops the gun against the wall of the lift, and then she's spinning around, her arm already outstretched, the barrel pointing down at me.

For a second we stare at each other, breathing hard. I am crouched between kneeling and standing, half-human, half-primate. The blood has reached the collar of her linen shirt, a maroon semicircle against the white.

An explosion of static from the speaker. I see Maeve's eyes dart to the panel on the wall. Does she want to get out of here after all? Does that scream mean she's not ready to give up on life just yet? But that is wishful thinking: it could have simply been the shock.

More static, interspersed with clicks. I fight the urge to scream at whoever is making the sound, to tell them to get me out of here right now. My eyes flick up to the ceiling, to that glass orb. There's still no light. Was there ever? I search my memory but come up short. Before today, I'd never thought twice about whether there were cameras. Never cared whether they were working or not.

'Sit down.'

Maeve's voice trembles and her hand is shaking. I do as she says, stretching my legs as I lower myself to the floor, trying to put as much distance between us as I can, even though I know the gun makes that meaningless. Whether the camera is working or not, I tell myself, this death-trap lift means there are people out there who know I'm in danger. They're trying to get to us as fast as they can.

'I've told you. We're not getting out of here.'

I swallow. My throat is so dry it hurts.

'Face it, Anna. It's not going to happen.' Her voice is uneven, but she's already recovering herself, already switching her focus back to me. She takes a step forward, her eyes dark. I see something in their depths and the breath catches in my windpipe. She's steadying herself to pull the trigger.

I have to make her stop. I have to say something. But my mind has gone blank. I can't think of any more stories.

'I promise you, I'll make it quick.'

I close my eyes. Will I see Mum? I wonder. Will she be waiting for me? Perhaps Dad, too. Perhaps I can tell them both how sorry I am.

'Stop crying. Be brave now.'

Mum and Dad.

Something stirs to life through the fog that fills my brain.

Mum and Dad.

Alistair let me keep the job when I told him Mum had died before my exams. But there was more to it than that, wasn't there? The night of the Christmas party, he'd been asking about Dad. And even on the day I'd sacked him, he didn't argue – but he did have questions. They just weren't about his job.

I open my eyes, see Maeve's white face above me. I can feel

the edges of something coming together, something that doesn't make sense yet.

'Alistair was asking about my father,' I say.

'What?' She cocks her head to one side.

'The day I did it – the day I had to let him go.' She pulls a face at the way I've phrased it. 'The day I sacked him,' I amend quickly. 'He was losing his job, but he didn't seem to care. There was something else that was bothering him. He was distracted, asking questions.'

'What about?' Her voice is sharp, suspicious that I'm dragging things out but too curious to resist.

'My father died in a car accident. It was a hit and run. Alistair was asking how it happened.'

I am aware that something has shifted in Maeve's expression, but I'm caught on my own thread now. I've spent so long fixated on the things I should have said that I haven't spent enough time thinking about what Alistair said to *me*.

'It wasn't the first time either. There was a Christmas party, a work thing.' I'm babbling, my thoughts now coming thick and fast. 'He was asking me about it then, about what had happened, when Dad had died. There was something strange about it, like it upset him.'

Maeve doesn't reply. Perhaps she doesn't believe me. 'It's true,' I say. 'I know I didn't handle things the way I should have. I know I should have told Alistair about the counselling service the day I fired him. I meant to, but I was distracted – I'm not making excuses. But it didn't seem like the job bothered him. The way he acted... It was almost like it wasn't important.'

And there was something else, wasn't there? Earlier still. Matt going to that conference, coming back saying Alistair had been weird on the train. That conversation they'd had about the wedding, how we were going to keep it small – it was when Alistair had found out Dad was dead.

I'm trying to put the pieces together, but I can't make out the picture yet.

'It wasn't his job he was upset about.' The moment the words are out, I know it's the truth. 'I think he knew something about Dad's accident. It was almost like...'

I trail off – I won't say that, not about Alistair. He drank, yes, he had problems. But he was a good man.

'Like what?' Maeve's voice is like stone. 'What are you saying?'

I shake my head. 'I would almost have thought he had something to do with it – with Dad's death. But that's not possible.'

And even now, the gun pointed at my head, I feel the memories come flooding back. Because I know something about the way Maeve feels, how it is to love someone and lose them. I know what it's like when the person to blame is out there walking around, living their life. How hard it is to try to move on. And suddenly the veil lifts for just a second, and I'm certain.

'Alistair knew what happened.'

Was that why he'd suddenly been acting so strangely? Avoiding me when we'd always been friendly? It had all started after that conversation with Matt. But according to Matt, all he'd told him was that my dad was dead. How could Alistair possibly have gone from that to thinking he knew who was responsible? And yet I know, deep on some instinctive level, that I'm right.

Maeve is shaking her head. 'You don't know what you're talking about.'

'He had family in Bristol, he told me. He must have been there when it happened, seen something. There was a witness. Maybe that was him.'

But no, the witness hadn't known who the driver was. All they'd been able to tell the police was that it was a woman wearing a headscarf. They hadn't even got the full car registration, just the last three letters as she'd driven away.

And yet I hear the words echo in my head. *Family in Bristol.* A woman driver. I stare at Maeve. It makes no sense. I don't understand it.

She is pale, the gun shaking in her hand. She moves to steady it, her other hand bolstering her grip. I watch the movement, and there it is again, the flash of silver at her wrist. And now for the first time I see it properly and the world tilts on its axis.

Maeve follows my gaze to where her sleeve has ridden up. 'Oh,' she says.

FIFTY-SEVEN

BRISTOL

Fifteen years ago

Siân's arm lay around my shoulders and I could smell her perfume, something light and floral. It wasn't her usual scent. Perhaps it had been a birthday present. I hadn't remembered, hadn't got her anything. The days had slipped past without my noticing. I hadn't even realised until I saw the cards on her mantelpiece. I'd said I was sorry and she'd told me it didn't matter. I should have done better, though. After everything she'd done for me.

'Miss Morgan? Anna.'

I looked up. The police officer who had spoken looked like he was expecting a response.

'I'm sorry, what?'

'We have good reason to be confident we'll find the driver. A witness has come forward.'

Siân's arm tightened around me. 'That's good, isn't it, love?'

'Someone saw it happen?' I tried to make sense of it, but my mind was loose, wandering. It occurred to me that I might be in shock.

'I realise this is a very difficult time for you, but it's important that we move quickly...'

His voice faded in and out. Something about a car, part of a registration plate. 'No,' I heard Siân say. 'No, I'm afraid not.' I shook my head too.

'The chances are the car will have been abandoned. But we have a description of the driver. A female.'

'A woman?' Siân's voice was sharp, incredulous. Like me, she'd been imagining a man, a boy probably. Someone reckless, risk-taking.

'She got out of the vehicle, but the witness was unable to see her face.' A pause, loaded with significance. 'She was wearing a headscarf.'

'And jeans.' It was the second officer. The way she said it carried the hint of a rebuke; but we all knew what the first officer was thinking, his focus on the headscarf. *Muslim*. And in this part of Bristol, perhaps *immigrant*.

The male officer cleared his throat. 'We also found something at the scene. We think it likely it was dropped by the driver.'

He held out a photograph and I felt every muscle tense. But it wasn't what I'd feared. Dad wasn't in the picture.

No one was.

It was just a close-up of a small object, an L-shaped gauge alongside it to show the dimensions.

I stared at it, the irony of its symbolism some kind of cosmic joke. It took me a moment to find my voice.

'I'm sorry,' I said, 'I've never seen that before.'

NEW YORK

Now

The chain glints on her wrist. From it dangles a series of silver hearts, each one with a blue enamel centre. She follows my gaze, twisting her hand as she does so, and I see the gap. The space where one of the hearts is missing. The small silver object I'd last seen in a photograph fifteen years ago, an L-shaped gauge lying next to it.

'How? How could it be you?'

My mind is racing. Words, ideas spinning so fast I can't grasp them. All I can think of is that this is her. The woman I've imagined so many times. The woman I've dreamed of, bending over my father's body.

And now the picture sharpens, new details coming into focus. Blonde hair escapes from the side of the headscarf. She stretches out her hand. It is pale, fine boned. She reaches out to touch him, draws back. A silver heart falls from her wrist, drops soundlessly onto his body. The clue they'd thought would find her, but never did.

This woman killed my father. This woman who is also Alistair's sister.

She doesn't speak and I am filled with such sudden and total rage I no longer care about the gun pointed at my face. 'How could you?' My voice shakes with fury. 'How could you do something like that? Just hurt him and leave him to die? Like he was nothing. Like he was a piece of rubbish on the road!'

Still she doesn't reply.

'Why didn't you call an ambulance? Why didn't you help him?'

I thought she was brave, this woman I've been stuck here with. I admired her, struggling to breathe through all these hours, but managing to keep it together all the same. But I was wrong. She's anything but brave. Too scared to take responsibility for what she did. Too pathetic to do the right thing.

'You're disgusting,' I say. 'You're a coward.'

She regards me steadily. Her hand isn't trembling now. She's nothing like the woman I'd imagined. I'd pictured someone reckless, unthinking. Someone who couldn't process what she'd done. Who'd fled the scene terrified of facing the consequences. But Maeve – reckless? Maeve, unthinking?

And then something slides into place, and I sway, the nausea almost overpowering.

'Oh God.' I hear my voice as if it's muffled through glass. 'It wasn't an accident.'

FIFTY-EIGHT

NEW YORK

Now

'You don't understand,' Maeve says. 'I had no choice.'

The bracelet glints against her wrist. I can't take my eyes from those silver hearts. The hand now holding the gun reached out to my father as he lay dying on the road. Then it pulled away and left him there.

'No choice?' I repeat. 'How can you say that? You killed him!'

And still I can't take it in. *It wasn't an accident.* This woman didn't just kill my father. She murdered him in cold blood.

She says, 'He was threatening me. He left me no alternative.'

'Threatening you?' Dimly I am aware that I am repeating her again. 'No. Dad wouldn't threaten anyone.'

'I didn't do it for me. I had to protect Alistair.'

'What are you talking about?' Every word is taking me

further down the rabbit hole. 'What did it have to do with Alistair?'

She draws herself up straighter, shakes her head. 'None of this is important. What's done is done.'

'No. You can't say that.' The anger has replaced my fear. 'You don't believe *what's done is done.* That's why you're here! You blame me for Alistair's death. And you know what? You're right. I blame myself too. Every single day.' She looks like she's going to interrupt, but I don't let her. 'But at least you know what happened. At least you understand why. Can't you do the same for me? Can't you give me that much?'

For a moment, there is silence. Maeve shifts the gun from one hand to the other, but right now I don't care what she does with it. I just need her to tell me what happened that day.

'Are you sure you want to know?'

'What do you mean?' *He threatened me,* she said. But no, Dad wasn't like that. 'Are you saying' – I swallow – 'are you saying he hurt you?'

She hiccups a laugh. 'He didn't hurt me. Not in the way you mean. He didn't have the stomach for anything like that.'

She's talking as if she knew him. But of course, she must have done. You don't plan to kill someone unless you know them. Unless you think they've done something to you.

'That was the problem,' Maeve continues. 'He was weak. Too weak to do what was necessary.'

I want to defend him – but isn't it what I'd thought myself? That he'd been too weak to help Mum. Too weak to stay with us. That he'd taken the easy way out, abandoning us both, starting a new life with some girl. The thought strikes a chord, a distant connection that I reach for but can't grasp.

'What do you mean, then? You said he threatened you?'

'I trusted him. I told him about something I'd done. It was a mistake. He told me if I didn't go to the police, he'd tell them himself.'

The dread comes upon me like a virus. I feel it in my stomach, not able yet to put a name to it. 'What did you do? Why would he have gone to the police?'

'It would have been all right, I expect.' Her voice is thoughtful. 'I think I could have made them see things the right way. But you see, I couldn't risk it.'

She's looking at me as if she expects me to understand. 'I don't know what you're talking about,' I say. 'You're not making any sense.'

'If it went wrong, I might have gone to prison,' she says. 'I couldn't have that. Alistair needed me. He wouldn't have coped without me.'

'Why?' The word is a whisper. 'Why would you have gone to prison?'

'It was an accident.' Her voice too is soft. 'She was out of control. I was defending myself.'

'Who was?'

The moment stretches, lengthens to a lifetime. A lifetime where everything I thought I knew was wrong. I watch her throat move as she says the words.

'Your mother.'

FIFTY-NINE

BRISTOL

Maeve, fifteen years ago

'We need to talk,' Paul said. He brushed past Maeve into the kitchen.

She followed, directing her questions to his back. 'Are you okay? How was Anna?'

He was busying himself at the fridge, taking an open bottle of white wine and pouring himself a glass.

'None for me, thanks,' she said sharply, ignoring the butterfly wings in her stomach. She'd been about to put the kettle on, but apparently he was in need of something stronger.

He didn't respond, tipped up the glass, almost draining it. Then, 'Come and sit down, Mae. Please.'

He left his glass on the worktop and pulled out a seat at the kitchen table. Obediently, she took her place opposite. 'So how did it go? How was she?'

He looked at her intently. 'Not good. Not good at all.'

'Oh, Paul.' She reached across to take his hand, but he pulled away.

'She said the police had been asking her questions.'

'What?' The butterfly wings beat harder. 'But we've had the funeral. Surely they can't still be raking over it all?'

'No, no. Before all that.'

She allowed herself to breathe. 'Then I don't understand. It's over now. The inquest, the funeral. I know how hard it is—' He shot her a glance. 'Okay, I can *imagine* how hard it is for her. But going over it all time after time isn't going to help anyone, least of all Anna. She has to try to find a way to move on.'

'She said...' He paused and when he spoke again, his voice trembled. 'She asked me if I'd had something to do with... with...'

She watched him struggle to compose himself. Finally he took a shuddering breath and looked her square in the face. 'My own daughter asked me if I'd pushed her mother down the stairs.'

Maeve's hand flew to her mouth. 'Why would she think something like that?'

'The police. They were asking about me and Bethan. Whether I'd ever been violent. Violent!' He threw up his hands. 'Me!'

'But I don't understand. They knew she was drunk. She was drunk and she fell. I don't understand—'

'It was how she fell, Maeve! I told you that first day they came here. They as good as said it was all wrong. I knew it then. I knew they were after me for it!'

She shook her head. 'But that doesn't make any sense. I told them you were here with me.'

His voice was cold. 'I imagine that means they didn't believe you.'

She was on high alert now, the energy fizzing through her

veins. 'But if they thought you'd done it, they'd have charged you! They never even asked you to go to the station.'

'That's only because they couldn't prove anything. That detective.' He snapped his fingers. 'Laker. She was round here all the time, wasn't she? Just one more question, one small detail to sort out... I knew what she was thinking. I just didn't think she'd try to poison my own daughter against me!'

'Anna doesn't believe you'd do that, Paul, I'm sure—'

'How would you know?' He jumped to his feet. 'You didn't see the way she looked at me!' He took a step towards her, and something in his eyes made her shrink back against the chair.

'Look,' she said, making an effort to speak calmly, 'it's going to be all right. Anna's heard the coroner's verdict, the same as the rest of us. She's lashing out because she wants someone to blame, and she can't face blaming her mum. Just give her time. She'll come around.'

His eyes were fixed on hers with an intensity she hadn't seen in him before. 'I know she will,' he said, 'because I'm going to tell her what really happened.'

SIXTY

NEW YORK

Now

'Mae,' I breathe, and it's as if the voice is coming from someone else. 'Mae, short for Maeve. You're her. You're the one he left us for.'

She nods, as if I've just asked her whether it's the day to put the bins out. 'That's what Paul called me. I liked it.'

I stare at her dumbly. I had so many questions for this woman once. Did she love my father? Were they happy? Did she think that made what they'd done all right? Was it worth destroying our family for? But there is only one question now. One question I never knew I needed to ask. 'What did you do to my mum?'

She tuts. 'You're just like your father. I didn't *do* anything to her. She was drunk. She fell.'

'But you were there.'

'I'd gone over there to see her, try to make her see sense. She was calling Paul all the time. Every night, at all hours. It had to stop.'

I can't breathe. 'You killed her.'

'I told you, it was an accident.'

'You killed her. You killed my mother!'

Somehow I am on my feet, no longer caring about the gun. She takes a step backwards. 'We got into an argument. We were at the top of the stairs and she tried to grab me. I twisted out of the way and she fell.'

'You could have called someone! You could have got help!'

'No.'

And I see it, there, in that single word: she wanted Mum to die. 'You wanted her out of the way.'

She doesn't reply.

'You pushed her, didn't you? Don't lie to me! And you just expected Dad to go along with it!'

'No. It didn't happen like that.' Her voice is flat. 'But you don't believe me either.'

'I blamed him.' The words catch as they leave my lips, and I choke back a sob. 'I accused my own father of killing my mother.'

She looks at me blankly. 'I know. He told me. That's why he arranged to meet you. He was going to tell you it was my fault. I couldn't let that happen.'

I press my hands over my eyes. This can't be true. This can't be what happened.

'I bought a car, the cheapest I could find. Wore a headscarf and sunglasses so no one would recognise me. It was a risk, but I didn't have a choice. Even if I'd persuaded Paul not to go to the police, I knew I wouldn't persuade you. And I couldn't go to prison. Alistair needed me. He wouldn't have survived without me.'

I look up at her and I see she believes it. She doesn't regret a thing.

'So in a way,' she says, 'it was all your fault.'

BRISTOL

Maeve, fifteen years ago

Paul had told Maeve all he wanted was the truth. That was all. That he knew she'd seen Bethan that day. That if she told him what had really happened, it would be all right. That they'd get through it together.

Something tugged at her insides as he said it, but she wanted to believe him. He loved her, after all. He'd understand she'd only been trying to keep them both safe.

She told him about going to the house, explained that she'd done it for him. 'I couldn't stand seeing how she upset you,' she said, 'phoning all hours of the day and night. You could never switch off. I wanted to talk to her, make her understand it had to stop.'

She replayed it all, the mess downstairs, the stinking bedroom. (She didn't mention finding his clothes in the drawers: there was no one left now to get the wrong idea.) She told him about Bethan attacking her, the scuffle at the head of the stairs. The moment she fell.

'Her foot slipped, Paul,' she said, searching his eyes to see what he was thinking; but his face was a mask. 'It was an accident, a terrible accident. And I'm so, so sorry I couldn't save her.'

She wanted him to reach for her, hold her, tell her that he understood. But that wasn't how it went.

'Tell the police,' he said. 'Tell them what happened, or I will.'

She thought at first he was bluffing, tried to make him see

sense. Knowing what happened wouldn't make Anna feel any better, she reasoned with him. There was nothing to be gained from dragging everything back up.

That's when he lost his temper. She'd never seen that side of him before. He snarled at her, his face red, spittle flying from his lips. His daughter had called him a murderer, he said. His daughter thought he'd killed her mother. And then Maeve knew: no matter what she'd thought once, he was tethered to his wife and child. She'd never come first for him.

He stormed back into the hall and she followed, watching from the kitchen doorway as he rifled through the pockets of the jacket he'd left hanging there, a feeling of dread growing inside her like a tumour.

'What are you doing?' she said, but he didn't answer. The jacket slipped from his hands, and he dropped to his knees, pawing at the fabric.

'I'm not going to the police, and neither are you. You'll just make things worse. I'll deny it all and Anna will think you're trying to deflect the blame from yourself.'

His back was to her as he knelt on the floor, still fussing with the jacket. 'There's no proof, Paul. Everything will be just your word against mine. Don't do that to us. Don't do it to Anna.'

He pulled his hand from the pocket. There was something in it, a crumpled piece of paper. For a moment she didn't understand. But then she saw the triumph in his eyes and her stomach lurched as the pieces came together.

'Go to the police,' he said. 'Tell them what you've told me. Because if you don't, I'll do it for you. And I'm pretty sure they'll believe me when I show them this.'

He held out his hand, staying far enough away that she couldn't grab what it contained. *All this time*, she thought. *All this time you've kept it, and you never said a word.*

She decided in that moment. From the second he held out

his hand, the scrap of envelope covered in creases, as if he'd carried it around with him, folded and unfolded it to read the words she'd left that day.

I've gone to have it out with Bethan. Don't follow me. I'll be back soon.

She saw the words and she understood the depth of his betrayal. There was no going back for either of them now.

SIXTY-ONE

NEW YORK

Now

She's standing too close – the scent of her chokes me. But it's not just here. She'll never be far enough away. Never sorry enough. Never lonely enough. Never hurting enough for what she's done.

Maeve watches me, her arm trembling with the weight of the gun. She thinks she's won. Thinks she has me cornered.

She's wrong.

When the doors of this elevator open, only one of us will walk out. And though she doesn't know it yet, that person will be me.

I move quickly, reach out. Metal against my skin—

The noise and the burning are one, fire spreading up my arm. I look down and see red blossoming through my sleeve. I put my hand over it, and warm liquid spreads beneath my palm and between my fingers. The strength leaves my legs and I am on the floor, my hand pressed to my arm.

I have never done well with the sight of blood.

Maeve is staring at it too. But it won't trouble her. There was blood when my mother fell. It smeared across the wall at the foot of the stairs. Got into the cracks between the floor tiles. Siân arranged cleaners, and they assured us not a speck of it was left. But when I went back to the house, I knew it was there. It called to me.

'Stay back,' Maeve says. She sounds frightened, though I'm the one who's bleeding. 'Don't move.'

At any moment, she will finish this. I'm surprised she hasn't already. My arm throbs, the pain keeping time with my heartbeat. It should be a distraction, but my mind is clear. I won't be walking out of here after all. I'm sorry, Mum, Dad. I should have done better. She was too much for me. She was too much for all of us.

And through the pain, the picture is finally clearing. I've been wasting so much energy trying to find a way out of this that doesn't exist. Now all hope is gone, it's as if my brain is setting itself to another purpose. And at last, I understand. Mum, Dad, Alistair. It's all connected. I feel the symmetry of it as the pieces come together.

'What is it?' Maeve says, and I hear the panic she's trying to hold in check. She feels it too, though she doesn't yet know what it means. 'What are you smiling about?'

Her hands are trembling, but she's still standing. She doesn't know what's coming. I lick my dry lips.

'At least there's one thing I don't have to blame myself for.'

She wants to finish me, but she can't resist. 'What?'

'Alistair didn't kill himself because of me.' I look into her eyes so I can see the moment my words connect. 'He did it because of you.'

LONDON

Eight months ago

Across the desk from me, Alistair's fingers drummed against his knee. 'Someone saw her?' he asked. 'What did she look like?'

I checked my watch: if I left now, it would be quiet at the chemist, little chance of running into a colleague on their lunch break. 'They couldn't see much. She was wearing a headscarf.'

'That's all they said?'

'Alistair, what is it? Why does this matter to you?'

'Nothing else?'

He was looking at me expectantly. Answering would be the quickest way to bring this to a close.

'There was something on Dad's body. The police thought the driver had dropped it when she went back to him. A heart. A silver heart with a blue bit in the middle – enamel. They thought it had come off a piece of jewellery.'

He stared ahead. The knee stopped jiggling and he sat perfectly still. And then I told him he was fired.

At the door he paused, one hand on the doorknob. 'I'm sorry,' he said, his back to me. 'I'm so sorry for everything.'

SIXTY-TWO

NEW YORK

Now

Maeve stares at me like she can't take it in. 'I told him about the silver heart,' I say to her again. 'The one they found on Dad's body. He knew what it meant, didn't he? He knew it was yours.'

She shifts the gun to her other hand again. 'You're lying.' But her voice is shaking.

'Why would I do that? That's what he was upset about, the day I let him go.'

'No. You fired him and he was desperate. He gave everything to that place.'

But it's not true. I remember it so clearly now, every word of that conversation burned into my memory. All the times I've replayed it, imagining it going differently, inserting the offer of counselling. But it wouldn't have mattered. I see that now. I'm free of that burden. For however many moments I have left, I will be grateful for that.

'He didn't care about his job, I told you that. I was telling him he had to leave the building, and the only thing he asked about was the accident. Except it wasn't an accident, was it? It was murder. And he knew that. He knew his own sister was a murderer.'

The gun shifts again, right hand to left, left to right. 'You don't understand anything.'

'He told me he was sorry. I didn't know what he meant then, but I do now. He was sorry for what you'd done. He was ashamed of you.'

'It's not true.'

But I'm barely listening to her. The pain in my arm has burned away the confusion. I see it all now, remember it all. I remember what Alistair said in that final conversation. *When you told me about your mum...*

'He knew, Maeve! He knew everything.'

It all makes sense, all those things he said, the things I didn't understand at the time. *I tried to tell myself it was a coincidence. Your name. The Bristol connection.*

'He knew what you'd done to Mum from the start. Or he suspected. That's why he let me keep my job when he found out about my CV. He thought he owed me. He was trying to make up for what you'd done.'

'No. Just shut up.'

'God, poor Alistair! To carry that all this time. He as good as told me, only I didn't understand what he meant.'

She's shaking her head. 'No, you're lying. You're trying to make yourself feel better. It was your fault. Ali needed that job.'

'He didn't care about the job! He didn't ask a single question about it. Not about money, not about a reference—'

'He had debts. He was scared what would happen if he couldn't pay. He thought they'd come after him. After me...'

She's clutching the gun in both hands now, trying to keep it steady. But she's shaking too much. Her finger trembles against the trigger. In a moment, this will all be over.

'He told me he was sorry.'

'No.'

'I thought he meant about what he'd done at work – coming in drunk. Being obnoxious. But that's not what he said.'

'Shut up.'

'He said, *I'm so sorry about your parents.*'

'Shut up! He was trying to protect me. He left a note. He told me—' She stops short.

And I watch her face crumple as understanding dawns behind her eyes.

*

NEW YORK

Maeve, now

The walls of the elevator shrink away and I am falling, back, back to that dreadful room.

The men and women in their fluorescent jackets have been and gone. Not even the echo of their presence remains. The silence is deep enough to drown in.

They tried to make me leave, asking if there was someone they could call. I told them I'd see to it myself. One of them looked doubtful, but they were busy people. Other calls to go to. Lives that could perhaps be saved.

Afterwards, I went to the fireplace, picked up the photograph on the mantel, stared at the smiling faces – our faces, Ali, yours and mine. A few summers before, a picnic in a nearby park. It had been a beautiful day, the sky a deep, clear blue, and you'd asked a girl walking her dog to take the photo. I saw it on my next visit, printed out and placed in a silver frame. It was a precious thing to us, we who had no photos from our childhood, no family mementoes to anchor our past.

It wasn't until I went to put it back that I saw the piece of paper tucked behind, a single sheet folded in half, my name sliding down the page. I could see at once that you'd been drunk when you wrote it. Later, I took it to the police, still imagining that they might care.

I feel it beneath my fingertips now, the flimsy paper, the indentations left by your pen. I run my fingers across them, as if they could call you back to me. The words dance before my mind's eye. I know them now by heart.

> I'm so sorry, Maeve. I know you always did what you thought was best. But I can't do it anymore, so I'm going where I can't hurt you. It's my turn to protect you.

I thought then I'd understood it all so clearly. You were drunk, overwrought. In trouble with your debts, worried there was no way out now you'd lost your job. Scared of what they'd do to you. Terrified of asking for my help, though all I'd ever wanted was to give it.

It's my turn to protect you.

It had seemed so obvious: you'd thought you were putting me in danger. That the person who'd come to your door that time, the one you'd accused of harassing you, would come after me if you couldn't pay. Or perhaps you believed you were the one I needed to be saved from – your distorted self-image of the weak man, the failure, the one who always needed me to stand up for you. Hadn't you realised, I thought then, that I didn't care about that? That for me, looking out for you was as natural as breathing? That you were never weak, never a failure to me – only and always my little brother?

But I got it all wrong. You knew about Paul – that silver heart, the one with the blue enamel centre. The one that had fallen from the bracelet you'd given me, the one I'd had to stop wearing. All those questions at Christmas, the photograph you'd kept of the flat, the viewing I'd dropped out of, asking me why I'd cancelled, what I'd been doing. There in the corner, the date pinned to the image with those orange digits. And I'd begged you to tell me what was going on, why you'd started drinking again, even though I thought I'd worked it out myself.

I'll help you if I can.

And what had you said in reply? God help me, I know.

I feel the cold creeping over me. It sinks into my bones. My limbs begin to tremble. My teeth chatter in my skull.

How could I have failed then to identify the look in your eyes? Not shame but disgust. Disgust at me, at what I'd done.

I can't do it.

I believed your note meant you couldn't ask me to pay your debts again. Assumed they were more serious this time, that it might have meant remortgaging my flat, maybe even selling it. But I got it all so wrong. You meant you couldn't cover up what I'd done. That I was the driver who'd killed Paul and left the scene. That you couldn't live with the guilt of it.

The memories pull me back again, further into the past. Our last Christmas. You and I seated in the living room. I'd found some fairy lights by then, strung them across the mantelpiece, tried to inject some festive cheer.

You hold up a newspaper – but no, it is a supplement of some kind. 'Have you read this?' you say, turning it so I can see the title.

MY DAD WANTED TO LEAVE US HIS HOUSE. ALL WE GOT WAS HIS OLD SCHOOL TIE.

I frown. 'What about it?' It wasn't the kind of problem we'd ever been troubled with. Our parents had left us little enough. I doubt our father ever owned a school tie; if he had, he certainly wouldn't have kept it.

'The man writing this thought he was going to inherit all his parents' money,' you say. 'Took out loans to send his kids to private school. Thought he'd be able to pay them back when he inherited.'

'Nice,' I say, disapprovingly. 'I'm guessing he was disappointed?'

'His mother died first, and his father married again. Left everything to the new wife.' You study me over the top of the newspaper. 'This guy's furious. All those plans, and they came to nothing.'

I snort. 'That'll teach him to be presumptuous.'

For a moment you are silent. Then, 'You wouldn't do that, then? Rely on someone leaving you something in their will?'

'You'll outlive me, brother dearest. And I can't imagine who else I'd rely on.'

'So you wouldn't do it? Make a commitment and rely on a legacy to meet it?' Your eyes are fastened back on the newspaper but there's something in the way you're waiting for me to respond, as if the answer matters to you in some way I can't fathom.

I force a laugh. 'I hope you're not planning to bump me off, Ali. There won't be much left after the mortgage is paid off.'

I expect you to laugh too, but you don't. A silence forms between us, grows uncomfortable.

'What is it?' I ask. 'What's bothering you?'

You turn the page of the newspaper. 'Nothing,' you reply.

And now at last I understand. The knowledge breaks like a wave, fills my senses, the horror of it sending me to my knees, acid rising in my throat.

That line in your note that never quite made sense. I know you always did what you thought was best.

You thought I'd done it for you. You thought I'd killed Paul expecting to inherit his money. That I planned to use it to pay off your debts. The tears in your eyes that day when I implored you to tell me what was wrong, told you I'd help you if I could. God help me, I know.

Somewhere there is a noise of desolation, an animal keening. I cover my face. I never want to open my eyes again.

SIXTY-THREE

NEW YORK

Now

The gun falls as Maeve sinks to the floor and I flinch, wrap my hands over my head, waiting for the explosion, the pain tearing into me. There's nothing. The only sound is Maeve. 'No no no,' she says, 'no no no.'

I unfold myself slowly, raise my head. She is curled forward, her head bent over her knees, her fingers thrust into her hair. The chignon has been torn to pieces and tendrils cover her face. I don't want to look at her. Her grief is all sharp edges. It will cut me if I get too close.

And then I see the gun. It lies to the side of her right foot. The handle – the stock, I think? – is towards me. An invitation. I stare at it, running the calculations in my mind, trying to ignore the pain in my arm, trying to learn from last time.

But this is different. Maeve is different. For now, at least, she is somewhere else, lost to the moment. I reach forward, inch by inch. My arm throbs but I ignore it. She is rocking backwards and forwards, still mumbling her incantation. Another inch, another breath.

I grab the gun. It's damp from Maeve's sweat and I want to wipe my hand, be rid of any trace of her on my skin. But I don't relax my grip. Instead I wrap my other hand around it too and point it at her, my elbows locked to stop it shaking.

She hasn't even looked at me. I should stand, but I don't trust my legs to hold my weight. I shuffle further away until I feel the doors of the lift at my back. My eyes stay fixed on her the whole time. Her hands still work at her hair – I can see bands of it stretched taut around her fingers. The bracelet glints at me, its blank space like a missing tooth.

There is a sound from above, a clank of metal against brick. It's close. They are coming for us. I have only a little time.

'Alistair knew,' I say. 'He worked it out. Tell me you understand.'

She closes her eyes, and a tear rolls down her cheek.

'He knew what you'd done. That's why he was asking all those questions. He couldn't stand it, could he? Couldn't bear knowing his sister was a murderer.'

She's frozen, the tears streaming from her eyes. And without really knowing what I'm doing, I am on my knees, shuffling back towards her.

'He was a good man, a kind man.' I am next to her now. I reach out with my good arm and place the gun next to her skull. Feel the bone beneath the hair. Imagine the pulse of her blood. 'You killed him too. You know that, don't you? You killed him, just like you killed my mum and dad.'

My voice breaks on the words. My parents are gone because of this woman. All the time we should have had together, wiped out. Every moment I've wanted to pick up the phone to Mum, to tell her about my day, laugh over something stupid – every time I've had to remember that I can't do that. That I can never tell her anything again. And Dad. All those nights I lay awake telling myself that if only I'd agreed to meet him earlier, if only I hadn't been so stubborn, so resentful, he might still be alive. But that's not true. None of it would have made a difference. She is to blame for all of it.

'Yes,' she says, so softly that at first I think I've imagined it. She turns her head slowly, looks straight at me. 'You're right. I loved my brother, and he's dead because of me.'

'And my parents.' *And my baby.* 'I'm alone because of you.'

'Yes.'

A thud and a clatter. Footsteps. Someone on the roof of the lift. I can't help it – I look up. And then I feel the gun move in my hand. I try to snatch my arm back but I'm too slow. Maeve has the barrel in both hands. She's strong – she's going to wrestle it from me. She'll kill me just like she killed my parents.

But that's not what's happening. She pulls the barrel closer, presses it against her forehead. 'Do it,' she says.

Someone above is shouting something, but the sounds melt into each other. I stare at the woman in front of me. At the metal next to her skin.

A clank, a whir. The whole lift vibrates. Someone is drilling into the roof.

'You need to make it right,' Maeve says. And I see sparks rain down as I remember Mum's smile, the way she'd stroke my hair. Dad taking me on his knee, the feel of his jumper against my cheek. I'll never see them again. Never talk to them. Never touch them.

Maeve looks at me, and though her eyes are swimming with tears there's determination in them too. 'Do this for them,' she says.

The sparks have died. The whirring stops. They are here.

I know what I have to do.

SIXTY-FOUR

BRISTOL AND SOMERSET

Now

It's a bright, cold day, the sun silver in the white sky. I don't know if I'm in precisely the right spot. But the road is straight, uniform. Whether here or further along, she would have seen him from a distance. Enough time to change her mind, to brake. Enough time to accelerate, to make sure there'd be no mistake.

I reach across to the passenger seat to collect what's there. The sudden pain in my arm makes me catch my breath. The nerve there was severed by the bullet; I'm told it won't heal. I take a breath, wait until it passes. Then I open the door and step onto the tarmac. The 1980s block of flats I've stopped outside is plain but homely, not the kind of place I would have pictured for Dad. I turn away from it – there's nothing left of him there. Instead I make my way down the road, imagining walking in his footsteps, wondering what he was thinking that final day. He had something to tell me, he said; I know now what that was.

A few steps on, there's a lamppost, an ordinary streetlight.

Something is taped to it, and when I get closer I see that it's a poster for a band. They're playing in a pub this weekend, the kind of music Dad would have dismissed as 'noise'. The thought brings a smile to my lips, and I stoop and lay the flowers at its base. I haven't written a note. I don't have the words yet. But I close my eyes and touch my fingertips to the pavement, feeling grit against my skin. When I open them, the daffodils are the first thing I see, their sunny faces full of the promise of spring. I leave them there, a splash of colour against the grey.

Back in the car, I'm fastening my seatbelt when I hear the buzz of my phone in my bag. I reach inside and fish it out, scan the message.

How long are you here? Would be great to meet up if you come to London.

Matt and I are on better terms these days. He swears to me he knew nothing about Maeve coming to Holbrooke and Dean, nothing about Elise telling her where to find me. The two of them split up not long after I went to New York, apparently, though I don't think I had anything to do with that. I suspect they both missed the sweetness of forbidden fruit.

I take a moment to compose a reply, wanting to get the tone just right. I'll be heading to the office next week, I tell him, a coffee would be lovely if he's around. There's no reason, after all, not to say hello, but I won't be there long. I want to talk to Grace, to put in place the final arrangements for Jay's secondment to the London office. She'll get the best out of him, I think, the role she has lined up a better fit than the job he was doing in New York. The team will suit him better too: sometimes it's as much about the chemistry as it is about the CV. He's excited about it, he says. He wants to make a go of it. That, after all, is half the battle.

I turn the key in the ignition, pull out slowly, checking my mirrors. I drive carefully, sticking to the speed limit, mindful of the children who could run out between the parked cars. Somewhere along the street, I pass the place my father died.

It's another hour before I turn into the long gravel drive, shaded on either side with trees. The way is narrow, and I almost missed it on my first visit. But I am practised now. Today will be my third time here, and I remember every curve of the road.

I have phoned ahead – it is important to do that here – and the iron gate swings open before I bring the car to a stop. I glance at the camera as I drive through. I do that every time now, checking for signs of life. I want to know when I'm being watched. A small red light eyes me beadily.

There are always plenty of parking spaces to choose from, and I pull up close to the entrance. I leave my handbag and take only the carrier bag of magazines with me. The front door is solid wood, a brass buzzer to one side. I press the button and speak my name into a grille. The door swings open silently.

At reception I present my passport and it is checked as carefully as always, though by now they know who I am. I wonder how widely the story is known. What they think of me coming here. The woman behind the desk gives nothing away, just checks the contents of the carrier bag. 'You know the way?' she asks, and I nod.

I'm wearing soft-soled shoes and my footsteps make barely a sound as I walk down the corridor. I stop outside the door, peer through the strip of glass that runs down one side, wire mesh crosshatching my view. Today she sits in the chair beside the bed, her face turned to the window. Her hair is loose and clean, neatly brushed. They take good care of them here, Pearl Associates' money well spent. Grace's doing, no doubt: she may not know what happened in that elevator, but she's a shrewd woman. This is a small price to pay to protect the firm's reputation.

For a moment I watch, waiting for a clue. Then I knock softly and make my way inside. I know there's no point waiting for an invitation.

'Hello, Maeve,' I say. She doesn't stir, but I sense something switching on inside. There is a second chair in the corner, moulded plastic discouraging long visits. I pull it to the other end of the window, close but not too close. 'I've brought you some magazines.'

I take them out of the bag, hold them out to her. She continues to look out of the window. 'I'll leave them here,' I say and place them on the bed. I settle into the chair, following her gaze onto the grounds. The grass is beginning to grow, and here and there crocuses flash orange and purple against the green. 'It will get warmer soon,' I say.

I study her as the minutes slip by. She has lost weight, her cheeks hollow, the bones sharp against the skin. They say she eats, but it can't be enough.

My mind wanders back to that day, the moment they opened the hatch in the roof of the lift. I dropped the gun, kicked it away from us both. I didn't know then what they'd seen, whether the cameras or the mic had been working. I was waiting for Maeve to say something, but she just sat there. I told the man who dropped into the lift that she'd had a panic attack. He was fussing about my arm, radioing that they needed an ambulance. I said it was an accident. And through it all, Maeve didn't say a word – not then, and not for all the months since.

It turned out there'd been no video, no sound. The camera was dead, and those bursts of static had been messages to us to keep calm, that help was on the way. But the sound had worked no better for them than it had for us, all part of the massive systems failure that had apparently affected everything from the lifts to the aircon. Some kind of virus in the software controlling the building. There were fulsome apologies, offers of compensation in return for signing an agreement not to take legal action. I signed, less for the money than to make them go away.

At first, I'd planned to tell the police everything that had happened. They were there waiting for us when we finally got out, asking questions about my arm. They didn't seem bothered by the gun, but I suppose they see things differently on that side of the pond. I was all set to tell them, to say that Maeve had slipped past security, that she'd gone there with the express purpose of finding me, taking revenge for what she believed I'd done to Alistair. And of course, I was going to tell them about my parents. That she'd been the woman in the headscarf who'd mown down my father. That I was certain she'd pushed my mother to her death.

But then I was taken to hospital, and somewhere in the hours that passed in X-rays and questioning, white coats and long corridors, I changed my mind. I thought about how it would be for Siân, having to hear that her sister had been murdered. That she'd been killed by the same woman who'd killed her brother-in-law, who'd nearly killed me too. It would have broken her all over again. She deserved more from me than that.

So when the police officer appeared in my room, asking what had happened, I found myself repeating the lie I'd told the man in the lift: that it was an accident. I told him Maeve had been looking for her inhaler, that she'd been struggling to breathe, had started to panic. She'd taken out the gun as she was rummaging in her bag. It had gone off. It had all been an unfortunate mishap, nothing more.

He didn't believe me, I could tell. I didn't know it then, but Maeve still hadn't spoken, hadn't reacted to anything around her. It wouldn't have taken a genius to work out that something more than what I was describing had gone down in that lift. But he was a busy man, no doubt, and my injury wasn't serious. I stuck to my story, and he gave up soon enough. What else was there to do?

And now I'm back here, watching her the way I always do. I'm not sure why I come. Dr Welmar asks me, and I can't answer. 'Your thoughts create your feelings,' she tells me. 'Your feelings create your actions. So we need to work backwards, identify the way you feel when you're with Maeve.'

I look at Maeve now and I find it hard to put into words. I remember how I felt then, there in that lift, the moment when I held the gun against her head. I was going to do it. I was a hair's breadth from pulling the trigger. I looked at her and anger and hate filled every cell of my body. I thought I couldn't go on if she was in the world with me. That what she'd done demanded retribution.

It's what she believed too. I remember the way she looked at me: 'You have to make it right.' She believed in punishment, and she wanted to be punished. Not for Mum and Dad – I don't believe she ever saw what she did to them as wrong. But Alistair – Alistair was a different matter. Perhaps in the end that's what stopped me – not any finer feelings, simply the idea that I'd be giving her what she wanted.

But I don't hate her now. Not most of the time. I remember those hours we were stuck in the lift, the way we relied on each other. She shared her water with me. I helped her breathe. Elemental things, two people trying to get each other through. And I remember that I didn't do it. No matter how much I wanted to pull that trigger, I didn't do it. I hold on to that. I hold on to the difference between us.

When thirty minutes have passed, I get to my feet and collect the crumpled carrier bag.

'Goodbye, Maeve,' I say. There is a flicker then; her head turns a fraction towards me. 'I'm going back to New York, but I'll be here again in eight weeks.' I wait in case there's a response. But she remains silent.

Outside in the corridor I see a nurse, the same guy I saw on my last visit. He smiles. 'Heading off?'

I nod. 'It's a long drive.'

He raises a hand in farewell, turns to the door. I'm halfway down the corridor when he calls back. 'She likes seeing you, you know.'

I stop, turn to him. 'She never speaks. She doesn't even look at me.'

He shrugs. 'That's the same with all of us. But she's calmer when you've been. When I go in there now, she'll be reading those magazines you brought.'

He smiles again and then his shoulder is against the door and he's gone.

I make my way back to the entrance. The woman at reception says, 'Bye then, see you soon,' and I wave at her as the door opens and I step outside into the cold sunshine.

Your thoughts create your feelings. I think tomorrow is going to be a good day.

SIXTY-FIVE

SOMERSET

Maeve, now

There is a small section at the boundary of the lawn where the trees thin out enough to see the drive beyond. I watch it, waiting for the flash of red that is Anna's car. There it is, gone the next second. So fast it might have been a dream.

I turn in my seat, not rising, stretching out my arm to the magazines left behind on the bed. I pick up the one on top, hold it in my lap. Run a finger gently down the crease at the edge.

Don't do it, Maeve. You promised.

But your voice is a memory. You come to me only when Anna is here. It's the reason I welcome her visits, though I know you're not real. The real Alistair has gone. You left me.

I believed at first that it was my fault. Blamed myself for having broken the promise I made. But that promise was old, threadbare. No longer fit for purpose.

Go outside, Ali, *I whisper.* Go and play in the garden for a bit.

And I am there again, in that dirty, cluttered house. Our father has dragged himself upstairs to sleep it off, but I know this mood. Know how it will be when he wakes up. Unless I stop it. Stop it once and for all.

It was easier than I'd imagined. A momentary distraction, a sharp push. Now he lies on his back, one foot on the bottom step. He struggles to focus on me as I place one hand over his mouth, pinch his nostrils tight with the other. The fall has broken him. It is a kindness to finish it. More than he deserves.

His right foot jerks twice, three times. Then it stops. I gag as the smell hits. The final indignity of death.

Maeve?

Perhaps it was the noise that brought you inside. It was louder than I'd expected, though there was only a single cry, cut off abruptly as his head hit the floor. Our father is – was – a heavy man.

Maeve? Is Daddy asleep?

Your bottom lip is trembling. I pull back my hands slowly. He's gone, Ali. He can't hurt you anymore.

Later, much later. Another house. A sobbing child. You stand between me and the boy nursing his wrist. You can't do this, Maeve. Promise me. Promise me you won't hurt anyone else.

He has to learn. He can't push you around and get away with it.

Promise me you'll stop. Please, Maeve.

But promises have a use-by date, and this one has passed. Died alongside you. And I understand, now that I've had time to think it through, that I mustn't blame myself. It was all her fault.

Anna.

If she hadn't lied to you to get that job, then bleated about her dead mother to get herself off the hook, none of this would have happened. You might have had doubts about what happened to Paul's wife, but you'd always let them lie. We'd been happy, hadn't we, you and I? And then Anna came along and stirred everything up. All the time she was working with you, she was like a ticking bomb. And finally she exploded, telling you about her father's death, about what they found on his body.

Now you're dead and I'm as good as, stuck here, every day the same. And that woman comes to gloat, talking about her life, bringing her magazines. My only comfort is that you come with her; I see your face in the window. The first time it happened, I cried and turned to greet you – but there was no one in the room but her. I tried to ask if she'd seen you too, but the words wouldn't come. They've abandoned me, just as you did. Because now I know: you're not real. I see you only in the reflection of the glass, your eyes never leaving mine while that woman drones on about the weather, the seasons, the condition of the grounds.

You promised, Maeve.

I open the magazine at the centre, my fingers tracing the crease between the pages. I find what I need, slide a fingernail beneath it, pull, twist, straighten, pull again.

I know you don't want me to do it, but you've never understood. That easygoing nature – it's the blessing of the younger sibling. You've never had to be the one to make things right. Never had to learn that you can't just let things go. That was our mother's way, the line of least resistance, and where did it get her? I won't make that mistake. I fought my corner, yours too. I won't stop now.

I repeat the process – slide, lift, twist, pull. I examine the objects in my palm, close my fist around them. With my other hand I turn the page, pretending I am reading. People watch me, I know, though I have lulled them into complacency with good behaviour.

Please, Maeve. You promised.

I sit here, turning the pages until I reach the back cover. Then I replace the first magazine with the second.

The afternoon light is starting to fade as I close the final glossy page. I get up and place the magazine on top of the others, neatening the stack then moving them to the bedside table with those from her last two visits. I am allowed a hairbrush and some hand cream, and these I place on top of the pile, a gentle discouragement to idle browsing by the nurses. Then I sit on the bed, swing up my legs so I'm propped against the pillows, let one arm fall over the edge.

In a moment it is done, my hand sliding into the gap between the mattress and the bed frame, pushing the contents of my palm into the groove in the metal. Four magazines. Eight staples to add to my collection. Sharp. Sharp enough to cut.

I'm not sure yet of the final design, how I'll find a way to turn these tiny pieces of metal into the weapon I need. But there is time enough to think about that. Eight weeks, that woman said. Eight weeks until she's back, and this time I won't hesitate. I know I won't see you again after it's done. I must make my peace with that before the end.

You promised—

I close my eyes, breathe deep until I no longer hear your voice. Because wrongs have to be put right, Ali. Injuries repaid. The balance has to be restored. And then maybe, maybe I can rest.

A LETTER FROM CLAIRE

Dear reader,

I want to say a huge thank you for choosing to read *The Elevator*. If you enjoyed it and want to keep up to date with my latest releases, just sign up at the following link. Your email address will never be shared, and you can unsubscribe at any time.

www.bookouture.com/claire-cooper

One of the best – and scariest – things about writing a book is that, at some point, it's no longer only yours. Your story and characters head out into the world, and you're left waving to them from the front door, hoping they'll find their way to those who'll love and understand them.

So there's nothing better than hearing from the people who've let them in, given them their time, and formed their own opinions of them. You're part of my book family (and I promise I'll never make you play charades at Christmas).

If you enjoyed *The Elevator*, it would be wonderful if you could spare a few moments to leave a review. I'd love to hear your thoughts, and it makes such a difference helping new readers to discover one of my books for the first time.

And if you'd like to drop me a line, I'd love to hear from you. You can get in touch on Twitter or Instagram.

Thank you for reading, and warmest wishes,

Claire Cooper

ACKNOWLEDGEMENTS

This book has been a long time in the making, and I'm very grateful to the many people who helped it on its journey.

To my lovely beta readers, Lisa Oyler, Henry Tam, Kath Thomas, Barry Upshall and Vicky Blackwell: thank you all for being so generous with your time and thoughtful feedback. I can't imagine doing this without you.

Special thanks to Melanie Sturtevant, who read this in the midst of serious illness, and still managed to find time to give me both detailed comments and heartening encouragement. I felt monumentally selfish asking for your help, but I just couldn't resist – you're too good at this! I'm deeply grateful.

Thank you to my former agent, Hannah Weatherill, for taking me on before moving to pastures new, and huge thanks to Diane Banks, Elizabeth Counsell and Natalie Christopher for seamlessly picking up the baton. From the moment I joined Northbank Talent Management, I've felt in the safest of hands.

Thank you to my dear friend Lisa Goll, for organising the inspirational London Writers Café, for introducing me to Hannah, and for all those life- (and lockdown-) enhancing discussions about writing, the universe and everything. I couldn't ask for a better birthday twin.

Thank you to über-guru Sophie Hannah, whose Dream Author coaching is a continual source of positivity, calm, and reassurance to me and, I know, to many, many other writers. The words 'Sophie says...' get used a *lot* in the Cooper household. Special thanks for your invaluable support for this book.

The most massive thank you to my editor, the brilliant Ruth Tross, for bringing me to Bookouture, and for making the editing experience such a joy. And to Kim Nash, Peta Nightingale, Noelle Holten and all in the Bookouture family – thank you for making me feel so welcome. My sincere gratitude also to Hannah Wann at Little, Brown, who read an early draft and provided invaluable feedback.

Thank you to the Lunch Buddies, and all the other wonderful writers who offer so much support and kindness, often unlooked for and at the moments where it's most needed. With you around, writing doesn't seem like such a solitary endeavour.

Thank you to my friend and spiritual (if no longer literal) neighbour Souki Kanagasingam, for helping me stay sane, and forcing me out for fresh air and exercise. We might not live next-door these days, but you don't get rid of me that easily.

My deepest gratitude to my dad, to whom this book is dedicated. You showed me the wonder of storytelling and made me a writer. Thank you for the magic.

And finally, to my husband, Mark. You're the luckiest man in the world, you know that, right? Oh, and the best human being I've ever met. Thank you for all of it.

Printed in Great Britain
by Amazon